Suddenly the lights went out. Completely out.

The "Happy New Year!" shouts died, abruptly. It was very dark, and unexpectedly quiet. A couple people laughed nervously. Even the emergency exit lights were out. It was like being in a cave.

Spirit wondered if this was supposed to be part of the evening, even as Burke held her hand even tighter. But nothing happened, and even the nervous laughter died out.

She got a strange, horrible, sick feeling in the pit of her stomach, and a cold chill went down her back that had nothing to do with the cooling air of the room.

Something was wrong. And something very bad was about to happen. . . .

Mercedes Lackey and Rosemary Edghill

Shadow Grail 2

CONSPIRACIES

TOR
TEEN

A Tom Doherty Associates Book

New York

SHADOW GRAIL 2: CONSPIRACIES

Copyright © 2011 by Mercedes Lackey and Rosemary Edghill

A Tor Teen Book
Published by Tom Doherty Associates, LLC
175 Fifth Avenue
New York, NY 10010

www.tor-forge.com

Tor® is a registered trademark of Tom Doherty Associates, LLC.

ISBN 978-0-7653-2823-6 (hardcover)
ISBN 978-0-7653-1762-9 (trade paperback)

4621 8235 8u

Printed in the United States of America

0   9   8   7   6   5   4   3   2

Shadow Grail 2

CONSPIRACIES

ONE

It was Christmas morning, and as she woke in a bed that still seemed strange, Spirit White had never in her life felt less festive.

It didn't help, of course, that this was her first Christmas since . . . The Accident. Her first Christmas without Mom and Dad and her baby sister, Phoenix. As she lay there half asleep, Spirit expected to feel the thump of Fee bouncing down on her bed and demanding she get up right now, it was Christmas, come on. And that would never happen again, because on a summer night less than a year ago, her sister and her parents had died in an accident that never should have happened. That alone was enough to make Spirit want to burrow into the covers of this bed and sleep until New Year's Day. At least. But adding to her sense of dislocation was where she was. If someone had told her this was where she'd be twelve months ago, Spirit would have laughed in their face.

The middle of Montana was a place so unlike her Indiana home that she could have been on another planet. And she was living at Oakhurst Academy: a luxurious boarding school—an *orphanage*—that invested more money just in sports equipment than most people made in a year. But the most unbelievable thing of all was what Oakhurst taught, and *who* the school taught, and why she was here.

Oakhurst taught *Grammery*—magic. And the only people who were allowed to attend Oakhurst were future magicians. *Orphaned* future magicians.

But Oakhurst was no happy, cozy place that nurtured young wizards and witches with feasts and magical competitions and quirky living quarters. Oh no. Being at Oakhurst was like being in one of those teen slasher movies where only the most competitive survived. And she meant that literally—because some of her classmates *hadn't* survived.

Only three days ago, she and the few friends she'd managed to make here—Oakhurst didn't want its students to make friends or keep them—had managed to defeat the evil force that had been killing Oakhurst students for almost forty years. And no one had realized this was going on, because everyone—well, all the students anyway—had just assumed that the missing kids ran away, or got too sick for the Oakhurst medical facilities to treat, or were sent away for some other reason. Until Spirit arrived at Oakhurst, no one had counted up the missing and come up with the truly scary total that she and her friends had.

The five of them shouldn't even have realized anything was wrong. Everything about Oakhurst, Spirit had realized, was designed to distract you, to make you come up with some sort of plausible explanation instead of looking for the real truth. Spirit wasn't really sure what had made them look past the convenient smoke screen. Was it because she and Loch were new here? Was it because one of the kids who vanished had been a friend of Muirin's?

Was it because she, Spirit White, didn't have the magic powers every other kid here had? The teachers—and Doctor Ambrosius—told her she did. They'd told her that *her magic* was why she was here.

At least Burke had said that everybody's magic didn't show up at the same time. He was being kind—Spirit knew that—but at least not having magic had one advantage. Everybody who *did* have magic could sense each others' presence. It had been Loch who, knowing she didn't have magic, had used that to defeat the thing that had been killing Oakhurst students. . . .

As the sounds got closer, Spirit could see Jeeps, SUVs. The vehicles were rusted and burned out, as if they'd come from some supernatural junkyard. Lashed to every grille or hood was a set of antlers: deer, elk, even moose, and each vehicle held passengers. Some leaned out the sides of doorless, roofless SUVs. Some stood in the beds of pickup trucks, whooping and hollering and urging the drivers onward. They were dressed in the ragged remains of hunting clothes— hunter's orange and red-and-black buffalo plaids and woodland camo.

Skeletal hands gripped roll bars and steering wheels and door frames. Eyeless skulls covered in tatters of rotting flesh gazed avidly toward their prey. Every single one of them was dead. . . .

✦

The Wild Hunt was supposed to be a myth, a folktale, a legend: a ghostly troop of riders—a *hunt*—that galloped across the sky, capturing or killing anyone it met. It hadn't been supposed to be real. Spirit wanted to think she and her friends—Loch, Addie, Muirin, and Burke—had actually managed to *destroy* the Wild Hunt, but she was pretty sure they hadn't. They couldn't possibly be that lucky.

At least they'd made it go away. Spirit burrowed deeper under the covers, shivering at the memory. They'd been crazy to try taking on the Hunt by themselves. It was a miracle they'd won. And their reward for doing the impossible had been a pat on the head from Doctor Ambrosius, Oakhurst's headmaster.

And that was an odd thing that stood out even in the middle of the general weirdness that was Oakhurst. On the day she and Loch had arrived, Doctor Ambrosius had told them that they—everyone here at Oakhurst—had enemies, and that a final showdown was coming. That was why he brought all of them here after their parents died. That was why he was training them in magic.

So if that's true, wouldn't he be a little more interested in the fact that there is a band of ghosts or demons or elves running around outside his magical shields?

They'd already figured out that the Hunt had been raiding

on the campus as well as off it. Oakhurst was surrounded by an invisible magical barrier—its wards—that wouldn't allow anything that didn't "belong" at Oakhurst to come in. For the Hunt to be able to raid on campus . . .

There had to be someone *at* Oakhurst—one of the teachers or one of the staff—letting them in.

And they had no idea who that might be.

At least we're still alive to try to figure it out, Spirit thought glumly. *That beats the alternative. I guess.*

Then again, the alternative was Christmas at Oakhurst.

There were no real "holidays" here, only a few days in which they didn't have classes, and despite the fact that there was a town only a few miles away, the students here were as isolated as if they were in prison: no television, no Internet—no junk food!—and the only movies they could watch were on the "approved" list. The rules were relaxed—just a little—at the school dances. That seemed to satisfy most of the kids. It only made Spirit think of how much she'd lost.

I hate this place, she thought numbly. *And not because Doctor Ambrosius turned me into a mouse during my "Welcome to Oakhurst" interview, and not because I'm the only one in the entire school who can't cast spells, and not just because even the teachers here are trying to kill all of us, and not even because I'm pretty sure this whole place wants us to all hate each other. I hate it because they even turn the holidays into work.*

The month of December had been packed not only with classes—and everybody's course-load was brutal—but with preparations for their so-called week of vacation. It wasn't really.

There were a lot of requirements, like snow and ice sculptures, including a snow castle and a snow maze. You'd think stuff like that would be just for fun, but it wasn't. It was a *course requirement* for the Water Witches, who were graded on *Grammery*, art, and architectural design.

Way to suck the fun out of playing in the snow, thankyew, thankyew very much, Spirit thought mockingly.

The Water Witches weren't the only ones with "vacation" homework. The music classes rehearsed for a Christmas concert. The English classes rehearsed a play for New Year's Eve. The athletic teams practiced for yet another series of demonstrations and contests. And everybody rehearsed for Christmas Day, which included another of Oakhurst's hideous "formal dinners." Even the carol-singing was mandatory.

Even if no one else is as depressed as I am, by the time today comes, everyone should be so sick of getting ready for it, all they'll want is for it to be over.

Suddenly Spirit's pillow was snatched off her head. She made a grab for it, but Muirin held it out of reach.

"Up!" the redhead commanded. "You're going to miss breakfast!"

Spirit responded by pulling her blanket over her head. "Wake me when it's New Year's," she muttered. "And you aren't supposed to go into somebody's room without permission," she added sulkily.

In reply, Muirin pulled the blanket off the end of the bed. Spirit yelped at the blast of cold air. Oakhurst believed that sleeping in cold bedrooms was good for you. Now she was completely awake, and there was no point in trying to out-stubborn Muirin. With a growl, she tossed back the covers, grabbed her robe, and stalked into her bathroom, shutting the door on Muirin's smug look of triumph.

She stalked out again a few minutes later, damp from her shower, and stomped into her closet. It was big enough to dress in—her whole bedroom here had luxuries she'd never imagined owning, like a flat-screen TV and her very own microwave—and it was the same as every other student's. They all had private rooms, and their own computers, and . . .

Pretty much everything they wanted, except privacy, freedom, and their families back.

A few minutes later, she came out of the closet, dressed—in an Oakhurst uniform, of course—for another wonderful day on Planet Oakhurst. Almost everything she owned—after The Accident, and its aftermath—was an Oakhurst uniform. She was really tired of brown and gold. Since the fancy formal dinner was going to be fancy and formal, she couldn't even wear pants (even though you usually could during vacation), but she could still make her feelings known. She chose a brown skirt that went down to mid-calf, brown tights, brown shoes, brown sweater, and brown blouse. There. She looked like a Mennonite. A *dowdy* Mennonite. All she needed was the little white hat.

Muirin rolled her eyes at the sight of her outfit. "You don't *really* want Burke and Loch to see you in *that*, do you?"

Argh. No, she didn't. Burke was sweet, and Loch was really cute, and—unlike most of the other kids, like Kylee and Dylan—neither of them had tried to kill her in the four months she'd been here. But she'd be damned if she was going to look "cheer-ful" when she felt so depressed. She set her jaw. Muirin gave a pained sigh. Muirin had fire red hair and vivid green eyes and was fashion-model skinny and the closest thing to an outlaw rebel that could survive here, since even if you didn't just "dis-appear," collecting enough demerits could make your life a living hell. Muirin despised Oakhurst's Dress Code, and had somehow managed to alter every bit of her own clothing so that it was just barely within school guidelines. How she got away with it, Spirit still didn't know. Maybe she cast an illusion over herself every time there was a teacher in sight.

Only that wouldn't work, Spirit thought in irritation. *Because if you have magic, you can tell when somebody's using it around you. The only one Muirin could really fool here . . . is me.*

"Come *on*, come on—they're having French toast and pan-cakes even though it isn't Sunday!" Muirin said, bouncing up and down at her. Muirin was a sugar addict, and one of her many grievances with Oakhurst was the lack of junk food on the school menus. Spirit really didn't miss anything but soda, but Muirin and Seth—he'd been one of the Wild Hunt's last victims—had set up their own smuggling operation to get con-traband into Oakhurst from nearby Radial.

The dining room was nearly empty. A lot of the school rules were relaxed a little over the Christmas holiday, so you didn't have to show up for breakfast if you didn't want to, though if you missed it, you had to starve until lunch. Today, missing breakfast meant you'd be stuck until about two-thirty, because the formal meals were always later than regular lunch. But even so, it looked as if at least half of the other kids had decided to skip breakfast in favor of more sleep. Not that it would be *much* more sleep, because there was a mandatory "spiritual education" service at ten. Any place else, it would be a church service, but Oakhurst was special. In the not-good way.

Addie, Burke, and Loch were already in the Refectory, sharing their usual table. Burke, as usual, was working his way through an enormous "healthy" breakfast: eggs and toast and sausage and potatoes and orange juice. Addie was crunching delicately away on a slice of toast, with a mug of tea at her elbow. Loch had a plate of bacon and eggs in front of him, but he was pretty much ignoring it to talk to the others. The moment Spirit slipped into her seat, one of the servers came around to ask her what she wanted for breakfast. (That was another creepy thing about Oakhurst. It was like living in a combination of Motel Hell and a fancy restaurant, because they had waiters and waitresses serving them at every meal.)

"Waffles!" Muirin said eagerly. "And cocoa, and orange juice, and bacon, and—"

"Just cornflakes, thanks," Spirit said, cutting Muirin off. At least during "vacations" you didn't have to eat a whole Healthy Breakfast if you didn't want to. The server nodded and walked away.

"Boy, *somebody* woke up in a bad mood this morning!" Muirin mocked.

Spirit glared at her, her blue eyes crackling with anger. "My parents are dead," she said, biting off each word. "My sister is dead. I don't even have any pictures of them because our house burned down while I was in the hospital having my third—or maybe it was my fourth—surgery after the crash. And now I'm here. And it's Christmas. So why don't you tell me what I've got to be perky about?"

"Well," Loch said, after a moment, "you don't have to go out and fight the Demon King of Hell today."

Addie gave a startled snort of laughter. It always seemed so odd when Addie made a rude noise. She was a plump girl with brown eyes and long, smooth, jet-black hair, and she looked a little like Snow White and a little like Alice in Wonderland, and a lot like somebody very prim and proper and maybe even stuck-up. And nothing could be farther from the truth, even though she was—Spirit had been stunned to discover—the sole heir to Prester-Lake BioCo., a pharmaceutical company worth literally millions.

"True," Addie said. "Unfortunately, you do have to attend the concert. Sorry," she added. Addie was in the Choral Society, so she'd be performing. Spirit was starting to suspect Addie'd joined the choir so she wouldn't have to attend the concerts. They were deadly dull.

The server returned with the plate of waffles and the bowl of cornflakes. Of course, since this was Oakhurst, they couldn't just be regular normal cornflakes. No, they were topped with slices of banana that had been dusted with brown sugar. Spirit picked up the milk pitcher and poured milk into her bowl.

"I know today's gotta be pretty awful for you—both of

you," Burke said, nodding to include Loch in the statement. "It'll get, I don't want to say 'better,' but you'll get used to it."

"Used to it *hurting*," Spirit said. She inhaled deeply, blinking against tears.

"Yeah," Burke said, and Addie nodded in sympathy. Addie had been orphaned three years ago, and Burke had been an orphan all his life—he had a set of foster parents in the Outside World that he talked about going back to once he graduated.

"I kind of wish it *did* hurt," Loch said quietly. Loch was the only other one of the five of them who'd lost his family recently, and all Loch had lost—as he'd be the first to say—was a father he hadn't been close to. Benjamin Spears had left his only son to be raised by a series of exclusive private schools. Oakhurst wasn't much of a change for Loch. Aside from the magic, of course.

At least Loch has his magic. I'm the only person at a whole school for magicians who can't cast a single spell.

It was true. The first thing that happened to you once you reached Oakhurst was getting tested to find out which School you had an "affinity" for. There were four of them: Earth, Air, Fire, and Water. The School you belonged to determined what kind of magic you had: Addie was School of Water, a Water Witch, while Muirin's ability to cast perfect illusions meant her powers belonged to the School of Air, and Burke's Combat Magery put him in the School of Earth.

Even Loch had passed his tests with flying colors. He had what they called minor Gifts from two Schools: Shadewalking, and Kenning, from the School of Air, and Pathfinding from the School of Earth.

Spirit hadn't had an affinity for any School at all.

"So . . . before the concert we've got that religious service, right?" Spirit said, just to change the subject.

"Not really religious, but yeah," Burke replied. "That's ten to eleven-thirty, then the concert's from twelve to two, then dinner at two-thirty. Fifty different spoons, the whole formal thing."

"It'll be fun," Muirin said, looking up from drowning her waffles in syrup to make a disgusted face.

Spirit nodded glumly. When it all came down to it, in the last year she'd lost her family, Loch had lost his father, Muirin had lost her friend Seth, and all of them had known most of the victims of the Wild Hunt.

There really didn't seem much to celebrate.

❊

The "religious service" made Spirit uncomfortable—and not just in the butt-numbing, having to sit on hard wooden pews for two hours way, but in a kind of soul-numbing way. She'd never been raised to be more than vaguely "spiritual," but services at Oakhurst always seemed wrong in a way she couldn't define, as if the entire thing was a smirky, mocking, yet somehow mind-deadening parody of a real religious service. Yet at the same time there wasn't a single thing that someone—whether they were devout or not—could have pointed to as being overtly insulting. She knew Burke was the only one of the five of them who was really religious, and even he couldn't say there was anything wrong with the Oakhurst services. They were all so *very* bland and inoffensive.

The concert that followed was pretty much identical to the one at Thanksgiving. Different music, but it sounded the same—like elevator music. *It's just like the Christmas service,* Spirit thought, with an odd air of discovery. *It's all stuff that might have started out being good or interesting but now it's had all the life sucked out of it. . . .*

By the time they were let out of the concert, Spirit was feeling like a marathon runner entering the final stretch of the race. *Only two more things to get through.* The Formal Dinner would have been okay if merely eating hadn't been an ordeal—and if Spirit had had any appetite for it. Like at Thanksgiving, there were place cards and assigned seating and extra-formal place settings, but even Dylan wasn't his usual vicious self. *I guess everyone thinks about their family at Christmas.* She took servings of everything she was offered—you weren't allowed to refuse anything, on the grounds that you were "broadening your gustatory horizons"—and just pushed it around on her plate with her fork until the potatoes and the vegetables were a beige mush. Then she covered them with the pieces of roast goose. At Thanksgiving, the meal had ended with pumpkin and mince pie. For Christmas, there'd be something called a Viennese Table set up in the dining room after the gifts were handed out. Spirit didn't think she'd have any appetite for that, either.

Now there was just one more thing to endure before she could go back to her room and indulge herself by being completely miserable and crying until she puked. One of the worst things about Oakhurst was that the Administration kept pretending that the school's money could make up for losing your family and your whole *life*. One of the ways they did that—*tried* to do that—was by giving all the students Christmas gifts, even though they didn't even bother to pretend anyone here knew you well enough to pick them out. No, the staff sent around a memo with guidelines and a list of "approved" gifts, and told everyone to pick three items. Not that they'd get all three. No. Despite the fact Oakhurst was rolling in money, each student got one "approved" gift from the Administration. They were probably told to pick three just so there'd be a little suspense.

I don't want an iPod or a pair of socks! I want Mom and Dad and Phoenix back!

Spirit wasn't even sure what she'd chosen from the list. Thinking about Christmas without her family had been so painful she'd just blanked on it and wasn't sure what she'd put down. Books and music, probably, to replace things she'd lost when her home burned down after The Accident. She wouldn't have come to the "gift-giving" at all if she could have avoided it. But she couldn't. *Everything not compulsory is forbidden,* she thought with a despairing flash of humor. *1984* had been one of Dad's favorite books, and he'd taught her to love it, too. She'd been surprised, on coming here, to find Muirin loved it as well. It seemed to be just as odd a choice for a Goth girl from New Jersey as it was for a reluctant hippie kid from Indiana.

✻

There were about a hundred kids here at Oakhurst. It seemed like a lot when you thought about the fact that they were going to be your nearest and dearest until you left

Oakhurst at twenty-one. *Or get sacrificed to demons. Hey, anything to get out of SATs, right?* It didn't seem like many when you thought about the fact that most high schools had about three times that many students.

It *really* didn't seem like many when they were all gathered in the Entry Hall and the place still echoed.

The Entry Hall was the first thing you saw when you came to Oakhurst. It was about sixty feet across, and its focal point was the biggest single tree trunk that Spirit had ever seen. It seemed to hold up the ceiling—which was at least thirty feet away. Behind the tree-pillar was a balcony stretching the breadth of the room with two half-circle staircases leading up to it. The rest of the ceiling was crossed with peeled-log beams—Loch had said the first time they saw it that Oakhurst was done in a style called "Arts and Crafts Lodge"—and between the rustic beams were panels of parquetry in vaguely Egyptian patterns. The floor was done in the same design, only in shades of green and gray stone instead of wood.

On the right side of the Entry Hall—as you came in—were the huge double doors that led to Doctor Ambrosius's office. On the left there was a stone fireplace more than big enough to park a horse in—or roast one. Hung above the fireplace was a huge banner with the Oakhurst coat of arms on it. Spirit hadn't liked the design the first time she saw it, and she liked it less now. (Loch called it "faux armigerous," whatever that meant.) The coat of arms appeared on everything at Oakhurst, including bedspreads, bathrobes, and towels, though most of the time it wasn't in color. The banner had the whole deal though: a red shield with a white diagonal stripe across it, an oak tree colored bright green and brown like a picture in a kid's book, and a bright yellow—or gold—snake coiled in the branches. On top of the shield there was a bear's head on a plate (brown head, silver plate, red blood). On the left side of the shield there was a gold upside-down cup, and on the right side there was a broken silver sword. *Way to impress the parents. Oh, I totally forgot. None of us has any parents to impress. . . .*

The log-and-leather couches that usually sat in front of the fireplace—though Spirit had never seen anyone sit in them—had been removed to make way for the Christmas tree. It looked like a tree in a movie, and that was another odd thing in a school that didn't believe in holidays: The Oakhurst tree was a gigantic blue spruce, tall enough to reach most of the way to the ceiling, and every inch of it was decorated. Not with a bunch of Kmart–Wally World plastic junk, either: The ornaments were glass, antique, and probably cost more than the last *Star Wars* movie.

All around it were presents, and Spirit saw, with a faint despairing disbelief, that no matter the design on the wrapping paper, every present under the tree was wrapped in the Oakhurst school colors: brown, gold, and cream. . . .

Since the couches were gone, there wasn't anyplace to sit. They'd all filed into the Entry Hall by the same alphabetical order they'd been seated at for the dinner, but once they were there, Burke beckoned to Spirit, and she saw that Loch and Addie were standing with him. Muirin joined them a few minutes later, looking—as usual—as if she were getting away with something. About half the other kids had shuffled around, too—maybe Oakhurst wouldn't care if you had friends on Christmas Day—but most of them still looked as if they were trying to pretend they didn't know anyone here. Conversation was kept to a subdued murmur.

That conversation died out completely with the entrance of Doctor Ambrosius. He was flanked by his assistants, Ms. Corby and Mr. Devon. Doctor Ambrosius looked like a venerable old college professor, white beard, flowing white hair, tweed jacket with leather elbow patches, and all. Ms. Corby and Mr. Devon looked—well, like bodyguards. Bored bodyguards. Ms. Corby was one of the few non-magicians here at Oakhurst. She was Doctor Ambrosius's personal assistant. Mr. Devon was also the supervisor of the Boys' Dorm Wing. Or, as they called them here at Oakhurst, "Young Gentlemen."

Doctor Ambrosius—and his bodyguards—walked over to stand in front of the fireplace. He gazed out at them for a moment, then cleared his throat meaningfully. Absolute silence descended.

"We are here to celebrate the end of another calendar year here at Oakhurst," he said, in a voice as smooth and reassuring as a documentary narrator on Discovery Channel. "Some of you haven't been with us long, and some are extended residents, but all of you are part of the Oakhurst family. Indeed, following the deaths of your parents, Oakhurst *is* your family now."

He beamed at all of them, but the moment his gaze had gone to another part of the room, Loch leaned over to whisper in Spirit's ear.

"Does he practice being that tactless, or does it come naturally?"

Spirit grimaced and shrugged.

"So, as the old year ends, and the new one begins, we pause for a time of remembrance. Remember—always—that it is your responsibility to live up to the high standards that other members of your Oakhurst family have set. An Oakhurst graduate who is merely average is one who has failed. An Oakhurst graduate soars where others plod. And an Oakhurst student can never rest on his accomplishments, for while he is resting, others are overtaking him."

He paused, and Ms. Corby signaled what was expected of them by initiating a patter of light applause.

"Now, in the generous spirit of the season and your family," Doctor Ambrosius concluded, beaming on them all again, "let us commence with the distribution of gifts."

While Ms. Corby and Mr. Devon handed out the gifts, Spirit stood there feeling a kind of bemused horror. She'd expected some kind of announcement about the Wild Hunt during the service, but when it hadn't come, she'd assumed there would be one here. But there wasn't. When the kids had disappeared— Seth and Camilla just since Spirit had come here, and that wasn't counting Nicholas and Eddie, who were alive but mind-blasted—Oakhurst had covered things up with lies that were meant to be reassuring. And maybe they'd had a good reason at the time, and maybe they'd even believed that Seth and Camilla ran away. But now that she and the others had defeated the Wild Hunt, and Doctor Ambrosius *knew* what had happened to everyone, Spirit had expected some kind of announcement. Wasn't the Wild Hunt a part of what they were being trained to defend themselves against? Didn't its appearance mean they should all be warned to be extra careful?

But there'd been nothing. Not one word about their classmates who were *dead*. Not one word about the fact that there were people here—and she'd even been one of them—who'd been marked for death at the hands of the Wild Hunt. It was just: too bad, so sad, you've lost your real families, people you knew, there's someone—probably inside the school!—that wants to kill you all, just forget about it, here's your iPod or your digital camera or your makeup kit or your Wii.

Even her own friends hadn't talked about what it all *meant*. Okay, maybe they were kind of in shock, but now they *knew*. Oakhurst wasn't safe. The enemies Doctor Ambrosius had talked about weren't out there. They were in here. Killing people. If the five of them wanted to live long enough to graduate—not to mention everyone else here living to graduate—they had to find out what was really going on. She knew they'd all been lied to. But adults lied to kids all the time, playing the "it's for your own good" card. Those kinds of lies were annoying, but they didn't mean the person lying to them was out to kill them.

But some people here were.

Who could they trust?

Muirin had mentioned a secret society within Oakhurst

called the Gatekeepers. Loch said secret societies were common at private schools and at colleges. There was Skull and Bones at Yale, for example, or the Seven Society at the University of Virginia. But if the Gatekeepers were—as the others seemed to believe—just a kind of "honor society," why wasn't it made public? The students here were encouraged—were forced, really—to compete with each other at everything. It didn't make sense that Oakhurst would miss an opportunity to make them compete with each other to join the Gatekeepers.

She hated the whole idea of seeing the world in terms of Good Guys and Bad Guys—as if she was living in a *Star Wars* movie, and you were either a Sith Lord or a Jedi Knight. But there didn't seem to be a lot of middle ground. Were the Gatekeepers Good Guys or Bad Guys? What did they have to do with the Alumni who visited here every summer?

What happened to all the kids who—supposedly—graduated? They never wrote to their friends. Nobody here got any mail.

They had to start figuring out what was going on. *Now*— before whoever it was who had been behind the Wild Hunt came up with a new way to kill them.

Could they trust their fellow students? Maybe some. But which ones? Could they trust the teachers? Doctor Ambrosius? Half the time he was scary as all get-out, ranting on about the Final Battle. The other half of the time he was a doddering old man who couldn't even remember your name. Was he another victim of the Bad Guys? If so, how could they possibly rescue him?

She was so lost in her own thoughts that it wasn't until

Loch nudged her sharply in the ribs that she noticed Ms. Corby standing in front of her with a look of impatience and irritation on her face. She was holding two small boxes wrapped in gold paper with a cream-and-brown design on it (the Oakhurst coat of arms, of course).

For a moment Spirit locked eyes with Doctor Ambrosius's assistant. She wanted to say that she didn't want Oakhurst's gifts and she didn't want to be here, either. But she didn't quite dare. She reached out for the gifts. Ms. Corby held on to them, staring at her meaningfully.

"Thank you, Ms. Corby," Spirit said, flushing angrily. Ms. Corby smiled in triumph and handed Spirit the boxes before turning away. Spirit's last name began with "W," so there weren't too many more gifts to hand out.

Spirit looked around at the others. Addie had a long flat box under one arm. It was about the size and shape of a board game. Burke was holding a large square box, a cube about twelve inches on a side. Muirin had a small box about three by three by ten.

And Loch had two boxes identical to hers in every way— except for the fact that they were wrapped in dark brown paper with the design on them in cream and gold. She and Loch exchanged a look, and for the first time today, Spirit felt like smiling. It really was idiotic for anyplace to be so logo-obsessed that it even had *wrapping paper* with its coat of arms on it. In half a dozen different designs, no less!

Loch brandished the larger of the two boxes.

"iPod?" Spirit mouthed.

Loch was about to answer, but Mr. Devon had stepped up in front of the fireplace.

"Every winner—and you're all winners here at Oakhurst—knows that one of the sweetest fruits of victory is the chance to kick back and enjoy what they've won. All of you have worked hard this year. Now is the time to enjoy yourselves. A dessert buffet is set up in the Refectory. Enjoy!" he added, clapping his hands together and smiling brightly.

Spirit thought it was the creepiest thing she'd seen—at least in the last few days.

Ms. Corby strode off ahead of Doctor Ambrosius, and Mr. Devon followed. When Doctor Ambrosius's study doors closed behind them, everyone began to shuffle in place and head in the direction of the Refectory. Muirin was off like a flash, of course. Unlimited sugar.

"Yup. iPod," Loch said, unwrapping the larger of the two boxes. "It's the Gift du Jour."

The "Gift du Jour" was brown, with the Oakhurst crest engraved on the back, and his name: *Lachlan Galen Spears*. Loch made a face, and Spirit winced in sympathy. It was awful to have a dorky name.

"They come in gold and cream, too, of course," Addie said kindly. "If you don't have one when you get here, you're pretty much guaranteed to get one for your first Christmas."

"Huh," Loch said, sounding surprised. "It's charged. And preloaded."

There was no real point in trying to push through the mob of students heading for the Refectory, and one thing Spirit could say for Oakhurst was that when it decided to let them fall off the healthy diet bandwagon, it didn't stint on the junk food. There was no need to hurry—there'd be more sugar and chocolate than all of them could eat in a week.

Bread and circuses. For a moment she could hear Mom's voice in her head. Mom had—used to have—a saying for every occasion. In Ancient Rome, the emperors used to keep the people from making trouble by giving them free food and free entertainment. Bread and circuses.

That's what we get, Spirit thought. *Every few weeks there's another school dance, and a lot of candy, and most of the kids don't look past that, to all the things that are wrong with this place. . . .*

"What color is yours?" Loch asked. With a feeling of resignation, Spirit unwrapped the larger of the two boxes. Her iPod was cream-colored. Same crest cut into the back, and her name: *Spirit Victory White.* She didn't bother to complain, even mentally, that now everyone at Oakhurst would know her middle name. "Victory" was just about as awful as "Spirit"—she'd always hated her name—but maybe someday she could just tell people her name was "Vicky" or something. She woke her iPod and looked at the preloaded playlist.

"Ah, I recognize this," she said mockingly, scanning the start of the list of titles. "This is next semester's Music History stuff."

"Heaven forbid we should actually use these for recreation," Addie said, her voice dripping with irony. "That would be frivolous. However could we expect to excel?"

"Ah, but you forget. We're all already winners here at Oakhurst," Loch replied, deadpan.

"Come on," Burke said. "It's cleared out a little, and we should go find the Murr-cat and stop her from eating herself into sugar shock."

"Fat chance of that," Addie answered.

🌸

The Refectory was full, but not crowded. Most of the crowd was around the dessert buffet, and Spirit had to admit it looked pretty. There were cakes on stands, pies, plates of brownies and blondies and cookies, pyramids of perfectly round scoops of ice cream frozen so hard that it would take them at least half an hour to melt, boxes of chocolates and marzipan shaped like fruit, and—because this was a school full of teenagers—stacked cases of soda.

The four of them, by mutual consent, took one of the empty tables at the opposite end of the room from the buffet table. Muirin saw them, waved, and came over, carrying two plates heaped high with goodies, including a stack of brownies topped with scoops of ice cream, hot fudge, and whipped cream.

"I don't see how you can eat all that," Addie said with a sigh as Muirin plopped down at the table opposite her.

"Practice," Muirin answered. She pushed the second plate toward them. It was stacked with plain brownies of various kinds.

Spirit picked up the top one—marbled and studded with M&Ms—and bit into it. She didn't have much of an appetite, but hey: chocolate. *Bread and circuses,* her mother's voice whispered in her mind.

"So, come on, open your other one!" Muirin urged around a mouthful of fudge and ice cream.

Spirit had almost forgotten about the second box. Why had she and Loch both gotten two when no one else had? She tore the paper off quickly. Inside it was a pasteboard box, and inside that was a tiny wooden jewelry box—a ring box—with the Oakhurst crest (what a shock) laser-cut into the top.

She opened it.

Inside, on a bed of black velvet, was what looked like . . . a class ring. Well, a really *nice* class ring, not the cheesy ones the high school kids back in Indiana had, the kind with fake stones, set into rings made out of some cheesy-yet-fancy-sounding made-up metal like "Valadium" or "Endurium." She lifted it out of its box and inspected it curiously. It was gold—when she looked inside the band, she saw it was stamped 24K—and felt heavy, very heavy. On the sides of the band were the broken sword and the inverted cup from the Oakhurst coat of arms. The bezel of the ring said: ABSOLUTUM DOMINIUM.

"Absolute dominion," Loch translated. He'd opened his own box and was looking at his ring curiously.

With everything else about the ring being so lavish, Spirit would have expected the stone to be something she recognized, something real. But to her surprise, it looked like something "lab created." It was opaque like an opal, a strange glittery sort of opalescent blue, the kind of thing that made you think there were other colors in it, only no matter how hard you looked, you couldn't see them. . . .

Spirit tore her eyes away with an effort and stuffed the ring back into the box and closed it. It made her uneasy for reasons she couldn't quite understand. She saw Loch slip his on—of course it fit perfectly—and bit back the impulse to cry out a warning. Against what?

"Oh, they gave you your rings," Muirin said offhandedly.

"Our rings?" Loch repeated, staring at his hand as if he was fascinated.

"Hey, open your stuff first!" Muirin demanded. "Look what I got!"

"You'd think they wouldn't want to encourage you," Addie murmured, as Muirin brandished the kit of makeup brushes and manicure tools. But she ripped the paper off her box gleefully, revealing a Monopoly set. It was the fanciest one Spirit had ever seen, with a wooden box and gold-colored counters.

"I get really tired of using the ones in the Games Library," Addie said, grinning. "There are always a couple of pieces missing, and not enough Monopoly Money to get through a full game."

She looked at Burke expectantly. He opened his gift methodically, prying the tape loose from the ends and folding the paper carefully.

"You got a *football*?" Muirin asked in disbelief. "This place has footballs coming out of its . . . ears."

"Yeah, but not like this," Burke said. "This is the old style, the one they stopped using around 1930. The modern one is more lightweight and streamlined." He hefted it appreciatively.

"Okay," Loch said, in tones that made it clear he didn't really get it. "But about the rings . . . ?"

"Okay. Class rings. We all get them at some point in our first year at Oakhurst," Burke said.

"Why don't you wear them, then?" Loch wanted to know.

"Because they're dorky," Muirin said with contempt. "I mean, come *on*. Class rings? That's so Fifties!"

"But—"

"Come on, Murr-cat," Addie said decisively. "You guys guard Muir's sugar-hoard. We'll be right back."

Muirin rolled her eyes, but followed Addie out of the room, while Burke continued. "You don't have to wear them, except for a couple of times a year—like Alumni Days, when we're doing the full School Uniform thing, with the blazer and scarf and everything, like we were—"

"—on the playing fields of Eton," Loch finished for him, in a broad fake English accent. Burke grinned at him.

"Some people wear them all the time, some don't," Burke continued. "The point about them is that they're . . . kind of magic. The stone changes color until it matches your School of Magic."

Great. A wizardly mood ring, Spirit thought.

"It does?" Loch stared at his hand again. "Try yours, Spirit," he urged.

Reluctantly, she reopened the box and slipped it on. It felt cold and heavy against her hand—much colder and heavier than she thought it should.

A few minutes later, Muirin and Addie returned; Muirin

thrust her hand under Spirit's nose and wiggled her fingers. Her ring was identical to Spirit's, except for the fact that the stone was a pale lemon yellow. It seemed to have faint sparkles caught down in the stone. "School of Air," she announced.

"Mine's green," Burke said. "Earth, you know? Addie's is blue, but a deeper blue than—"

Suddenly, Addie squeaked. She smothered the sound immediately, but thrust her hand at them. "Look!" she whispered, half in excitement, half in alarm.

Just as Burke had said, the stone in Addie's ring was a deep translucent sapphire blue instead of the pale opal blue of the stone in Spirit and Loch's rings. But as Spirit stared down into it, she could see there was an image in it, too. It looked as if it had been engraved on the underside of the stone.

It was the image of a goblet, just like the one on the Oakhurst coat of arms.

"Holy Toledo, Addie!" Burke breathed. Spirit had never heard him sound so shocked.

"I know . . ." Addie gulped, staring at her hand. "I have a Destiny."

"A what?" Spirit was puzzled. Addie'd said it as if the word "destiny" was capitalized. Did that mean you were especially powerful? She could sure believe that of Addie. . . .

"Oh hey," Muirin said, trying not to sound impressed and failing. Out of the corner of her eye, Spirit saw Muirin slip her own ring off and stuff it into her pocket.

"Is this like a 'it is your Destiny, Luke,' thing?" Loch asked.

"Kind of," Addie said hesitantly, staring at her hand.

"I heard a couple of the seniors talking about it a while back," Burke said. "It's something Ms. Groves teaches you about in your last year here. You can ask her about it if you like."

"No thanks," Spirit said. "I've already had enough extra assignments dumped on me." Ms. Groves taught the "History of Magic" courses, as well as teaching magic itself. Any time she thought you weren't interested enough, you got hit with an extra assignment on top of the stunning amount of homework the Oakhurst faculty already assigned.

Burke grinned a little at her comment. "So anyway, what I know is, if a Destiny appears in your ring, it means your future is pretty much set. Fixed. Unchangeable."

"It's not always good," Muirin said, her face unreadable. "Trailer Trash had a Destiny."

"Trailer Trash" was Muirin's cruel name for Camilla Patton—one of the victims of the Wild Hunt. "She showed me once. She thought it meant she was going to turn into a wolf. Stupid b—"

"Hey, look," Loch said, interrupting Muirin—probably on purpose. "My ring's already starting to turn!"

Sure enough, the pale blue was starting to change. Right now it was a pale greenish color: Loch's main Gifts came from the School of Air, so his stone would probably turn as yellow as Muirin's was.

Spirit looked down at her own ring. The stone remained a cool, serene blue.

тwo

It took Muirin about half an hour to wolf down three heap-ing plates of gooey sugary treats. On her last trip back to their table she brought two more plates heaped so high with brownies and chocolates that Spirit was amazed they didn't spill. It was obvious Muirin was settling in for the long haul, and with good reason: You couldn't take anything out of the Refectory—though you could eat as much as you wanted while you were here—so most of the other kids were hanging around, too. Spirit didn't have any appetite for the desserts, but the chance to mainline as much Diet Pepsi as she wanted was too good to pass up.

When Addie said she wanted to try out her new Monop-oly game, it didn't take much coaxing for her to get all of them to agree to play, because really, it was a game with them Ad-die wanted for Christmas, not the set itself. Addie chose the

Moneybag token (with a faint smirk), and Loch chose the Top Hat (with an ironic bow). Burke chose the Race Car (he was from Indianapolis, home of the Indianapolis 500), and Muirin (surprisingly) chose the Scottie Dog. Spirit didn't care what piece she picked, so just reached in and grabbed one at random. It turned out to be the Cannon. *I wish I did have a cannon,* she thought with irritation. *I'd blow up Oakhurst.* Unfortunately, that wouldn't really solve anything. She tried to concentrate on the game, but her mind kept wandering—and not to good places. She was just as glad she'd taken her new ring off again—Loch hadn't, and he kept looking at it with an expression of pleased wonder that was kind of sick-making. She wondered if Loch would find a "Destiny" in his stone when it finished changing color. Hearing about them had absolutely creeped her out.

And at least part of what creeped her out was that no one else seemed creeped out. She wouldn't have known if the other kids were—from what Burke had said, you weren't even supposed to know what a "Destiny" was until your Senior Year here—but even her friends just seemed to shrug the whole idea off.

That wasn't all they were shrugging off, either. They'd defeated the Wild Hunt *three days ago.* They should still have been trying to deal with their very-near-death experience at the cadaverous claws of a collection of ghosts, demons, and—oh yeah—evil elves. She certainly was! She'd had nightmares about the battle in the snow every single night. But from the way the other four acted—and everything they said—it was as if that fight had happened three years ago, not three days ago. And that was just crazy.

She wanted a break. Needed a break. They'd taken on one of the nastier things in Celtic mythology—and won—and an all-expenses-paid month in Disney World—anywhere but here!—was the least of the things she would have liked as a follow-up. But she had the horrid feeling that things were only going to get worse from here on in. And fast.

So . . . get a break? Shoot, she hadn't even gotten enough time to sit down and *think*. Too much wasn't adding up, and that was terrifying. If the Wild Hunt showing up the way it had was the start of the wizard war, why wasn't Doctor Ambrosius stocking up on magical nukes and having everyone build barricades? (Or, hey, just warning people, because that'd be nice.) And if the people here were the good wizards, where were all the bad wizards coming from? Didn't anybody care?

She frowned, tuning out the sound of Loch and Muirin arguing—just as if it mattered—about whose turn it was, and whether or not Loch owed Muirin rent. There was another thing that had been bothering her for a while. If the only kids allowed here were magicians, but all the children of former Oakhurst students were eligible to come to Oakhurst, where did the kids who weren't magicians go? Was there another school—a kind of Shadow Oakhurst—where the non-magical kids were sent?

"—so I got permission to have Admin ask the Trust peeps to send my formals, and—*quelle surprise*—she actually did, and I only fit the black one anymore," Muirin was saying, as Spirit tuned back in to the conversation. "But that's okay, since the others are like so last century and you gotta know if I fit one of them, that'd be the one Ms. Corby'd say I had to wear." Muirin shuddered. "Seafoam! Come *on!* Maybe if I was thirteen and still into Magical Girl animé!"

Spirit frowned harder. *Formals?* What was Muirin going on about?

"The Trust sent me another new one," Addie said, sighing faintly. "Just like the old one, only blue this time."

Spirit glanced around the table. The guys were exchanging "I hope they're not going to talk about dresses all night" looks. *Formals? We escaped death three days ago and they're talking about—*

"You guys seriously aren't talking about the *New Year's Dance* are you?" she asked incredulously.

Muirin gave her a slanty look. "Why not? We get graded on it, you know. Ballroom dancing, deportment, blah blah blah."

"Don't worry. You won't get graded on the dancing, Spirit," Addie said in a kindly tone of voice. "You weren't here for the Summer Term, so you didn't get Ballroom Dance. They only give it in the Summer Term."

Spirit was so shocked all she could do was stare at the two of them with her mouth slightly open. "But we—But you—" She gathered her scattered thoughts. "But— We can't just go on as if nothing happened! It isn't over! You know it isn't over!"

She would have said even more, but suddenly a sharp pain in her ankle interrupted her—Loch had *kicked* her!—and his equally sharp elbow hit her in the ribs for the second time that day.

"Let's get something to drink," he said. "That diet stuff might be okay for *some* people, but *Real Men* want *real* high fructose corn syrup." He grabbed her wrist and practically hauled her out of her seat and off toward the Viennese Table. By now there wasn't a mob of kids surrounding it, but about half the Refectory tables were full. They weren't the only ones here playing a board game, and she glimpsed some kids playing card games, or just reading books and listening to music, either on Oakhurst iPods (easy to spot, since they were in custom colors) or on ones of their own.

Loch dragged her past the table, over by the kitchen doors. It was about as private as they could get without leaving. And the others would notice that—their table was right by the door.

"What do you think you're—" she began, as soon as he stopped.

"Leave them alone, Spirit," he hissed in an undertone. "You deal with stuff your way, let them deal with it their way."

She blinked at him. This was the last thing she would have expected to hear, from the last person she'd have expected to hear it from. "But, Loch—"

"Don't you 'but' me, Spirit White! Yeah, the New Year's Dance is stupid, but if that's what they want to focus on, *you let them*. Get it? If they want denial, whose job is it to tell them they can't have it? Yours? Are you some kind of super-shrink now? Are you going to tell me you can help them deal when you can't even stop moping around over your family and *that's* half a year ago? Okay, we saw awful things, we almost died, but we won, game over, now let it go."

The injustice of Loch's accusation made her want to erupt with anger—just because he didn't care whether or not he'd been orphaned didn't mean she hadn't loved her family and didn't still miss them—and it took all her willpower to answer him instead of slapping his face and storming off. "But it's not over! Loch, you *know* it's not over! We still have to—"

"I don't know any such thing." Loch pulled himself up to his full height and folded his arms over his chest. "I know none of us—including you!—knows what Doctor Ambrosius and the teachers did after we told him what happened. I know they're a million times better magicians than we are. And I know all this time he's been *telling* us there's danger out there. So what do you know? Did you follow all of them around for the last three days and see they *aren't* taking what we told them seriously and beefing up the security? Have you got some kind of super Magic 8-Ball you can listen in on the meetings with?"

"But— But—" *But why do you think they'll take it seriously now when kids were vanishing for the last forty years and nobody cared? Why do you want to trust them when we know one of them was in league with the Wild Hunt? How can you think they're going to take us seriously after you saw the basement, with all the dead kids' stuff stored down there and their school records stamped "Tithed"?* How could she explain any of this if he was so determined to deny what he'd seen with his own eyes? How could she make him see she wasn't being crazy or paranoid, that all of her instincts were shouting at her that this wasn't the end, it was only the beginning. *What am I going to do if I have to do this all alone?*

At the expression on her face, Loch's softened a little. "Look, Spirit, I understand why you're doing this. Your magic hasn't developed yet and you feel like you're the only normal kid in Super-Hero High. And you *did* get us all together and get us to see there was something wrong, and I know that had to feel pretty damn good. And it must have felt even better to face down those things *without* magic—and I'm not lying when I say if you hadn't been there, we'd all be dead now. Nobody wants to take that away from you. But you have to accept that, well, you *did* win. It's over. And trying to relive it and make it happen again so you don't have to think about not having your magic yet is . . . it's *unworthy* of you, Spirit. Just be patient. Your magic will show up soon enough. Meanwhile, it's time to let go and stop trying to get attention and make yourself feel special by coming up with crazy conspiracy theories." He smiled faintly. "We like you whether you have magic or not."

He thinks this is all about me? That I'm just thinking of myself, and about not having magic? That this is all some sick way for me to try to get attention by crying wolf and making up imaginary enemies? She was so outraged by his accusation that for a moment her voice wouldn't work.

"Is that what you *really* think?" she finally choked out. "That I'm acting out because I *don't have magic?*" She stared hard into his eyes until he was the one who had to look away. "Well. Then what about this: Someone set up all those kids as sacrifices to the Hunt. It didn't get here all the way from Ireland or Wales or whatever by itself. And someone opened the wards so *it could get onto the school grounds.* And whoever that was, *we never found them.* Do you think they're going to stop now? Do you think the Administration can find them? What if it *is* the Administration—or some of it?"

"I—" It was Loch's turn to be at a loss for words. "I don't know—"

"Whoever called the Hunt has been doing it for *years*, Loch! And Doctor Ambrosius hasn't figured out who they are, either! He would have stopped them a long time ago if he had!"

"We don't know that—" Loch said weakly.

"Yes we do!" she snapped. "We know it had to be someone inside the school to take down the wards, because they were taken down and put back up—not broken. So—if you're right, and the teachers are handling this and not telling us—who on the staff isn't here anymore?"

"Uh . . . We wouldn't notice someone gone from the kitchen or maintenance—" Loch said helplessly.

"Oh, give me a break," Spirit said in contempt. "You think someone from the kitchen or maintenance is that good a magician? We don't even know that any of them even *are* magicians—do we?"

He withered a little under her glare. "I— Um— Well—"

Now she was the one crossing her arms over her chest. "I'll take that as a 'no'—that the Housekeeping Staff *aren't* magicians. And none of the teachers or the Admin staff have 'left to pursue other opportunities' in the last three days. So? Still think I'm creating crazy conspiracies to get attention?" It made her sick with anger to think he'd actually accused her of that.

"Look, just cut Addie and Muirin some slack," he finally said. "It's not like they—*we*—aren't cutting *you* plenty."

She started to snap back at him, then forced herself to nod. As much as it galled her to admit it, there was some justice in that. All four of them had put up with a lot from her since she'd arrived at Oakhurst. And she had to admit they'd all been on board with finding out what was hunting Oakhurst students and putting a stop to it.

"Having a good Monopoly game is making Addie happy. Stuffing herself with cookies and candy until she's sick and babbling on about what she's going to wear to the prom is making Muirin happy," Loch went on. "It's Christmas, for heaven's sake, Spirit. Give them at least one day off from being The Mystery Gang. You owe them that."

Her throat suddenly filled with a big lump. "As long as I don't have to be the goofy mascot," she managed to whisper.

Loch gave her his sunniest smile—looking relieved, she thought. "Nah. I always thought of you as more the 'cute cheerleader' type."

All she could do after that was nod, and let him lead her back over to the soda table, and fill her arms with cold cans.

She followed him back to their table, still gulping back tears of grief and humiliation, and if she couldn't manage to smile and chatter cheerfully, she could at least pay attention to the game to give Addie a good one, and nod when Muirin went on about what an ordeal and a torture session the New Year's Ball was going to be.

Because, yeah, Loch was right.

She did owe them that much.

But they owed her, too.

The next day—Boxing Day—was the day when the students at Oakhurst traditionally exchanged their "personal" gifts with each other. Spirit had made book covers and matching bookmarks out of felt. Privately, she thought the gifts were a little cheesy, but they were all she could manage, and she'd wanted to give her friends something, at least. When the other girls on her floor had seen Spirit's bookmark-and-book-cover combinations, some of them had asked her to make some for them. She'd done it, even though it had taken precious time from figuring out how to destroy the Wild Hunt, because she'd been terribly conscious of needing to behave as if everything was completely normal. And since the student body at Oakhurst had a flourishing barter economy going, it had meant she at least had some pretty and colorful paper to wrap her gifts for her friends in.

By prearrangement, the five of them met in their favorite student lounge, the one beside the Library. Spirit had been worried she'd receive gifts far more elaborate and expensive than the ones she gave, but the one good thing about the draconian way Oakhurst ran things was that nobody could give expensive presents, even if they had a lot of money waiting for them in the outside world. So Loch gave her a flash drive full of music, which surprised and touched her, since she missed her music collection, and Loch had taken pains to track down (and trade for) most of her favorite songs, and Addie (who knitted) gave her a scarf that *wasn't* cream, gold, or brown: It was knitted out of soft wool and striped in every color of the rainbow. Spirit was surprised to get a second gift from Muirin, as Muirin had already given Spirit her Christmas gift a few days earlier. But now Muirin presented her with one of the Oakhurst blouses, which would have been an insulting kind of gift if Muirin hadn't covered it with intricate embroidery on the collar, the cuffs, the placket, and the back yoke. Spirit was grateful, but she couldn't help wondering if it was some subtle Muirin-type commentary on her fashion sense.

Burke gave her a necklace. He'd made it in Wood Shop, he told her after she opened it: It was a pendant in an oval shape, about two inches long, made with elaborate marquetry work and polished to a mirror smoothness.

"Figured you might like to have something to wear that, well, wasn't Oakhurst-y," he said awkwardly.

"I love it. I do," she answered, reaching out to give him an impulsive hug.

Muirin applauded mockingly—drawing irritated hisses from the other kids in the lounge, since even on Boxing Day there were always people studying—and Burke pulled away, blushing.

"Um, so, it's kind of stuffy in here, isn't it?" he said clumsily. "Want to go outside and—uh, look at the stuff?"

"What, go out where it's cold enough to freeze your assets off and pretend the snow statues haven't been there for the last three weeks?" Muirin mocked. "No, thanks. *I* am staying right here where it is nice and warm."

"I—" Loch began, and to her astonishment, out of the corner of her eye Spirit saw *Addie's* elbow connect with *Loch's* ribs, hard and fast. After what had happened Christmas Day, it was actually gratifying to see Loch on the receiving end of a "shut up" elbow. But why? . . .

"You two go out and freeze your toesies off in the nice healthy subzero air," Addie said cheerfully, as Loch gave her a look of blank astonishment. "The rest of us will keep the fire going for you."

Burke hadn't missed the byplay, either, Spirit noticed—the color was back in his cheeks. If she'd met him back in Indiana (while she'd still been going to public school, before Dad decided the School Board wasn't fit to raise hyenas, let alone set curricula), she'd never have given him a second glance. Sure, he was really good-looking—in a football-player way—but he was also quiet, bashful, self-effacing, and devout. *So* not what she'd been looking for in a boyfriend!

But that had been when she was fourteen, not almost seventeen. When she'd still had a family, when magic was something you only found in books, before she'd come to Oakhurst and found out she'd been drafted into a wizard war and there were people out to kill her. She hadn't made up her mind about whether she wanted any boyfriend at all—let alone Burke Hallows—but now she didn't automatically dismiss him as too boring to be likable.

Burke walked her down to the Entry Hall, where the two of them separated to get their coats—and in Spirit's case, to get every other warm thing she could think of to bundle up in, because nothing in her life had prepared her for the cold of a Montana winter—and then met up again just inside the front door. Most of the Winter Carnival was on what would be the "front lawn" of any other place, but in the case of Oakhurst, it was the "front acreage." It was almost as if the school was trying to shout to any (rare) visitor, "Look! See our Happy Students! See them Frolic at the Winter Carnival! And see how they are so much better at this than *your* kids are!"

No wonder everyone from Radial hates us, she thought sourly. *A few visits to Oakhurst and they'd have to be thinking we're a bunch of stuck-up rich kids.* She supposed they were lucky that Radial was twenty miles away as the crow flew—an odd expression she'd never understood—and thirty-five by road—when the road was even passable, which it really wasn't for a lot of the winter. There was a reason everybody at Oakhurst used the private railroad set up by Arthur Tyniger, the nineteenth-century railway tycoon who'd built the place.

She stepped out the front door, blinking at the bright glare of sun on snow. When she'd gotten here four months ago, the front lawn—the Oakhurst literature referred to it as the "Grand Lawn," big whoop—had been as green and flawless as Astro-Turf. When it started to snow, it had been just the same (only white)—a smooth sloping expanse leading down to the front gate.

Now? Now it had been turned into a showpiece, a set piece, and once again Spirit wondered just *who* the Oakhurst Staff and Faculty were trying to impress, because really, there wasn't anybody here but them. Even the Alumni didn't visit until summer. Despite that, it was almost obscene, how professional—how *posed*—the scene before her looked.

First of all, the whole Carnival had been carefully laid out beforehand by the teachers, with each piece of the Carnival to be placed exactly so. None of the ice sculptures were allowed to be an inch off the centers of their allotted spaces, and they all had to face the carefully sculpted and groomed avenue that threaded through them. Spirit supposed (grudgingly) the avenue was a good idea, since it was carpeted with pale blue AstroTurf so no one slipped and broke something. The thing was, Spirit had seen pictures of professional competitions in Sapporo and Montreal that hadn't looked any better than this, and she wished she could stop wondering what invisible watchers Oakhurst was trying to impress, but she couldn't. *Maybe they're just trying to suck all the fun out of it,* she thought. Loch liked to quote something he called "The Litany Against Fun" (it was from a parody of a science fiction novel he liked): *"I must not have fun. Fun is the time-killer. I will forget fun. I will take a pass on it. When fun is gone only I will remain—I, and my will to win . . ."*

She wondered if Oakhurst had read the same books, because not only was the Carnival laid out with all the spontaneity of a chessboard, all the kids who had to do the Carnival (three-person teams, whose Gifts were mostly from the School of Air and the School of Water, though there were a few Fire Witches involved) were given a theme and not allowed to deviate from it. This year's theme was "Famous Statues and Monuments" (Spirit had seen it because Addie had to compete, of course) and the handout had been very clear that the statue of the little Belgian boy taking a whiz—the *Manneken Pis*—was *so* not on the list. So there was the armless Venus de Milo, and the headless Winged Nike (Addie's team had done Laocoön and His Sons, but Spirit was already pretty much on board with the idea that Addie was a major-league overachiever), the statue of the Little Mermaid from Copenhagen, the Sphinx from Giza (with its face miraculously restored, though Spirit thought it would have been more of a challenge to reproduce the battered and eroded version), the Lincoln Memorial from Washington D.C., and—probably the most ambitious of all, because of the almost-unsupported "zodiacal zone" ring—the reproduction of Prometheus, who loomed over the Oakhurst skating rink just like he did over the one at Rockefeller Center.

In keeping with Oakhurst's general suck-all-the-fun-out-of-this tradition, there was a little plinth in front of each statue, and each plinth had a waterproof notebook on it, and each notebook contained a five to ten page essay about the original statue, with the pages inserted neatly in clear plastic sleeves to protect them from the weather.

Not that anyone was reading them.

Behind Prometheus (extending out toward the side lawn) was the maze, a duplicate in snow of the hedge maze at Hampton Court Palace. (Spirit knew the Jaunting Witches teleported snow from all over the place so there'd be enough for everyone to work with at Oakhurst, and frankly, she thought it was a wonder there was any snow left on the ground anywhere in McBride County.) And on the other side of the maze was the snow castle.

It could have been fun. Even with all the regimentation, all the rules, all the grading as a class assignment, it *still* could have been fun. But even now, the teachers prowled among the statues taking notes, and watching the skaters, and she just knew they were even being graded on that—though she couldn't imagine what the grades were in. Advanced sense of balance? Intermediate speediness? Whether or not the Chicago Black- hawks would like to recruit you?

I am so not getting out there on the ice, she decided.

"So, um, you want to skate?" Burke asked.

She did her best not to facepalm. Guys! Every time they started to learn to read minds, they always got it completely wrong! "Not with the teachers watching," she said truthfully. "Can we just walk and pretend to read the essays? Maybe get lost in the maze?"

"Sure!" Burke said, more cheerfully than her suggestion really called for.

The two of them walked along the AstroTurfed path, pausing at each plinth to leaf through the essay books as if they were reading them. Even though Burke was carefully not touching her—not even getting too close—he kept glancing over at her with this soft puppy-dog look, and she was starting to get the idea that he was working his way up to talking about Feelings. She wasn't ready for that conversation right now, and she wasn't really sure whether she ever wanted to have that conversation, but the thought of what it might involve gave her a warm flut- tery feeling in her stomach. She wondered what he was going to say. She wondered what she'd say back. She wondered if—

"Hey! Burke! Spirit!"

Oh . . . damn. So much for finding out what Burke's feelings were. Or hers, for that matter. It was Kelly Langley—one of the nicer proctors—but she wasn't alone. She was more-or-less herding another girl along, kind of like a determined sheepdog with a stubborn sheep. Kelly was a Fire Witch, so she was out in only a jacket and a knitted gold Oakhurst cap, but the girl with her was bundled up to the eyebrows in so-new-it-crackled Oakhurst gear with no personalizing touches. Her shoulders were hunched, her collar was up, and her face was buried in the scarf that swaddled her almost to her ears.

New girl? Spirit wondered. Belatedly she realized she'd heard the train during breakfast this morning. But there hadn't been any kind of an announcement. . . .

Well, maybe they never make an announcement. How would I know? Loch and I were the last kids to come here. There hasn't been anyone after us. . . .

"This is Elizabeth Walker," Kelly said briskly. "She just got here this morning. Lizzie, this is Burke Hallows and Spirit White." Spirit tried not to roll her eyes; poor kid, whether or not she *liked* the nickname "Lizzie," she was going to be stuck with it now.

"Hello," came the voice faintly from behind the wool.

"I need to report to the coach, so I'll just leave her with you. I know you can show her the rest of the place," Kelly said, and without even waiting to hear them agree, she turned abruptly and strode off, not quite running, but at a "walking" pace that would leave most people gasping in her wake.

The three of them just stared awkwardly at one another for several minutes. Spirit couldn't see much of the new girl, just brown eyes and light brown hair that looked as if it was probably long. She was an inch or two taller than Spirit—which meant she'd tower over Muirin and be just about Addie's height—and in her stiff heavy coat it was hard to tell whether she was plump or thin. After the silence had stretched so long Spirit wondered if they were all going to stand there silently until they froze, Elizabeth said, in a wispy voice, "You don't have to go to all that trouble. I can find my room from here."

"No, it's okay, Elizabeth." Spirit was half amused, half miffed to see that Burke was putting on his best "big, friendly dog" routine. "We don't mind, do we, Spirit?"

"I only got here this fall myself," she admitted, a little relieved because Elizabeth's arrival had saved her from the Feelings conversation, and a little irritated for the same reason. Then, for some reason even *she* couldn't fathom, she suddenly blurted out, "I hate this place. I'd give anything to—"

Then she stopped. *Don't drag anyone else into this mess.* It was almost Loch's voice Spirit heard in her imagination, but Loch wouldn't say anything so sensible. *Especially since you don't even know her yet.*

Elizabeth nodded in a jerky sort of way. "It's not home," she said softly. "And it won't ever be. And Doctor Ambrosius . . ." She cut off whatever she was going to say, glancing skittishly from side to side as if she was looking for something. Or someone.

"Did he give you the 'Oakhurst is your family' lecture?" Spirit asked, bitterly.

Another jerky nod. Burke snorted rudely, surprising Spirit. She kept forgetting that Burke wasn't the rah-rah "Be True To Your School" guy he seemed so much as if he ought to be.

"I— They were all out on snowmobiles. Out on the lake. I

didn't go 'cause I had Hamthrax. Um . . . flu. You know? The ice was supposed to be really thick. It *was* really thick! There were fishing shacks out there with ice-holes a foot or more thick!" Elizabeth's voice shook, and when she put her hands up to her face to push the scarf out of the way, Spirit could see her hands were shaking, too. Spirit felt her own grief welling up in her throat again, and she felt a fierce uprush of pity for Elizabeth. "They said it was a freak warm spot that thinned the ice, and you couldn't see under the snow. The temperature was twenty below. They didn't have—" Her voice broke in a sob that called answering tears from Spirit's eyes. "They didn't have a chance in the water—"

Spirit made an abortive gesture toward her, wanting to show sympathy, but Elizabeth wrapped her arms around herself as if trying to protect herself and backed away. "I—I'm sorry. I—I'll just go back now—" And she turned and scuttled away, head down, shoulders hunched.

Burke and Spirit looked at each other. Burke looked as if he wanted to say something, then just shrugged. "We can try talking to her later," he suggested. "She sure seemed skittish though."

Spirit sighed, watching Elizabeth pull open the door just enough to slip inside. "But not the pep talk Murr-cat and Addie gave me when I got here," she said, a little acidly. "And do you blame her for being nervous? I wonder how Doctor Ambrosius tortured *her?* She probably expected us to turn into wolves and vampires."

And it won't do her any good to hear that the ice probably wasn't thin, and her family's death probably wasn't an accident. It's nothing

I can prove, anyway—any more than I can prove what I know I saw the night our car went off the road . . .

Burke had been staring after Elizabeth. Now he turned back to her. "I don't know. You know this place. She's going to have to toughen up fast or—"

Spirit sighed. "Yeah. Or she might as well be surrounded by wolves and vampires for real." She made a face. "Well, I'm cold. Mind if I go inside?" She was kind of hoping Burke would go with her, but it looked like the mood was broken, because he shook his head.

"You go ahead. I need to hit the gym for my workout, and since I'm halfway there I might as well do it now." With a cheerful wave, he trudged off in the direction of the stand-alone Gymnasium complex.

Spirit's mood soured even more. She shoved her hands in her coat pockets and turned toward the terrace door that Elizabeth had vanished through. She had some vague idea of tracking Elizabeth down and—

And what? Trying to make her feel better? Like that would happen! She hugged herself tightly, trying to warm up. With Burke gone, it seemed even colder out here. She might as well go in and tell the others there was a new inmate in the asylum.

Once she stepped off the AstroTurf carpet, her feet crunched through a heavy crust of snow. It came all the way up to mid-calf, and the drifts were even higher—even in her snow boots she was freezing. She couldn't wait to get inside, and the two of them had walked so far that the terrace entrance was closer than the Entry Hall entry she and Burke had come out through.

But as she started along the side lawn, she saw a sudden flurry of snowballs appear in the distance. "Appear" was exactly the right word: One moment there'd been nothing, the next, the air was full of snowballs. Hovering. It was hard to decide what Gifts were involved in the snowball fight, though it was pretty clear most of the "combatants" were School of Air: Jaunting, Telekinesis, and just plain Weather Witchery combined to turn what might otherwise be an ordinary snowball fight into something more like a snowball *apocalypse*.

No way was she walking into something like that, even if it did mean spending a lot longer out here in the cold. Grumbling under her breath, Spirit turned around and trudged back to the main entrance.

When she got there, she struggled up the steps—everything she wore was caked with snow by now—and pulled open the enormous (pretentious) heavy oak door with a certain amount of struggle. Burke made it look easy. Of course, Burke made *everything* look easy, even living here.

For a moment she indulged herself in the wistful fantasy of *not* being here, but still having met the other four. Would they still have been friends if they hadn't been stuck here in High School Hell? She thought she and Burke might have been more than friends—Loch was dazzling, and she liked him a lot (maybe loved him, maybe just crushed on him), but Loch came from an entirely different world. She and Burke were a lot alike, really. She thought about having a boyfriend. A real boyfriend. Her first.

And suddenly she realized she didn't dare.

It didn't matter if it was Loch, or Burke, or even someone she hadn't met yet (hard as that was to imagine)—Oakhurst didn't even like you to have *friends,* let alone a *boy*friend. The fact that she and Addie and Muirin were friends had been a secret they'd needed to hide as carefully as they'd hidden the knowledge that their fellow students were dying, not "leaving to pursue other opportunities." If Oakhurst realized you had friends, they did everything they could to destroy the friendship.

Suddenly she realized she'd been thinking "Oakhurst" and not "the teachers" or "the Administration." It was as if Oakhurst itself was some kind of malevolent entity.

It's like that hotel in that horror novel. The haunted one that everybody who stayed at went insane.

She shuddered faintly, and distracted herself by stomping her feet to get the last of the snow off her boots. The Entry Hall was completely empty—it wasn't a place people lingered—and even the fire roaring in the fireplace couldn't make it look cheerful and inviting. The huge cheerless Christmas tree only made things worse, somehow. She wished they'd take it down now, but Burke said it would be up until after New Year's. She didn't see why. It wasn't as if any of the students spent their time admiring it. And a thirty-foot tree? *Quelle* overkill. She wasn't even sure how they'd gotten it in here. *Maybe it's always here, and they just make it invisible for the rest of the year. Maybe old Mr. Tyniger built the place around it.*

As if anyone would want to build a room around a tree. . . .

Then she blinked and shook her head. *What the—?* Because,

of course, this room *was* built around a tree. And for one moment, staring at the Christmas tree, she had utterly and completely forgotten that, even though the tree Oakhurst was built around was there, right in front of her—that huge oak trunk in the middle of the Entry Hall.

It should have been the focus of the entire room, actually. And it . . . wasn't.

She tried to stare at it—really tried—and after a very little time she found her eyes sort of shifting away from it. For some reason, after glancing at it, she kind of found herself dismissing it. As if it was nothing more imposing than a lamp. Instead of being a tree trunk at least twelve feet in diameter and two stories high.

She would never have thought about that twice—she certainly didn't when she first got here—except for the whole Hunt business. *The Wild Hunt was another thing people should have noticed immediately and didn't* . . . Little alarms went off in her head. If something was making her "forget" about an oak tree that an entire building was built around, she wanted to know why.

Slowly, she walked across the inlaid stone floor toward it; warily, with a creepy feeling as if she was halfway expecting a door in the trunk to open and some horror-movie monster to pop out. When she got up close to it, she studied it, only to see that there were marks all over its smooth time-polished surface. They were faint—but they were there.

And they'd been *made* by someone. Or something. She would have dismissed them as natural—and a part of her really wanted to do that, because didn't worms and beetles crawl under tree bark and leave marks on the wood?—but there was something about the marks that kept her from doing that. She couldn't swear to it—not exactly—but she had the vague feeling the marks on the wood looked *familiar*.

That was even creepier.

Well, one thing was certain. She didn't want anyone to catch her looking so closely at that tree or those marks. She was pretty darn certain that if they had something to do with Oakhurst tradition that the kids were supposed to know, Doctor Ambrosius or the teachers would have been all over the story at every given opportunity.

So— They weren't. And maybe she needed to find a way to look at those marks without being seen.

She moved along, as if she'd been on her way back to her room all along, and resolved to tell the others. With any luck, one of them would have an idea about the best way to get a really good look at the Oakhurst Oak—and its marks—without anyone noticing. With a little *more* luck, she might be able to get them to wake up to the fact that there was still a lot going on here at Good Old Oakhurst that was just not right.

†HREE

At lunch, Elizabeth stood out by not standing out; she picked the table farthest from the desirable spots—which put her at the window, where it was freezing cold—she ate quickly and without really talking to anyone. Even by Oakhurst standards this was odd, and Spirit wondered if she was going to find herself sharing the back of the class with Elizabeth. At Oakhurst, there was competition, and fierce competition at that, for the seats at the front of the room. Everyone wanted to be noticed.

Because, hey, we are all winners, right?

She watched Elizabeth leaving the dining room and wondered where she was going. Her room? Probably. When your family had just been killed, it wasn't as if you were really in the mood for a Winter Carnival.

She was still thinking about Elizabeth when she got back to her room and found Addie and Muirin waiting for her.

"What do you think of the new kid?" she asked, putting her books beside the computer in the order she was going to do the homework assignments (and why call it "homework" when they never left the campus?).

"Uh, Eleanor? Elsie?" Muirin said, without any interest. "Why?"

"Elizabeth," Spirit corrected. "She's in most of my classes. So what do you think of her?"

"I think she's a wimp," said Muirin dismissively. "Limper than a shoelace. She's going to get run right over in this place. Or become invisible, like that song from *Chicago*." She did a shuffle-step and sang a couple lines from "Mister Cellophane."

"I didn't know you liked musicals," Addie said, surprised.

Muirin smirked and appropriated the computer chair. "It's got gangsters and murder and prison numbers, what's not to like?"

"Well, what do *you* think of her?" Spirit said to Addie, interrupting before they could get off on a tangent.

Addie shrugged. "I think she's just really shy. Why are you so interested in her? You didn't get assigned to her."

By now Spirit knew that the proctors set up an informal "safety net" for the new arrivals; it irritated her, as if Addie and Muirin were her friends only because they'd been assigned to be—as if that were possible at Oakhurst. "I don't know," Spirit replied, a little fretfully. "It just seems like there is something important about her, but I don't know what it is, and it's making me crazy—"

"—er," said Muirin. "Craz*ier*."

Nettled, Spirit counted to ten before she snapped back. "If it's crazy to think we're all still in danger—"

Then she stopped as a new thought struck her. "You know, maybe that's it. She acts like she's scared. Like she already *knows* there's something here out to get all of us, and she doesn't know who to trust!" Crazy as the idea was, it just might explain Elizabeth's behavior.

Muirin rolled her eyes, but Spirit wasn't going to give up this time. "Look, the Hunt didn't come out of nowhere. It didn't migrate across half the world from Ireland by itself. Someone, and it was probably someone right here in this school, set kids up as sacrifices for it!"

"Right, but we chased the Hunt off." Addie lay back on Spirit's bed, staring at the ceiling.

"We might have chased the Hunt off, but we didn't do squat about whoever is right on this campus. I went over this with Loch. Someone set it up, or at least kept it going by supplying sacrifices. Someone dropped the wards so it could get in. Even if Doctor Ambrosius decided to do something after we told him about it—I don't know about you, but I didn't see anybody missing from among the adults here—either he hasn't done squat, or *he* couldn't find the person, either!" She didn't say *so there,* but she sure felt like doing it.

Muirin turned around in Spirit's computer chair and gave her an odd look. "Huh," she said.

Addie sat up. "Well even if that's true—and I'm not saying it is!—since you talked to Loch about this, he had to tell you *cui bono*."

Muirin made a face. "Yeah. Or for us normal people, 'follow the money.' Who here would benefit from killing us off? It's not like Oakhurst is in our wills or like that—sure, Daddy Dearest left me a little trust fund, and Addie's an heiress, and even you probably have an insurance settlement waiting for you back in the world—but the only way Oakhurst gets any of it is if we live to graduate, get our hands on it, and feel generous."

For a second, Spirit's attention was diverted. She'd spent all this time thinking she was a pauper, but Muirin might be right—about part of it, anyway. She knew Mom and Dad had insured everything—the house, the car, her and Phoenix's lives—and Oakhurst had paid all her hospital bills from Day One. . . .

Then she shook her head and went back to the important subject. "I don't think it's about money, Muirin. We saw the records. *You* saw them. This . . . This *Tithing* went back maybe to the beginning of Oakhurst, and that would be more than thirty years. So what if the wizard war that Doctor Ambrosius told us about is already going on?"

"And he hasn't mentioned anything?" Muirin asked dubiously.

"Well, wouldn't you freak if he did? I know I would." Spirit chewed a nail.

"Don't do that, it's disgusting," Addie said automatically. "And you're already freaking."

"Well *someone* should!" Spirit hoped she sounded resolute instead of hysterical, but in her own ears she sounded shrill.

"Okay, let's break this down." Addie ticked off a *one* on her fingers. "Oakhurst has been graduating kids since the seventies. So some of them were our parents. And when we were born, we automatically became Oakhurst Legacies, so when we were orphaned, we ended up here. So, if this wizard war has already begun, everyone here is an orphan. And if it *hasn't*"—she ticked off a *two*—"some of the kids here have *live* parents and were sent here for training in magic. Because Oakhurst is safe."

"But didn't Doctor Ambrosius just give us that speech about how Oakhurst is our real family?" Spirit replied, more confused by the minute.

Muirin snorted. "Every fancy school I've ever been to gives you that speech. It's supposed to build togetherness."

Addie nodded her agreement. "And who talks to each other here? I mean the way we talk. How much do you know about Jenny or Claire or Kristi or even Brendan? Cadence is one of my closest—well, I can't even call her a 'friend,' really—here, and I don't even know what city she grew up in, or if she had any brothers or sisters. When Burke told me about his family, I was *shocked*. Yes—shocked! Because nobody here tells anybody else anything real. Half the student body could have families, Spirit, and none of use would ever know."

"Maybe everyone here with families just *wishes* they were orphans," Muirin suggested mockingly.

"So either the wizard war has started and we're all orphans—

because of the Evil Wizards—or it hasn't and we aren't." Addie looked pleased with herself. "Logic is your friend."

"Thanks so much, Mister Spock," Spirit replied. She frowned, thinking she was missing something. Whatever it was, she'd have to hope it would come back to her later. "So . . . how do we find out about people's families? Set up an online poll?"

Muirin grinned gleefully. "We hack the school computer and get into the student and graduate databases, of course! I've been wanting a really good excuse to do that for ages!" Then she jumped to her feet and grabbed Spirit's hands. "But meanwhile, there's something vital we need to take care of right this minute, or it's going to be too late."

✦

Spirit shivered in the cold of the storage room and eyed the double rack of dresses with dismay. She *liked* clothes. She did. That was why she'd wanted to learn to sew. But getting set up to make your own clothes was almost as expensive as buying them—she could mend, and embroider, and make alterations, but that was about all. But she liked clothes. So she should've been in heaven. Right?

These aren't clothes. These are terrifying implements of torture.

Pastel pink warred with hot pink, eye-searing blue, turquoise, deer-hunter-orange, and a lot of sequins and metallics. The one thing there *didn't* seem to be here on the Isle of Misfit Dresses was anything knee-length or shorter. *I guess Oakhurst doesn't consider anything that's not down to the ground to be formal enough.*

"So as you see, this is where bridesmaid dresses go to die,"

Muirin said scathingly. "The New Year's Eve thing is a formal dinner and dance. That's *full* formal, meaning floor-length. And if you don't have your own formal you have to get one from here. You can see why Addie and I had ours sent. What size are you? Hopefully things haven't been picked over too much yet."

Addie snorted disbelievingly, which only made Spirit more depressed.

"Um . . . Four? Six?" She tried not to fidget. And here she'd thought the Christmas Dinner was bad. The New Year's Dance was going to be hideous.

Muirin and Addie dove into the mass of tulle, glitter, and satin at the far end of the racks. "Seafoam: Eighties. Fuchsia: Eighties. Nineties' Hippie revival, oh noes, not unless we want you to look like a flower child." Muirin rejected one dress after another until Spirit wondered if staying in her room was an option.

"But hark! Is that a plain white something I spy?"

Addie finally hauled a candidate out where Spirit could see it. The dress was white, yes, but it had some sort of bizarre rainbow-colored tulle ribbon poof stuck to one hip, some sort of weird scarf-like thing in the same material wreathing the neckline, and matching poofs at the shoulders. And shoulder pads. Big ones.

"I think these are supposed to be flowers," Muirin said critically. She started poking and prying at them. "The basic dress is all right . . ."

Spirit could not imagine how anyone could describe that horror as "all right."

"It's the only one with classic lines in her size," Addie agreed.

Muirin and Addie exchanged an enigmatic look. "Three hours, tops," said Muirin, in answer to an unspoken question.

"Have they told us anything about not cutting things up from here?" Addie asked.

Muirin shook her head smugly, then dived back into the racks to grab a black-and-silver thing that was even worse than the rainbow poof dress—and not even in her size. She couldn't imagine anyone her age—anywhere, *ever*—wearing that horror.

"I'll get this stuff deconstructed before they have a chance to tell us not to get creative, then it'll be too late for them to do anything about it." Muirin glanced down the row of dresses at Spirit, who was wearing a look of utter horror. "Trust me," she said, knowingly, waving the silver-and-black dress like a flag of triumph. "I might have to cover up where I take Rainbow Brite's corsages off. You'll love it."

For one moment Spirit contemplated telling her not to bother, that she'd pick something out by herself. Then she looked at the other choices. And realized there *were* no other choices. "Um . . . thanks," she said, faintly. She only hoped she wasn't going to end up wearing something held together with safety pins.

Then, as she followed the other two out, she could have hit herself. What was wrong with her? They were all still in deadly danger—and she was worrying about a *dress*? She'd started her conversation with Addie and Muirin wanting to talk about

Elizabeth, who behaved as if she knew she was in danger. She'd wanted to talk to them about the danger she *knew* they were all still in. And she'd ended up down here picking out a prom dress as if she didn't have anything to worry about besides who'd dance with her at the ball!

This was the last thing that should have been on her mind. Maybe it wasn't just shock and denial. Something was going on here. Maybe they were all being manipulated into forgetting what had happened at Midwinter, and even she was falling into the trap.

She started to say something to Addie and Muirin—and then stopped herself just in time. Because telling them—again—wouldn't help. She couldn't prove there was some sort of Jedi mind-trick stuff going on, and saying there was would only make her look more paranoid.

No, somehow she had to get them to see it for themselves.

Maybe investigating the oak in the Entry Hall would help. She had to start somewhere.

Muirin showed up to dinner a little late—not so much that she got in trouble, but enough so that a couple of the proctors gave her a glare. There were bits of white and black thread on her skirt, so Spirit knew she had made good on her plan to cut the two gowns up, and the cat-in-the-cream look on her face told Spirit that she was happy with the results. They kept the conversation to perfectly ordinary stuff over the food, but once they were free for the evening, they all retired to their favorite nook and Addie brought her Monopoly board from her room.

"I've been thinking about the Hunt," Loch said, reluctantly. "And, yeah, it doesn't belong here. And, yeah, somebody had to summon it."

Spirit managed to not say "I told you so." She practically held her breath as she waited for Loch to continue.

"It's mostly Celtic in origin, so we're looking for someone who really knows Celtic tradition, the genuine old stuff, as opposed to—oh, Nordic, or Native American or Chinese. So that's as good a place as any to start," he continued.

But Addie sniffed. "Oakhurst isn't exactly the Rainbow Coalition," she pointed out. "Most of the students and *all* of the teachers are whiter-than-white WASPs. That doesn't much narrow down who could be the summoner, since practically anyone could have known about the Hunt."

Spirit blinked a bit in surprise. Addie was right, and somehow she hadn't noticed. Why hadn't she noticed? Was this something else they didn't want you to think about? But why? What difference could it possibly make?

Loch grimaced. "You've got me there, but it's the only thing I can think of. Maybe if we can find someone doodling in ogham or something . . ."

Thanks to all the research they had done, Spirit knew what he was talking about, and—hadn't those marks on the oak tree looked a bit like ogham? "I noticed something I hadn't before. Two things, actually. You know the big oak tree the Entry Hall is built around?"

"You mean the Christmas—" Burke began, then blinked, looking puzzled. "Now why would I think that? Especially when you said 'oak tree' . . ."

"That's my point exactly!" Spirit said, excitedly. "What I noticed was that there's something about the oak tree—it's hard to remember it's there even though it takes up *tons* of space!"

Both Addie and Muirin shook their heads, not as if they were saying "no," but as if they were trying to shake something loose. "Okay. That *is* weird," Muirin admitted grudgingly. "Really, really weird."

"And wrong," Addie said firmly. "Why would anyone here want us to not look at the tree? Why not just wall it up or plaster it over or something in that case?"

"I don't know, but I decided that if something or someone didn't want me looking at the tree closely, then I was going to." At least now she had their attention. "There wasn't anyone around, so I went up to it and stared at it for a while. There's marks on it, and they didn't look natural to me. But it was hard to make them out, and there was more weirdness, because right after I left the room I couldn't remember them well enough to try and sketch them."

Burke mulled that over for a moment. "I don't think it's a good idea to go and stare at it," he said, eying her as if he expected her to object. "I mean, if by some crazy chance you're right, and there still is someone here after the kids—us—you never know how they could be watching."

Spirit tried not to bristle at the *if by some crazy chance* part. "Well, how can we get a good look at it then?"

"Actually, I think I can," Addie piped up unexpectedly. "My Art Class is supposed to be doing sketches around Oakhurst all vacation. I can sketch the tree. I bet no one else is."

Spirit felt a chill of alarm at the idea of Addie sitting alone in that room, sketching something that had deliberately been protected in some way. What if someone saw her?

Addie must have read what Spirit was thinking from her expression. "Relax," she said, with a little chuckle. "I'll keep our sketch hidden by using an onionskin overlay. I'll sketch the tree without the marks, and then draw the marks on a piece of onionskin that I can hide easily. And I won't just draw the oak, I'll draw the Christmas tree, the fireplace, and the Grand Staircase, too."

Well, that seemed safe enough. "Thanks, Addie," she said with relief. "I should know by now you're too smart to get into trouble."

"Oh, I wouldn't say that," Addie demurred, but Spirit could tell she was pleased at being called "smart." "You can all make it up to me by actually playing this game instead of faking it."

✦

For the last three years, Elizabeth Walker had wavered between thinking she had a really vivid imagination, and thinking she was going crazy. But it wasn't the kind of crazy she could actually talk to anyone about. She wasn't anorexic, she didn't want to cut herself . . . no, the problem was, since the morning of her thirteenth birthday . . . she'd been *remembering*.

It had all started with a bang; she'd woken up from a dream so vivid she'd expected to find herself in a stone-walled room, looking out of a narrow little window that had no glass in it toward a harbor and the sea beyond. But the ships in the harbor—in her dream—bore no resemblance to anything she knew; they were all boats with sails. Not sleek racing yachts, but rough and wooden things like something from a movie about Vikings. The harbor itself was little more than a rocky cove with a single wooden pier.

Her head was weighed down by the two thick braids that hung as far as her knees. She could feel the stones of the floor through her thin leather slippers. And the dress she'd been wearing had been impossibly heavy, made of thick wool—she somehow knew—and trailing down to the ground.

She'd felt . . . older. In her dream, her body felt foreign to her in ways she didn't have the words to describe, but that were very confusing. She'd ached for things she couldn't put a name to, which was why she was looking out the window. Waiting for someone. Longing for someone.

Behind her, there'd been someone moving. She didn't want to turn to look. Her body—the person she'd been in her dream—didn't like the person behind her, the person in the bed she'd risen from at the first rays of dawn.

The person behind her said something. It was as if he spoke

a foreign language: Elizabeth recognized only one word. *Yseult*.
Her dream-body turned, knowing this was her name.

That was when she woke up.

She'd been almost as confused on waking as she'd been in
the dream. Her pink canopy bed, her pink and cream bedroom,
the dolls and bears she knew she was outgrowing but couldn't
quite bear to be rid of—these all seemed strange, alien, *wrong*.

She'd shaken her head, and then everything settled back
into place. The room was hers, of course, and whatever she had
dreamed about was, of course, nothing but a dream. She thought
about telling someone, because her parents would praise her
imagination and her friends would all get a big laugh out of it,
but something held her back.

It was the first dream. The first memory. But it was by no
means the last.

After that, the dreams came more and more frequently.
Soon they filled all night, every night—all of her sleeping
hours. They were as consistent as if they weren't dreams, but a
biography, and eventually, fearfully, Elizabeth Walker came to
realize that this was what they actually were. A biography. The
life of someone she had once been.

Except, of course, that was impossible. There was no way
she could've been a sorceress named Yseult. She could not
possibly have helped to create magic armor and weapons for
her uncle, a giant of a man named Morholt. She couldn't have
spent her days learning magic and healing from the Queen.
Magic didn't exist. This was some amazing—terrifying—fantasy

created from far too many viewings of Lord of the Rings . . . though the castle Yseult—her dream-self—lived in didn't look much like the Elven castles of the *Rings* movies, and only a little like the ones the Riders of Rohan lived in. It was wood and stone and shockingly—to Elizabeth's eyes—small, though Yseult thought of it with pride and satisfaction, because all the floors were stone instead of being dirt on the ground floor, and because she and her parents had rooms of their own and didn't have to sleep in the big main room—the hall—with everyone else.

That she was actually dreaming about a time she knew nothing about—and had lived before, lived *then*—was impossible, but that magic was real was even more impossible. Or so she'd thought as she lived a double life, growing up as Elizabeth by day, living as Yseult by night. Although Yseult knew and did things that Elizabeth had not even in her wildest waking thoughts imagined—

—things that involved a man named Tristan, and Elizabeth grew to love him as much as Yseult did. So many mornings she woke up and started to cry, because Tristan wasn't real any more than Yseult was, but Tristan was everything she could ever want in a boyfriend: he was handsome, and kind, and smart, and he loved . . .

Yseult. Tristan loves Yseult, not me. And he isn't even real!

The things they did made her blush when she thought of them, even though she knew about them from movies and television she wasn't supposed to watch. And the last time she'd slept over at Marcie's house, Marcie'd had an actual DVD with real sex in it, and they'd all watched it, muffling their giggles and squeaks behind their hands. But Elizabeth had thought (privately) that the DVD had been kind of, well, *gross*. Not at all like what Tristan and Yseult did—when they could get some privacy, because Yseult's castle didn't have a lot of that.

She kept having to remind herself they weren't real. Sure, sometimes she thought she was going crazy. But it wasn't as if she was seeing things when she was awake. And it wasn't as if she believed in all the magic she—Yseult—was doing in those dreams. She had a good imagination, that was all. She began to think about writing her dream-life down as a story, and maybe it would be good enough to get published, like the boy with the dragon books had been.

And that was the way her life went while she turned fourteen, and fifteen, and sixteen. She never told anybody that she didn't dream about anything but Yseult's life, but she didn't think of herself as keeping bad secrets. Who did her dreams hurt, anyway? Nothing in them was really real, any more than magic was really real.

That was what she'd believed right up until three months ago.

September, and she was a junior, and head of the Cheer Squad for the Junior Varsity football team. They'd all been at the game when Terry Bishop, who looked a little like Tristan in the right light, jumped for the ball and got clotheslined, and there was an awful *snapping* sound, and he screamed.

She got there first, even before the coach, and she still didn't know how because she didn't remember moving. Terry's leg and knee were lying all wrong, and before anyone got there to stop her, Elizabeth put her hands on them, and did what Yseult had been doing in Elizabeth's dreams for months.

With a weird *snap,* the bones went back the way they belonged, and she felt a rush of something pouring out of her and into Terry. So much *something* poured out of her that she nearly passed out, and she hardly noticed when the coach and everybody else shoved her aside and told her to get back to the sidelines with the rest of Cheer Squad. She stumbled back to the sidelines, and she must have looked really wrecked, because Marcie told her she probably shouldn't do any of the stunts, and Elizabeth knew better than to try when she felt so awful. She sat through the rest of the game in a daze, then went straight home instead of going to the after-game party, and when she woke up the next morning she discovered she hadn't even taken her shoes off before collapsing on top of her bedspread and pretty much passing out. Mom had a few careful words to say to her at breakfast about drugs, and how she wasn't going to preach but she hoped Elizabeth would tell her if she'd decided to experiment because a lot of them were a lot more dangerous than alcohol, and Elizabeth had stumbled through an explanation about the game and seeing Terry get hurt. At least that explained her behavior.

The game was Friday, and normally she'd have had to wait until Monday to find out anything, but Marcie's older sister was dating Terry's best friend, so it only took Elizabeth one phone call to find out that Terry'd wrenched his knee and he'd be out for a couple games but not the season. That *certainly* didn't match Elizabeth's memory of a leg broken in at least three pieces, with the ends of the bone pushing against the skin and threatening to break through. She spent the rest of the day trying to convince herself that Daphne and Marcie were right—just a sprain—and she hadn't seen—or felt—what she knew she had. And when she tried, it seemed as if she could hear Yseult's laughter in her mind, affectionately mocking her attempts to blind herself to the truth.

So if the magic was real . . . were the dreams?

She wasn't ready to admit that. Not yet.

She began to experiment, using ideas taken from books she'd read, fantasies where magic was real.

Lighting a candle: easy. Seeing through the eyes of a bird: piece of cake. Putting magic into an object . . .

There was this girl at school who Elizabeth felt kind of exasperated with and sorry for at the same time. Janine was nice enough, but she'd gotten mixed up with this guy who controlled practically every moment of her life. She stayed with Tommy because he said he loved her—and she said she loved him even after she ended up in the hospital and had to stay for three days. She told everybody she'd "fallen down the stairs"— but everyone who knew Tommy knew what had really happened to put Janine into the hospital.

So Elizabeth decided she was going to do something about it. The magic that made people change their minds about things was pretty much always the same—according to the books— you just varied what you wanted them to do. Elizabeth swiped

Janine's sunglasses; they were expensive designer ones, but besides that, the girl *had* to wear them sometimes to hide her dark circles and even an occasional black eye. She returned them the next day—enchanted. "See him the way we see him," was the enchantment she'd put on them—appropriate for a pair of glasses!

It worked better than she had ever dreamed it would. The next day Tommy was in jail on assault charges, and Janine was wondering aloud what she'd ever seen in him.

But Elizabeth's triumph was short-lived. Because after that, *she* started seeing things—while she was awake.

At first it was just out of the corner of her eye. Something moving impossibly fast, something that wasn't there when she turned her head to look at it. Eyes in shadows.

But then she started seeing them clearly, in daylight.

They never showed up except when she was alone—when she was walking back from school was the first time she saw one by daylight. She had turned a corner, and realized the street was deserted, and too, too quiet. And there he was, standing in a challenging pose in the middle of the sidewalk, as if daring her to pass. A black blot that seemed to absorb all the sunlight, staring at her—he didn't wear the black-washed armor and helm of her dreams, but she knew him, knew what he was, as he stared at her from beneath the brim of a black hat, black trench coat down to his ankles, open to the breeze, and showing black jeans and a tight black tee.

She froze like a scared baby bunny.

Then a little mob of grade school kids came around the corner, laughing and shrieking, and she turned involuntarily. And when she looked back, he was gone.

He—they—were something she remembered from her dreams, the menacing Knights of the Shadow.

But he, or more like him, kept popping up, and soon they appeared whether she was alone or not. Staring at her out of a crowd of spectators at a game. Lurking outside the school, right where she would see him when she looked out the window. Cruising by in a black SUV. And nobody else seemed to see him—or them, if there was more than one.

At that point, she wanted to think she really was finally going crazy. Because being crazy would have been better than what her dreams were telling her, what her instinct and everything she'd experienced was telling her.

Her dreams weren't fantasy. They were truth. She'd been Yseult of Ireland, wife of Mark, lover of Tristan. Sorceress, healer. She was back—and so, somewhere, were Mark and Tristan. And so were . . . others. How many others, she didn't know for sure, but she knew of one, whose name she shuddered even to think about. The one the Shadow Knights served. The one who meant the Shadow Knights to claim her and make her kneel at his feet, surrendering her power to him.

Of course, her family stood between her and *him* and not even the Shadow Knights could do anything about that. This was the twenty-first century after all. Not even *he* could just waltz in and take her from her parents. So even if the dreams and all were true, she was safe—

Until he killed her family.

And now she was here.

Doctor Ambrosius was no protection; if he wasn't senile—which she was half convinced he was—he still had no idea what he was *really* up against. She knew Oakhurst was part of *his* plots—or she wouldn't be here—but was Doctor Ambrosius an unwitting dupe . . . or one of his henchmen? Without knowing, she couldn't warn him outright. He hadn't listened to her hints—and worse, she'd already heard some of the kids had already gone missing from this place, no matter what Doctor Ambrosius said. It wasn't nearly as safe here at Oakhurst as he claimed it was. It wasn't safe from *him*.

So here she was, in the middle of nowhere, no idea who to trust, and not a familiar face in sight. Except for Mark—who she did *not* want to meet again—and Tristan, she'd never known any of the other ones likely to come back. She wouldn't recognize them, so how could she find someone it was safe to trust her warnings to?

And even if she did figure out who they were—would they even listen?

❧

"Tell me I'm brilliant," Addie begged with a grin.

"You're brilliant," Spirit replied, going along with it. "You got the sketch?"

Addie nodded, and pulled a couple of sketch pads out of the bag she had slung over one shoulder. The others gathered around their usual "study" table in the lounge as Addie flipped the pads open and started passing them around as cover for the one they really wanted to see.

They all made appreciative or critical noises as she cast a cautious look around to see if anyone was watching them. She must have been satisfied that no one was, because she pulled a piece of onionskin from the back pages of the pad and laid it over the sketch of the oak tree. Spirit and the rest bent over it.

"You were dead right, Spirit," Addie told her, a little grimly, as they all studied the marks now made plain on the tree. "I could feel something kind of pushing my eyes away while I was working. There is some very powerful magic on that tree. What do you think, people?"

"These aren't natural," Burke agreed, his finger starting to trace one of the signs, then pulling away, reluctantly.

"They look familiar, but I can't place from where," Muirin observed, then shrugged. "Although for all I know, they might have come from the cover of a Death Metal album."

"You don't really think that, do you?" Spirit challenged.

"It's possible. Rumor hath it that this place was used by a biker gang before Doctor Ambrosius turned it into a school." As usual, Spirit couldn't tell if Muirin was serious, or trying to yank her chain.

"I don't think bike-gang signs would try to make me look away from them," Addie said firmly. "We need to research this. I made copies for all of us—by hand of course." She passed them all tiny paper cranes, which they all oo'd and ah'd over. "I'm going to check the photo archives in the Art Department and see if there are any pictures of the tree I can use to photo-enhance the marks. We need to find out what they mean."

Burke nodded. "I can check Norse," he said. "I've got a project I can twist around to cover Norse runes."

Muirin made her little crane "fly," bobbing her hand up and down. "I can check Celtic ogham because of the Hunt connection." She looked pointedly at Loch and Spirit. "That leaves you two."

Loch sighed. "Into the archives, again?"

"What else?" Muirin nose-dived her crane. "And who else? You two make the cutest little spies."

Spirit thought she saw a strange look pass over Burke's face. But in the next moment, it was gone, and she decided she had imagined it.

She sighed. "Archives it is. And hope we can continue keeping from getting caught."

FOUR

The Oakhurst storage rooms were beginning to feel as familiar as one of the classrooms.

At this point, Spirit felt that she and Loch had all this sneaking around stuff down to a fine art. They managed to meet up without scaring the pants off each other, and without either of them running afoul of anyone else. Of course, since Loch was a Shadewalker, that was relatively easy for him, and Spirit felt more than a little jealous, but being without magic did make her invisible to people looking for wandering magicians, so maybe it all evened out. And once down in the subbasement, Spirit felt a little more relaxed, maybe because there was only one entrance, so they should have plenty of time to hide if someone turned up.

This time they both had better flashlights than Loch's little penlight, and Loch had an LED work light as well. Spirit didn't ask him where he had gotten it, or how, but it was probably through Muirin.

They didn't need Muirin's skeleton keys this trip, because they weren't going to the hidden storage room yet, but to the regular storage rooms. Which was just as well because those hidden rooms gave her the serious creeps. Dungeonlike cells, an operating room, and boxes of the records and belongings of the students who had vanished . . . it was too much like something out of a horror movie.

Now if you were looking at things in the best possible light for Oakhurst, it kind of made sense to have prisonlike cells down there given what Doctor Ambrosius said about the wizard war. If you caught one of the bad guys you would want a place to hold and interrogate him, right? Doctor A. might be one of the good guys, but it was pretty obvious that he was no kind of angel; the way Oakhurst was run alone showed that the people at the top were pretty cold and businesslike when it came to doing "what needed to be done" to win this war. There was a Darwinian ruthlessness about the way that competition was encouraged here.

And on the good side, none of those rooms, at least during Spirit's cursory look around, had shown any signs of actual use.

But still . . . the fact that they were there at all was seriously creepy. And it began to strain things more than a bit to have all the personal belongings of all of the kids who had disappeared stored down there. But what really put the frosting on the cake were the records, all marked "Tithed." Who had marked them that way? Had it just been a frustrated guess on the part of one of the administrators? Or had it happened after the records were put down there, as a kind of smug "gotcha" by the person who had called the Hunt? And if that was the case, then why do something like that to alert Doctor A. that whoever-it-was walked among them?

It was way more complicated than Spirit could figure out.

This time they had something quite simple to dig up. Addie needed pictures, photos, of the tree. They all agreed that it was too risky to try photographing it unless one of them got a class assignment in art that involved photography with an open-ended "photograph what you want." You couldn't exactly line everyone up for a candid shot in front of the tree, because—well, why would you want to do that in the first place? As a memento of your friends? You were discouraged from having friends. To send to your family? Even if you had family, you couldn't e-mail them to your family, because you couldn't e-mail anyone. So until one of them got that sort of chance, it was better to look for existing photos.

In its ongoing attempt to make things look as normal as possible, Oakhurst had a yearbook—and, sporadically, a school paper. That, Spirit figured, and Loch agreed, would be where there were any free-roaming photos of the Tree.

It meant going through a lot of dusty boxes and leafing through a lot of books and six-page newspapers that pretty quickly started to look alike. But it did yield some pay dirt; occasionally some club or team actually *would* pose in front of the Tree. It was never quite the same shot, so the marks never looked quite the same, and it appeared that the marks had no particular aversion to being photographed. Interestingly, the best shots were by someone who was actually in the photo, meaning that he or she had set the camera on a timer, then run around to be in the picture—so the aversion communicated itself to the photographer, but not the camera. By the time she and Loch got to the end of the newspapers and yearbooks, they had been at it for two hours.

They looked at each other, then Loch divided up the stacks into two piles, and shoved one half of each over to her. When she looked at him, he just shrugged and didn't comment. So neither did she. Instead she took her stack, got herself up off the floor, and headed back to her room as quickly and silently as possible.

She dropped her stuff off at Addie's room on the way to breakfast, leaving earlier than she usually did to do so. While she and Addie nattered about the dance, Addie carefully stored the stuff with her art supplies.

"I think you'll like your dress," Addie said, as they closed the door to her room and headed for the dining room.

Spirit shrugged. "As long as it's not as ugly as it was, that's all I hope for," she said. "I just wish I didn't have to go in the first place."

"Well the only way you can get out of it is to be sick," Addie said warningly. "And I mean, really sick. And the way we're isolated out here, it's not likely you're going to get exposed to anything between then and now."

Spirit weighed the advantages and disadvantages of puking up her toenails versus going to the dance, and reluctantly concluded that the dance would be less miserable.

And caught herself again. Why was she even thinking about the dance? The dance was inconsequential—

But nothing has happened since we took on the Hunt, came the insidious little voice in her head.

Yet, came the reply.

⁂

The next night, she and Loch needed Muirin's keys.

Muirin had a ring of skeleton keys—she said they had been her father's because he was in the construction business, though she wouldn't say how she had gotten hold of them. Knowing Murr-cat, Spirit would not have been at all surprised to learn that she'd gone through her dead father's things the first chance she had gotten.

It was funny how you could still like someone even though the things they said and did sometimes seemed somewhat immoral, callous, and even cruel. Maybe because, in Muirin's case at least, she would then turn around and do something unselfish—like volunteering to make the dress—or brave—or both, the way she'd been right there taking the Hunt down.

Once again, Spirit armed herself with a flashlight, an LED one that wouldn't deplete batteries, and stuck Muirin's keys in her pocket before turning off her room lights and slipping out into the hall. Spirit hadn't expected any interference—but hey, paranoia. So when she went slinking down the hallway that led to the basement, she *didn't* get caught by Ms. Corby prowling the hall.

It was a near thing though. La Corby moved as quietly as

Loch, and she only used her flashlight intermittently, which was how Spirit spotted her. She was still about fifty feet away, so Spirit was able to backtrack to the kitchen and duck inside. She hid by squeezing into the utility closet with the smelly mops and brooms, and waited breathlessly while Ms. Corby played the light around the kitchen. Looking for late-night snackers, no doubt. Maybe.

Or maybe she was actually on the alert for real trouble. Maybe Doctor A. *was* taking the Hunt seriously.

Maybe she's just prowling around trying to get people in trouble. It seemed the most likely.

When Ms. Corby was gone from the kitchen, Spirit counted twice to sixty, then slipped out of the closet, padded quietly to the door, listened, then cracked the door open. Ms. Corby's flashlight stabbed through the darkness back down the opposite way Spirit wanted to go, and with a sigh of relief, Spirit scooted out the door and headed for the rendezvous with Loch.

He was waiting outside the Furnace Room door; without speaking, they both went inside and headed for the furnace itself. The thing was going full-bore to keep up with the arctic temperatures outside, but it was so well insulated it was barely warm to the touch at the back where they knew the round cast-metal door to the secret rooms lay. By the light of Spirit's flashlight, Loch picked out the right skeleton key, which Muirin had marked with a speck of blood-red nail polish. Like Muirin, Loch pocketed the padlock before he opened the door. Hopefully Ms. Corby wouldn't prowl all the way down here.

Once the door was closed—and it had quite the seal on it, almost airtight—Loch flicked on the light switch; there were no windows this far belowground to betray them. The bare bulbs lighting up the cement stairs down and the room beyond were painful after the darkness of the basement proper.

"Right," Loch said out loud, his voice making her jump. "We might be living in the digital future, but when Oakhurst was founded, it was all paper. We know there are paper records on former students here as well as the Tithed ones. At some point, probably early, they had to start sending the students that didn't have magic to the—well, call it the 'Shadow Oakhurst.' So we should start finding records of students transferred if such a thing exists."

"And if it does?" Spirit asked. "What then?"

"Well, then we'll know that every Legacy kid ends up *somewhere*. So if you had a brother or sister that didn't have magic, they'd go there."

"And?" Spirit prompted. "I mean, what then?"

This was where Loch fumbled to a halt. "I don't know. Except that it means Doctor A. isn't telling us everything."

We already know that, Loch, she thought, but she didn't say it out loud.

"If there is such a thing, I suppose we ought to find out just what they're telling those kids." She stepped carefully down the wooden stairs and headed for the storage rooms, averting her eyes nervously from those *other* rooms.

She headed straight for a stack of dusty boxes that didn't look as if they had been touched in decades, while Loch dove into the filing cabinets where they had found the records of the "Tithed."

She leafed through cartons of what looked like old tourist brochures and real estate magazines for a while, then glanced over at Loch, who was studying something in a folder.

He's really sweet, she thought, out of nowhere. *And cute. Really cute.* She remembered how nice he'd been to her in the limousine, and then in the plane on the way here. Of all of them, he was the one that seemed closest to her in a lot of ways. Addie was always distant, Muirin had a slightly sadistic side, and Burke—Burke was nice, but she couldn't tell what it was he really wanted from her, and he never, ever seemed vulnerable, not even when they were all in deadly danger. Burke was fearless; confessing her fears to him made her feel awkward and useless. Loch, on the other hand, was someone she could probably talk to about anything. He never seemed to have a problem with admitting he didn't know something, or asking for help. She couldn't even begin to imagine Burke doing that.

And like her, he didn't have anyone out there, either. Burke still had his foster family. The existence of that family was almost like a wall between them, because she envied him that more than she could ever admit.

"Ugh," Loch said suddenly, in a voice full of distaste. "They used to have a hunting club here."

"Like horses and chasing foxes?" she hazarded.

"Like guns and shooting down anything that moved," he replied. "I'm glad *that* stopped anyway."

"Why don't you like guns?" she asked, hesitating a moment before she asked the question. "I thought it was a guy thing."

"Not this guy." Silence fell between them for a moment, and Spirit figured that was the end of the subject until he coughed. She looked back up again. He was staring bleakly down at the files.

"I was at Carnarvon Academy," he said, as if he thought she would recognize the name. Then he added, "It's a prep school in Massachusetts. This was before I learned *parkour* and how to get away from the bullies. There was another guy, David, he was kind of my friend, because we both got bullied about the same amount. It got to him more than it got to me, I guess. I wish I'd known at the time how much it was getting to him."

He fell silent for a very long time. "One day . . . one day he dragged me into his room and said he was going to make it stop. For good. He'd got hold of a handgun somehow, I never found out how. I don't know if he managed to get off-campus and buy it, or stole it from his parents over break, or found it somewhere. . . ." His voice trailed off for a moment. "Anyway, he showed it to me. Said he was going to wait until the ring-leaders were all at lunch and come in and shoot them. I tried to talk him out of it."

Spirit *knew*, right then, that this was not going to have any kind of a good ending.

"Everything I said just seemed to make things worse." Loch shook his head heavily, as if there was a weight settling all over him. His voice grew hoarser, as if he was trying to hold back emotion. "I kept trying to tell him that, at best, he was just going to hurt someone and go to jail, and at worst, he'd kill someone and end up getting the death penalty or getting gunned down himself by the cops. He kept telling me he didn't care, that anything was better than trying to live like we were, and finally he said"—Loch's voice broke a little—"he said since I cared so much about *them* and so little about *him* there was no reason for him to go on anymore, and he put the gun in his mouth and—"

The silence pressed down on both of them like lead. She didn't know how to break it. "I'm sorry," just wasn't adequate.

Loch slammed the cabinet drawer closed. "So that's why I don't like guns."

He looked up, and she nodded a little, trying to look as sympathetic as she could. She didn't feel as if she dared say anything.

They leafed through files and boxes until almost three in the morning, and the only thing that seemed worth looking into was something Spirit found in a box half full of what looked like old receipts. It was a pile of identical leather-bound scrapbooks, each with gold tooling, an elaborate monogram, and a picture of the house inset on the front cover. Just paging through the first couple, Spirit quickly realized that they were older than anything she had ever seen about Oakhurst—that they dated from the time the first stone had been laid here. In fact, as she deciphered a couple of handwritten notes, it looked as if these were scrapbooks put together by the original owner.

As far as she could tell, he had documented every step of the construction, and then went on to collect every mention of it he could lay his hands on. In later volumes there were society columns from as far away as Chicago mentioning parties here, and the menus and guest lists from those parties, photographs of people posing stiffly on horseback or with guns or in clunky-looking masquerade costumes.

"Have you found anything at all?" she asked Loch, after turning the stiff pages of a third volume, and wondering how the women ever got their waists that tiny.

"Not a single record of a transfer," Loch replied, sounding a little more normal, if disappointed. "If there *is* another version of Oakhurst for the Legacies without magic, there's no record of it here."

"So where do they go?" Spirit wondered aloud, and thought, *And what happens when they figure out I'm never going to get any magic?*

"Maybe they don't go anywhere." She looked up, and Loch shook his head. "I am completely without a clue here."

"You don't suppose . . ." she gulped, but it had to be said. "You don't suppose that the ones without magic . . . die?"

That possibility had been haunting her ever since she got here; that the only reason that she had lived was because she wasn't "normal." And worse . . . that because she wasn't "normal," her family had gotten a big fat target painted on them. So in a way, the reason they were dead was because of her.

Loch looked her right in the eyes and nodded just a little. "It makes a kind of awful sense, doesn't it?" he replied.

She swallowed hard. She didn't want to think about it. Instead she showed him the pile of scrapbooks. "I found these. I think they belonged to the original owner of the house."

He got up and came over to where she was sitting, squatted down on his heels beside her and looked through a few pages of one. "These might have something for Addie in them, and I doubt anyone is going to miss them. We might as well take them upstairs."

She nodded, and shoved roughly half of them over to him. He picked them up wordlessly.

She still felt awkward after his revelation, and the awkwardness didn't pass once they were out of the Furnace Room. It was only when they got into the hallways near the kitchen that it was broken, when she thought she heard a faint footfall, and they both froze.

Loch put a hand on her arm, ran it up to her mouth, and tapped her lips, warningly. She nodded. They both held as still as they could, though it seemed to Spirit that her breathing was horribly loud, and surely her heart was beating hard enough for someone to hear it.

She also had the creepy feeling that there were eyes on her.

But if it was Ms. Corby, or one of the other teachers, why hadn't someone jumped out to confront them? They *were* breaking the rules; they shouldn't have been out of their rooms this late, and certainly not together.

Maybe it was another student. Maybe it was someone who was sneaking into the room of a girlfriend—or boyfriend.

They stood like that, unmoving, for so long her legs started to cramp.

Loch could have left her, of course. He was a Shadewalker, he was really in no danger of getting caught.

But he didn't. He stayed with her, hand warm against her arm, while she stood there getting all knotted up with tension, listening for another sound out in the dark.

Finally he squeezed her arm again, and tugged it a little before letting go.

They parted at the divide between the boys' and girls' wings; the entire time they'd been making their way back to the dorms, she couldn't shake the feeling that there was something or someone following them. But whatever, whoever it was, he, she, or it didn't make its presence known. She got back to her room and eased the door open and closed again without a feeling of relief. All she could do was find her closet by feel and shove the pile of scrapbooks into the back of it on the floor, behind the shoes and boots. She'd have to find a better place for them later; for now it was enough that they were out of immediate sight.

Then she got her pajamas back on and huddled in the cold bed, shivering until her body heat warmed it up, and she finally was able to fall asleep.

Elizabeth Walker wrapped her arms around herself in the hallway and stared at the door she had just seen someone enter. There had been two people down in the part of the house past the kitchen. One of them had been a boy, since he'd gone to the boys' wing. The other—she hoped she had counted the number of doors right; she wouldn't know who it was until daylight and she could check the nameplates.

What had they been doing down there? She was pretty sure it wasn't for making out. Who'd go make out in the storage rooms when everyone had his or her own private room and it would be just as bad to be caught out of bed as in it with someone? She thought she'd seen them carrying something, maybe two piles of books, but why? What could they possibly want that they couldn't get by daylight? Not student records, those were all kept on the computer, not in notebooks.

Maybe they knew something, too? Knew just enough, and were looking for more answers, maybe allies, the way she was?

Could it be two more of Them?

She didn't *think* there were any Shadow Knights among the students. . . .

But could she really be sure?

🌟

Spirit didn't get a chance to show Addie her pile of scrapbooks in the morning, because she was awakened by Muirin, who sailed in the door without even a knock, her arms full of—stuff.

"Up!" Muirin demanded. "I can't finish this now without fitting it on you."

"What?" After last night, Spirit felt as groggy as if she had been drugged, and she couldn't imagine what on earth Muirin was talking about.

"Your *dress,* doofus!" Muirin said. "I have to fit it to you if it's going to look decent. Up! I won't be seen with anyone that looks like she got her dress straight out of the storage closet!"

"Uh—" Spirit didn't get a chance to say anything else; Muirin ruthlessly pulled the covers off her, hauled her up to stand on a chair, pulled something like an inside-out gown over the top of her pajamas, and then poked and pinned and muttered while Spirit tried to wake up and make sense of what Muirin was doing.

She hadn't gotten more than a vague notion of what the dress was—maybe—going to look like, when Muirin finished pinning, yanked it up over her head again, and sailed out the door, muttering, leaving Spirit standing with the door open, barefooted, in a shower of pins, with her pajamas half over her head.

By the time she'd picked up all the pins so she was sure she wasn't going to end up with a toe impaled, she knew she was going to have barely enough time to get dressed to get breakfast without getting into trouble.

Loch, Burke, and Addie were just finishing as she squeaked in the door. Muirin was nowhere to be seen.

"She ate early," Loch said, without looking up at her.

Spirit blinked, and realized that must mean Muirin had gotten up to eat as soon as the dining room opened in order to have stormed into Spirit's room to fit the dress.

"She didn't sleep," Addie said, with a wry smile. "She was in a white-hot passion of creation all last night."

"Creation or caffeine." Burke shrugged. "Don't look at me, I'm a guy, I don't get all that froufrou stuff."

Spirit sat down, silently poured milk over her cereal, and began to eat. Her brain sluggishly began to wake up . . . and she looked down to hide her sour expression.

Because it certainly would have been nice if the others could be half as motivated about finding out who was behind the Hunt as they were about that stupid, stupid dress.

FİVE

Spirit sat on the edge of her bed in her slip, and reminded herself for the bazillionth time that this was just *one* night. Nothing was going to get done or undone in just one night. It wasn't as if this was even a Significant Night like the Equinoxes or Solstices. Not a thing had stirred, for good or bad, since the last night of the Hunt.

New Year's Eve was just an arbitrary night on a calendar; there was nothing magically special about it. Keep her guard up, sure, but there was no reason to be paranoid.

She'd never have gone to a dance, much less a formal dinner and dance like this one, if she was still at home. If she was still at home. . . .

It would have, could have, been so exciting. Fancy dress, a dinner right out of a movie? Way to go, Oakhurst, for turning what should have been a dizzying experience into an ordeal, and sucking every bit of joy out of it.

That was pretty much the way things went around here, though.

She took a deep breath. Okay, so this was going to be a night of tense misery alternated with pure boredom, but hey, at least there wouldn't be anything trying to kill her or her friends.

She was sitting on the edge of her bed in her slip because Muirin hadn't delivered the dress yet . . . and if she didn't hurry up and do so, Spirit was going to have to go to the formal dinner in whatever was left in the Little Closet of Horrors. Or whatever she could make look sort-of formal with her school uniforms.

And at this point, she wasn't sure she cared.

The door burst open and Muirin sailed through it, carrying a black-and-white dress over her head like a banner. Her expression was one of triumph and she looked absolutely fabulous, as if she was ready to step onto the Red Carpet at an awards ceremony.

"Sorry I took so long, my hair decided to have a mind of its own." Muirin handed the hanger to Spirit and closed the door. "Oh good, Addie did your hair already."

Actually, Spirit had done her own hair—she wasn't too bad at doing a French braid—but she decided not to say anything. Instead she stood up and held the dress out for a look.

She felt herself smiling. It was actually—nice! More than nice, it was elegant! It had nice straps—she had lived in terror that Muirin was going to make her go strapless, because she didn't *have* any strapless bras. It was kind of like the dress Audrey Hepburn had worn as Eliza Doolittle at the ball, fitted in from the chest to the hips and flaring out from there, except the black had been made into a couple of side panels that would make her look taller and model-slender. "Here," Muirin said, shoving something else at her, which turned out to be a wrap made of more black satin with white fur on the inside. "You're going to freeze otherwise. You got them to get you white shoes like I told you, right?"

"Uh-huh," Spirit replied, sticking out one foot to show, while she struggled into the dress. Muirin spun her around while she was still struggling, expertly tugged the dress down and into place, and zipped her up, all before she quite knew what was going on.

"A credit to my design," Muirin said smugly.

Spirit turned to look in the mirror and blinked. She looked . . . well, a lot older. Sophisticated. Not like she'd expected.

Next to her, Muirin was just amazing, all sleek and styled and a whole lot older than she actually was, with just enough Goth about her to keep her looking like herself instead of someone's trophy wife. All in black, of course. Even to the tiara in her hair, which was black crystals instead of the usual faux diamonds.

Then Spirit blinked at the tiara, because it didn't even remotely have that "fake" look to it, and turned toward Muirin to look more closely at it.

"Black star sapphires. Man-made. And the setting's only ten

carat." Muirin smirked. "The Trust isn't going to let me go *that* crazy."

She's wearing a gold and star sapphire tiara. . . .

Spirit didn't have any jewelry . . . but then again, what was the point? Everyone knew she wasn't rich. Self-consciously she patted her hair, took a last look at her makeup, and reached for the wrap to go.

"Don't forget your ring," Muirin cautioned.

Spirit blinked. "My—"

"Ring. Class ring. This is one of the times you have to wear it." Muirin held out her hand with a look of distaste. On it was her class ring, the stone reflecting golden-yellow. "Even if it doesn't go with the dress."

"Oh. Right." Spirit opened the drawer she'd tossed the box into the day she got it, and fished it out. She felt a distaste that matched the look on Muirin's face as she opened it, and a heavy reluctance to put the thing on.

It seemed to close around her finger as she did, and she fought back an urge to yank it off and throw it back in the drawer. Instead, she picked up her wrap, and waved at Muirin. "Age before beauty," she quoted wryly.

"Pearls before swine," Muirin smirked, finishing the Dorothy Parker quote, as Spirit had known she would. Spirit grinned, and followed her out.

The dining room looked even more formal than it had at Christmas dinner. Red velvet curtains hid the buffet line, more red velvet curtains closed out the view from the windows. Every table was set with the really, really good china with the school crest in gold, and a dozen different forks and spoons and knives. There were candles in silver holders on each table, the napkins were linen in silver holders, and there was a card at each place setting, in a silver holder. Spirit didn't have to pick them all up to know they were solid silver, not silver plate. There were four Waterford Crystal goblets for each place—Spirit knew they were Waterford because the instructions for the dinner had mentioned them. The rolls were in silver baskets lined with linen napkins. The butter was sculpted rosettes on ice in a cut-crystal bowl that sparkled and cast rainbow reflections. The salt and pepper shakers were crystal and silver, which did the same. One of the waitstaff, done up in a tux, stopped them at the door. He gravely asked Muirin her name, then consulted a list and conducted her to a table. He did the same for Spirit, who by this time was hideously tense. Who was she going to get stuck with?

No one awful, it turned out; just the regular gang plus an adult, which was such a relief. The waiter brought her to a table near the windows that held Burke, Muirin, Addie, Loch, and a teacher she only knew vaguely, a Ms. Campion, who taught Chemistry and Alchemy.

She started to reach for her chair, then remembered just in time to let the waiter pull it out for her. When she was seated, he handed her a menu. One of the glasses was already poured full of water, and with her mouth dry, she reached for it.

She looked up at the same time, and noticed Burke staring at her as if she was a stranger. She felt her cheeks getting warm, but in a good way.

"That's a very attractive gown, Miss White," said Ms. Campion.

"Thank you. Muirin made it for me," she replied, blushing, and Muirin grinned and winked.

"Muirin's creative ways with clothing are familiar to the staff," Ms. Campion responded dryly. Muirin grinned even harder, but managed to make herself look serious before the teacher glanced her way again.

Polite conversation. We're supposed to make polite conversation. . . . Spirit racked her brain for something to say. Not school, that wasn't sophisticated enough. The weather was too ordinary.

Addie saved her. "Are you a fan of classical music, Ms. Campion?" she asked politely.

"Very much so," the woman said, a little warmth coming into her smile.

"Ah! Well, I recently was introduced to the works of a composer new to me," Addie replied brightly, "through a movie Spirit recommended."

That managed to get a conversation started that they could all add to, the use of classical music in movies, and from that, to composers who specialized in movie music. Then the waiters delivered the appetizers, except the menu called it "First Course." It was—snails. She had never, ever thought she would find herself eating snails! But the other choice was raw oysters on the half shell, and at least the snails were cooked. So she dug the snails out of their shells with a special little fork, and managed to get two down by not thinking about what they were.

Then "Second Course," which was soup; she couldn't tell what it was, except it was creamy, orange, and didn't taste like tomato. Third was a little portion of fish with a pale yellow sauce on it and cucumber slices. Fourth was a little piece of steak and a couple of teaspoons of stir-fried vegetables, and she would have thought that was going to be the end of it, except the menu said, no, there was a lot more to come . . . all the portions were tiny, but with all the food that was on that menu, they would have to be, or you could never get through it.

Next, a slice of . . . she had to consult the menu . . . it was duck with orange sauce, some sort of fancy sweet potatoes, and peas. All in doll-tea-party-sized portions, of course.

Then they brought a cup of something that looked like sherbet. It was, kind of. Not very sweet. Tasted sort of wine-y.

Then half a little bird. The menu said "quail." With stuffing. She was terrified they were going to make her eat the bones, too, but no, she watched Addie, and Addie teased the meat off with her knife and fork and just ate that.

Then cold asparagus with a vinegar-y sauce.

Then something brown and little rounds of bread to spread it on. *Pâté de foie gras.* Goose liver paste. *Ugh.* But the rule was, you had to eat some of every single course and look as though you liked it. They were actually going to be graded on "apparent enjoyment." Well, not graded, "critiqued," but it might just as well have been a grade. She managed, somehow, mostly by scraping as little of it on the bread as she could.

And finally, at last, dessert. Bananas Foster, which she had never heard of, and which a waitperson made at the table with a lot of fanfare and flames. It turned out to be bananas in rum with sugar and cinnamon, cooked and set on fire and served on ice cream. Muirin's eyes just lit up when she saw it, though she didn't act the way she usually did when presented with dessert. It was good, better than the snails and the goose liver.

Every course came with a change of plates, different silverware, and a change of drinks. Not real wine, fruit juice, but it wasn't sweet, it was dry and tart. Red with the meat, white with the fish, sparkling with the duck.

She was glad it wasn't wine, she'd have been drunk.

They did get coffee, real coffee, with dessert. She was grateful for that, she needed the caffeine along with the sugar jolt. She never knew eating could be such hard work!

She was more than ready to go back to her room, pull on a sweatshirt, and watch a movie, but the evening wasn't over yet.

Never mind that they had been sitting there for three hours, from seven until almost ten!

Ms. Campion signaled the end of dinner by putting her napkin on the table and waiting for one of the boys to come pull her chair out. Loch picked up on what she was waiting for first, of course. It was then that Spirit saw that Loch not only had a tux, he had a *full* tux with tails, like something Fred Astaire would have worn! And he looked, well, amazing in it. He pulled out Ms. Campion's chair and she stood up. "There will be about half an hour for you to freshen up," she said. "Then the dance will start at ten-thirty. As always, you are expected to be prompt."

"Thank you, Ms. Campion," they all murmured; in the rest of the room, similar gettings-up and goings-out had started. Loch pulled out Spirit's chair, while Burke got Addie's and Muirin's.

Spirit would have liked nothing better than to go back to her room, pull off the dress, and pretend she was sick. But . . . no . . . there was no way she could get away with that.

Bleah.

❧

The dance was, of course, in the gym/auditorium. The decorations from the Winter Dance were back up, along with some balloons and streamers. She'd been in a kind of numb state at the time, and couldn't appreciate them then; now, well, on the one hand, they were pretty, all blue and white and glitter and crystals. But on the other hand, they looked cold, and not so much festive as "professional." Like this was some kind of theater or movie set, and they were all extras who were actually working and supposed to pretend they were celebrating.

Well, yeah. We are pretending. This wasn't our idea of a good time. Obviously if the kids had their way, this would just be a flashier version of a school dance. More and better refreshments, maybe costumes. Certainly louder music. And everyone would be using their powers, too.

The music tonight, however, was all Big Band, and none of it was swing or any kind of lively—it was kind of what you'd hear at an Old Folks Home "dance," Spirit thought.

People are going to go to sleep in the middle of dancing, she thought, which would be kind of amusing actually. She could just see it. Like a bunch of zombies.

Use of powers was completely forbidden. The teachers had been *so* adamant about that, without specifying what would happen if you dared try, that Spirit figured even the most rebellious were pretty cowed.

All she could figure was that this was supposed to be more "practice" for the leading roles in society they were all supposed to take when they graduated. You had to pretend you liked all the food, pretend this sort of music was your idea of a good time, because people were watching you, and if you didn't fit in, you wouldn't be invited back or to the private dinners where important things got done. Well, if this was what being a lead in society was like, she would be perfectly happy to go work at Mickey D's for the rest of her life.

For a fleeting moment she wondered just what she *was* supposed to do when she graduated.

Assuming I survive.

Unless Muirin and Addie were right and there was a big pile of money waiting for her somewhere because of insurance, it wasn't as if she had any money for college. Where was she supposed to go? What was she supposed to do? The others who didn't have money, well, they had powers, and there weren't any rules out there in the world telling them they couldn't use them. So they would, of course. And that made her think about something else; sure, there were plenty of honest ways to use your powers, but there were more that weren't. How many Shadewalkers were master thieves for instance? Or spies?

But, of course, she didn't have any powers.

Maybe she would have to work at Mickey D's for the rest of her life. She had a fleeting vision of herself serving burgers, living in a trailer . . .

Strangely, that fleeting vision almost seemed more appealing than being here.

She shook off the mood and walked all the way into the gym. There were more little tables set up around the dance floor, *also* with little name-plaques on them, but it was clear when Spirit spotted her that Muirin had somehow managed to swap a bunch so the gang got a table in a corner. Muirin was putting the last of the name-plaques on the table when Spirit saw her; Muirin looked up at her as she hesitated, just inside the door, and waved at her. With relief, she pulled the wrap around her shoulders and joined them.

It turned out that the refreshments were pretty sparse—but then again, only someone like Murr-cat would have room for any kind of snacks after that dinner. There was punch and there were soft drinks—but *not* in cans or bottles, you had to ask the "bartender" for one and you only got a cup at a time, unless you were a boy, getting a drink for a girl, too. The boys were supposed to do that. The girls were not supposed to do the same.

There were shiny gold cardboard tiaras for the girls and shiny black cardboard top hats for the guys, and noisemakers all bunched up in the centers of the tables, waiting, but hardly anybody even looked at those. No one was wearing them.

"Welcome to our joyous celebration," Muirin said, straight-faced. "Happy New Year. Be festive if it kills you."

Now that she wasn't concentrating on eating and making sure she did all the right things with the right silverware, Spirit got a chance for a good look at the other gowns, starting with Addie's. It was strapless, with a chiffon scarf, corset-like top, and huge, flowing chiffon skirt, all in a pale ice blue. Like Muirin's, it was pretty obvious that this hadn't come from the Little Closet of Horrors, either. Addie didn't wear jewelry, though she had matching silk flowers in her hair, and not the kind you got at a discount store; these would have looked real, except for the color. Bird-of-paradise flowers didn't come in blue—though, of course, if you had the right powers, you could turn them blue.

As she looked at the other girls sitting down or milling around, it was *really* obvious who had gowns of their own, and who had been stuck with the Closet. Poor Elizabeth was one of the latter, bundled into an ill-fitting seafoam horror that made her skin look yellow, and bunched up around her waist. It made her look fat, which was pretty hard to do, considering how slender she was. Elizabeth wasn't sitting down; she kind of hovered at the edge of the crowd as if she wasn't sure what to do.

It occurred to Spirit at that point that, unless some of the others had made their dresses—she supposed that was possible; after all, there was a theater group, and a costume shop, so there had to be sewing machines—this was a good way to tell who had money and who didn't. Anyone who *could* have a real formal clearly did.

Judging by the lack of Ugly, most of the kids, the girls, anyway, had money. . . .

"Do I get to keep this?" she asked Muirin. "The dress, I mean."

Muirin shrugged. "Put it in your closet. If they don't demand it back, it's yours. I don't suppose you know how to sew?" she added out of the blue.

Spirit flushed, because . . . well, that was one of the things her mom had insisted she learn along with her homeschooling. Most of her clothing was homemade. No, not *was*, had been, because it all burned up in the fire. The last two years before the accident she'd been making all of her own clothes rather than suffer her mom's tastes. The only thing they'd ever bought was blue jeans. "Uh, yeah . . ." she said. "Pretty well. I mean, not like *you*, but I can do basic stuff."

"Good. Your payment for that dress is to help me. No one ever wants to get stuck in the Bridal Rejects dresses twice." Muirin licked her lips. "I collect a *lot* of favors around October and November, and again before the Spring Dance at the end of the term."

Spirit blinked. "You mean . . ."

Muirin began pointing out the dresses she'd remade, refitted, or sewn completely from scratch. "There's a certain amount of raiding the Theater Department fabric that we can get away with," she said with a smirk. "Of course, they keep buying up Prom Zombies and sticking them in the closet, so I don't often have to resort to cutting up stuff meant for *The Importance of Being Earnest*."

Spirit began revising her estimate of how many of the girls had a lot of money sharply downward.

"Remember what I told you? There's a big trade in favors around here." Muirin nodded wisely. "Hey, you know what? If you don't want one of the jerkwads to mess with you, we'll offer to help his girlfriend with her party stuff for the Spring Fling, make sure he knows we did, and I guaran-darn-tee you he'll leave you alone. If I'd known you could sew before this, I could have saved you some grief."

While Spirit was blinking in shock over this revelation, Loch and Burke returned with drinks for everyone. Muirin seized on her soda with the look of someone dying in the desert seizing a cup of water, and blew a kiss to Burke, who gave it to her. "Loch, I cannot believe you have a fitted tuxedo with *tails*," Addie said with admiration. "You look fabulous! Is it bespoke?"

Spirit had no idea what Addie meant, but evidently Loch did.

"Yeah," he said, with a shrug. "Dad got invited to a lot of Embassy things, and during school holidays it was easier for him to haul me along than leave me behind. I think he got some kind of brownie points for having me with him. So here I am, with a tux, and no blue jeans, because everything that got shipped here was packed by Dad's secretary." He rolled his eyes. "I think all she did was grab what was in the closet in my bedroom, which was *never* stuff I actually wore much, because I was hardly ever home. God knows what happened to the stuff that was still at school. It probably got bundled up and sent to storage."

Burke, who was wearing what must have come out of the

boys' version of the Little Closet of Horrors, gave him a look of sympathy. Somehow, he made the boxy secondhand rent-a-tux look good. Then again, his didn't fit *too* badly. Not like a couple of the boys, whose trouser-waists were obviously somewhere in the vicinity of their armpits, and who were wearing cummerbunds to conceal that fact.

"Why won't you ever let me fit your tux to you, Burke?" Muirin asked, teasingly.

"Cause it won't fit next time I have to wear it," he replied, with calm logic. "Besides, you just want an excuse to tickle me."

"He's ticklish?" Spirit asked Muirin, who smirked.

"Very, if you catch him off guard. Which I never can. Addie did it once, and it was hilarious, he turned purple."

"Everyone got your dance cards?" Addie asked.

"My which-what?" Spirit was bewildered now. Addie shoved a little booklet-thing across the table at her; it had a brown metal foil cover with the school crest in gold stamped on the front, and a tiny little gold pen attached to it with a gold ribbon. She opened it. There was her full name in gold on the inside, and a list of numbers with the names of dances and blank spaces beside them.

"You have to dance at least five dances, whether or not you've taken Ballroom yet," Addie reminded her. "Your partner signs off on the dance. Or if you're really popular, guys come up to you and fill it in ahead of time." She made a face. "It's part of 'improving our social graces.' Yet another thing to get graded on."

"Next thing you know, they'll start grading us on how many dreams we have a night," Muirin said sarcastically.

"Oh . . ." Spirit swallowed. "Uh . . ."

"No sweat, Spirit." Burke plucked the card out of her nerveless fingers, and wrote his name in three of the spaces. Not to be outdone, Loch did the same. "There you go. One over the mandatory number, you're set." Then they both did the same for Muirin and Addie.

Muirin took hers back with a smirk. "Since I took Ballroom and I have a bigger quota, I'm going to go collect on some favors," she said, archly, and sailed off in the direction of the other tables. Addie laughed.

"But . . . I don't know how . . . ," Spirit began.

"Which is why we picked easy stuff." The music changed, and Loch held out his hand. "Come on. Just do what I do, backward."

It wasn't as easy as Loch had implied—but it wasn't as hard as Spirit had feared. He helped by counting it out under his breath—it was a cha-cha, a dance she'd only seen in movies. She managed to not trip and fall or step on his feet. He brought her back to the table, and since the next dance didn't have his or Burke's name after it, she sat and watched the others, trying to get the steps.

Loch was a very good dancer, and some of the girls started coming up to him to get him to sign their cards, which he did, readily. It seemed to Spirit that he was sad, though, and she couldn't figure out why. Okay, there was no real reason to be all that happy, but there was a melancholy look to him that was odd.

She couldn't get up the nerve to ask any of the boys to dance the way Muirin was doing, and anyway, since *she* hadn't taken the Ballroom Dance classes, she wasn't being graded on this, so she just sat and drank diet cola and watched in between being taken out on the floor by Burke and Loch, and felt a little envy when she watched Murr-cat being whirled around by Loch in a waltz. *That* looked like fun; Muirin was even smiling.

About ten minutes to midnight, there was a little stir at the door, and a moment later it was obvious why. Doctor Ambrosius strode into the room, though he spent a little time greeting the teachers at the "bar" end of the room. Spirit sighed. They were probably in for another speech.

She just hoped Loch would come get her for the midnight dance. That would be a nice sort of omen for the new year.

But it was Burke who came over to the table, and held out his hand, just a little awkwardly. She didn't want him to feel badly, so she got up and took it and let him lead her out onto the dance floor with a smile, even though she was a little disappointed. Still, at least she wouldn't be sitting out the first dance of the New Year. That would bite.

The music didn't start, though, and Doctor Ambrosius walked out to the edge of the floor, standing in a spotlight. Spirit tried not to sigh. *Here comes the speech. . . .*

The sixty-second countdown started before he could open his mouth, much to Spirit's relief. Ambrosius didn't even look annoyed; he had his "genial" face on, the one he'd worn when the presents were given out. She felt Burke tighten his grip on her hand, and in spite of it being pretty corny, she found herself counting down aloud with everyone else. Burke caught her eye and smiled. She smiled back.

She wondered if he was trying to work up the courage to kiss her . . . and she wondered how she'd feel about that, even as she called out the last few seconds. Did she want him as a friend, or as a boyfriend? Maybe it would be easier to keep things the way they were. But if he was her boyfriend, maybe he'd feel like he had to support her more. That would help while she tried to convince the others that they were still all in danger.

But would that be using him? Was that fair to him?

"Five . . . four . . . three . . . two . . . ONE!"

Suddenly the lights went out. Completely out.

The "Happy New Year!" shouts died, abruptly. It was very dark, and unexpectedly quiet. A couple people laughed nervously. Even the emergency exit lights were out. It was like being in a cave.

Spirit wondered if this was supposed to be part of the evening, even as Burke held her hand even tighter. But nothing happened, and even the nervous laughter died out.

She got a strange, horrible, sick feeling in the pit of her stomach, and a cold chill went down her back that had nothing to do with the cooling air of the room.

Something was wrong. And something very bad was about to happen. . . .

Maybe not, she tried to tell herself, a little desperately. *Maybe it's just a prank so people can kiss.*

But that horrible feeling in her stomach didn't go away, and neither did the sensation that made her want to shudder. The darkness wasn't at all comforting; it swallowed up even the little sounds people were making as they stirred nervously, engulfing the shuffling feet and edgy titters in a way that made her hair try to stand up.

There were uneasy murmurs now . . . whispers that didn't sound like people were using the dark to neck. Why didn't Doctor Ambrosius say something?

Why didn't one of the teachers?

"Something's wrong," Burke said, still holding her hand hard. "This never happened at the other dances."

"C-c-could it be a trick?" she whispered back, her voice shaking despite herself. "You know—a prank?"

"Not a chance. All the circuit-breaker boxes are in locked rooms to keep people from pulling stupid stuff; it has to be a power failure." Burke sounded very sure of that. "Maybe as far as town. There's no storm out there, though. Maybe someone from Radial got drunk and blew up a high tension tower."

"Do they do that?" she asked incredulously.

"Well, they never have before, but they're redneck cowboys, it's New Year's Eve, and they have easy access to dynamite . . ." his voice trailed off a moment. "Heck, it could be a cascade failure from as far away as Canada. Anyway, the power should kick back on in a minute. Oakhurst has big backup generators. We can make all our own power for as long as the diesel lasts, in fact, and there's huge storage tanks underground."

But he moved closer to her, and she to him, and all over the room people were starting to get an edge of fear in their voices.

"I'm sure Doctor Ambrosius and the teachers are getting the gennies going now," Burke said, but his voice sounded . . . uncertain.

But the power, and the lights, didn't come back.

The room was really getting colder.

And the sick feeling in the bottom of Spirit's stomach told her that the worst was yet to come.

SIX

Spirit clutched Burke's hand and strained her eyes until they actually hurt, trying to see in the darkness. Still none of the teachers spoke. What was *wrong* with everybody?

Suddenly, there was something—a spark of light. Then another, and another. For a moment she was afraid that she had strained her eyes until she'd torn something in there, but no— there were more and more of these little lights—

"What's that? What are those?" someone gasped, a girl with plenty of hysteria in her voice.

More and more of the lights winked on, hundreds of them now, all colors. Just tiny little sparks, not enough to do anything but break the pitch-black darkness. Spirit couldn't even tell for sure how close they were to her. Were they on the walls? Floating in the air? She glanced up; there were more overhead, anyway.

They weren't staying on steadily, either, they were flickering—you couldn't say "flashing," they were too dim and it was more like they were fading in and out. It was like a million multicolored lightning bugs were in here, but none of them seemed close enough to touch.

Somehow, though, there was nothing very comforting about them. It was more like the lights were watching them. Like eyes. And not friendly eyes, either. Like the lights were waiting for something to happen, and it was going to be bad when it did.

There was some nervous laughter. And just at that moment, it occurred to Spirit that she was in a gym full of magicians . . . and shouldn't *someone* be able to generate light? Or fire? Or something?

And why hadn't those people whose powers included that little parlor trick thought of doing it yet?

Does it matter? Maybe they're all just waiting for the punch line of this joke, only it's not a joke and they haven't figured that out yet. Say something!

She opened her mouth.

It was as if the mere thought had summoned up a terrible retribution. A wave of incredible terror washed over her, out of nowhere.

The words died in her throat, and the scream that tried to replace them choked off into a little squeak. She couldn't feel Burke's hand. The little sparks of light gleamed malevolently at her. Her heart was beating so fast it felt as if it was about to explode in her chest; she was burning hot and ice cold all at the same time. Her eyes burned, and she couldn't move, and even if she *could* have moved, she couldn't see where to move to. She felt her whole body shuddering with every panicked heartbeat, as if her body was rattling to bits.

The vision of the night her whole family died rose up in front of her; she could see the baleful sparks at the bottom of the holes that *thing* had instead of eyes glaring at her. Sparks of light, like the ones here, in the gym. The thing was here, with her, the thing that had killed her family! It was here, and it was looking for her, it had come to finish the job and it had brought a whole mob of friends!

Her throat ached, her chest ached, and it felt like her lungs were going to explode. She couldn't get any air, and yet she was panting as if she had just finished a kendo bout with Dylan.

Someone screamed, shrill, high, piercing the darkness.

Now at last a scream burst out of her, joining the other screams all around her, triggered by the first person to cry out. And instantly, everyone else in the room was shrieking in the same terror.

Her knees started to give. She couldn't think, she could only feel. Fear, fear, nothing but fear! She felt the screams coming out of her, but she couldn't hear them over the shrieks of everyone else. Her hands were clenched—on Burke?—but she couldn't feel them. Her hands were numb, she needed to run, to hide, but there was nowhere to run and nowhere to hide.

Her heart was beating so fast—it was going to explode. Or she was going to go insane.

Then—salvation. *Light!*

It happened like an explosion, and so painful to her dark-accustomed eyes that an instant headache burst into life at the back of her head. But at last, at last, the room erupted in light, the perfectly ordinary lights of the gym, high above all the decorations, glaring down on everyone with white fluorescence.

And the fear—vanished. It just disappeared, leaving her limp and exhausted and feeling like a used paper towel.

Her brain started to work again; the first thing she realized was that she and Burke were clinging to each other like a— well, a terrified couple. Right now, she didn't much feel like letting him go, and he didn't seem to want to let go of her any time soon, either. He was alert, though, his gaze flitting all over the place. Looking for something? Or just looking?

She tried to get hold of herself and do the same. Whatever had caused this, it was pretty clear as she looked around the gym that it had come as a complete surprise to everyone; everywhere she looked, students were clinging to each other, confused, as wrung out as she was, and a few still scared. Even that hulking brute, Blake Watson, was white and shaking, his eyes wild, fists clenched. Dylan Williams was passed out cold on the floor a few feet away, and he wasn't the only one who had passed out, either. As people managed to shake off the last of the fear and start to react, a couple little knots of people were forming around others. Spirit got sight of a poof of frothy pink skirt, a long trail of gold-and-black slinky stuff, and someone's legs in tux pants. From far across the gym floor came the sound of someone throwing up.

The teachers had been caught off guard, too; the first teacher she spotted, Ms. Holland, was white, thin-lipped, and still shaking, groping for a chair to collapse into. Over near the "bar," Mr. Krandal, Mr. Bowman, and Ms. Groves had just started to talk to one another, and at least Mr. Krandal was furious from the look on his face.

So none of them knew this was going to happen . . . .

Slowly, people were starting to throw off the lingering remains of the fear, and their reactions were as varied as the students and teachers were themselves. Spirit could hear, and see, people starting to cry; most of the adults were getting angry. Some people were very groggy, staggering or wobbling, acting as if they'd had a stroke or a concussion.

Whispers broke the silence, and a few sobs. Then more and more people started talking. Voices rose, echoing across the gym, then more and more joined in, until the babble was as loud as a storm over the ocean. Mostly people were saying the same thing. "What was that?" "What happened?" "Who did that?"

Then one voice cut across them all.

"Have done."

It had the volume of a drill sergeant without sounding as if the person speaking was raising his voice at all, and it had, above all, Authority. It was recognizable immediately, of course.

Doctor Ambrosius.

"He used Command Voice," murmured Burke, still making no move to pry her off his arm. "It's a minor Air Spell."

The babble cut off to nothing—well, almost nothing. There were still some people sobbing, and a couple murmuring drunkenly.

"Whatever caused this, no one has been seriously injured," Ambrosius said, his expression unreadable. "It's entirely possible it was a prank gone wrong, as I doubt any Oakhurst student intends to actually *challenge* the staff, and such an effect, *if* it were caused by a spell, would, of course, be properly taken as a formal challenge."

His eyes flitted over the crowd, as if he was looking for a guilty face, or someone who might at least know something. As he looked them over, he continued to talk, meaningless explanations, as if he was trying to hold their attention while *he* looked for something. Nothing of what he said made any sense, at least not to her. Ball lightning, Magnetic Resonance Waves, ancient Panic fear caused by the presence of a supernatural being . . . it seemed as if he was just babbling whatever came into his head while his eyes probed everywhere.

That was when Spirit realized that her ring was glowing.

So was Burke's.

"Your ring," she hissed at him. He glanced down and his eyes went wide.

She flashed a startled look across the gym and caught Addie's eye and, under the cover of her skirt, waved her ring hand at her friend. Addie's eyes narrowed, she looked down, and murmured something to Loch and Muirin.

Their rings were glowing, too. And near as Spirit could tell, no one else's was.

Addie quickly turned the stone into her palm and closed her hand over it; the other two did the same. Spirit tugged on Burke's arm, demonstrated, and he followed suit.

All the while, Doctor Ambrosius kept talking, his eyes searching, searching, searching. But whatever he was looking for, he didn't find it, so at last he gave up.

"All things considered, this was unpleasant, and an exceedingly rude way to interrupt the festivities, but the damage, such as it was, is minimal. Since it is clear that we can hardly continue the New Year's celebration, I am ordering all students back to their rooms, and all teachers into conference in my office. We *will* get to the bottom of this. And meanwhile, compose yourselves. Fortunately, tomorrow is not a class day; I will leave orders with the staff to keep a brunch buffet open until two in the afternoon so that you may sleep in and shake off the aftereffects of this. If anyone feels seriously ill, please report to the Infirmary."

He turned and left. Muirin, Addie, and Loch pushed their way through the crowd to Burke and Spirit, all three of them still visibly shaken. Muirin was so pale it looked as if she had done a full-out Gothic Vampire makeup job, and Addie's lips were pressed tight and colorless.

"Are you two all right?" Addie asked. Spirit nodded, and finally let go of Burke's arm, but still kept hold of his hand.

Addie shivered, and hugged herself, rubbing her arms. "I've never been through anything like that in my life. I wasn't even that scared when we were fighting the Hunt."

"I don't know what that was, but I'm kind of torn," Muirin put in. "On the one hand, anything that ends this funeral early is all right with me. On the other hand, I didn't get nearly enough soda." Her words were light—but her voice was strained, and her eyes were still so wide with fear that she looked almost comical.

"I can fix that." With an apologetic smile, Burke patted Spirit's hand until she let go of his hand. He shoved his way through the crowd to the bar, and when he came back, his arms were full of two-liter bottles of soda. He shoved the cola at Muirin, who took three bottles with a tremulous smile of thanks. He passed a ginger ale to Addie, a cola to Spirit, a bottle of something fluorescent-yellow to Loch, and kept a bottle of cola for himself. "Caffeine and sugar," he said by way of explanation. "Good for shock. That's what I told the bartenders anyway."

At this point, the teachers had completely shaken off the effects—or at least, enough so that they could follow Doctor Ambrosius's orders—and had started to chase the students out of the gym, stopping only to help the ones still sitting shakily on the floor. "We'd better go," said Addie. Spirit nodded.

"So much for a festive New Year," Loch said, dryly.

She cradled her soda bottle in her arms and followed Addie to the girls' section, Muirin beside her. It was a very surreal sight, all of these girls in their formal gowns, shuffling along like a bunch of shell-shocked disaster victims. Most of them still looked terminally confused.

"Net" mouthed Muirin, as she ducked into her room to stash her loot—or drink it all, there was no telling with Murr-cat. Having the dining room open with a brunch until mid-afternoon was pretty much license for her to go on a caffeine and sugar jag and sleep it off. Addie and Spirit nodded.

Whether or not caffeine and sugar were good for shock, Spirit's mouth was dry and she felt parched, and she was awfully glad Burke had snagged all that soda. Water just wasn't going to do it, and she did *not* want to go out into the empty halls to the communal fridge to replenish her depleted supply of bottled water and juice.

She put the bottle down, stood there a moment, exhaustion making her indecisive, then finally squirmed around until she could reach her zipper. She carefully peeled herself out of the dress and hung it up in the closet. Night of terror or no night of terror, she still wanted it; weird, but she did. Under all the fuzziness of exhaustion and the ever-present paranoia and the reaction to what had just happened was this little voice reminding her urgently that it was easily the most gorgeous thing she had ever worn, and she needed to put it away safe. Since that ridiculous little voice was the only thing giving her a direction at the moment, she obeyed it.

Net. Murr-cat said to get on the 'net. Right. She pulled on fuzzy Oakhurst-brown, polar-fleece jammies, poured herself a huge glass of Burke's bounty, and logged on.

The intranet, as she fully expected, was humming. As soon as she was on, she got an invite to a private chatroom—or at least as private as you could be with Big Brother probably keystroke-logging everything you typed. She sipped her soda, feeling the cold, acidic cola cutting through the layer of parched "desert" down her throat, and opened a second window to the school-wide chat.

It was scrolling almost too fast to follow. Everyone had a theory, some of them pretty out-there, even for someone as paranoid as Spirit. She only caught a handful of them; someone thought it was aliens (of course), citing the "paralyzing fear" that was supposed to overcome you when you were about to be abducted. Dylan's theory was that the government had finally figured out what Oakhurst really taught and was using

some sort of top-secret mind ray on them as a prelude to round-
ing them all up and incarcerating them in a death camp. He
was hysterically telling them all that they had to barricade
their rooms, block up the windows, hide in the closet, and get
ready for the commandos who were going to come over the
horizon in black helicopters at any moment.

*Huh, that's not as crazy as it sounds, except for the top-secret
mind ray part. I bet if the government really did know what was going
on here, they really would round us all up. Of course, it wouldn't be to
go to a death camp. We'd be too useful.*

Probably they'd all be recruited for stuff. Espionage,
intelligence-gathering, assassination. Somewhere, she thought,
the ghost of her hippie father nodded with approval at her
reasoning.

The flaw in Dylan's reasoning was that this place had Money,
and if she had learned anything from her folks, it was that the
government never, ever bothered anyone with Money. Wacky
cultists had "compounds" that could be raided. When people
with Money built the same sort of places, and stockpiled an
equal amount of weaponry, the places were called "estates" and
the weapons were a "collection" or a "private security arsenal."

She checked the private chat window.

Never seen or heard of any magic that would do that, Addie was
typing. It took everyone I saw by surprise, unless there are people
that are better actors than I think they are.

What was the point? Loch asked. Whatever happened, the question is, why did it happen in the first place? I could see it if something
had followed up on the fear, but nothing did.

Loch was right. If an attack had taken place, whether it was the Wild Hunt or Dylan's black-helicopter commandos, no one would have been able to do anything to protect themselves. But there had been no attack so—why?

In answer, Muirin pasted some lines from Elizabeth Walker.

EW: It only makes sense as a test. Otherwise something would have happened while we were all frozen. Maybe a test to see which of us could stand up to the terror.

Spirit emptied her glass, poured another, and thought about that. It was a good idea, actually. The only problem was that the teachers had all been caught, too.

Wait a minute . . .

It got the CHAPERONES too, she typed, putting the word in all caps so they remembered that not all of the teachers were there, chaperoning. Not more than half, so far as she could tell. So had the teachers who were not in the gym been affected, too? Or had they been the ones behind it?

But surely Doctor Ambrosius would think of that, first thing. And surely the absent teachers would be the first ones he questioned.

In brightest day in blackest night, Burke typed.

She blinked again, looked down at the ring with the stone still turned into the palm of her hand, and clenched her teeth. Their rings had glowed. And no one else's had. So what did *that* mean? She yanked it off, shoved it in the box, and shoved the box to the back of the desk drawer.

And what was it that Doctor Ambrosius had been looking

for, back there when he'd been babbling about Magnetic Waves? His eyes hadn't been down, as they would have been if he had been looking for glowing rings, but he had definitely been looking for something.

Maybe Elizabeth was right. Maybe it had been a test that Doctor Ambrosius himself had run, to find out who was able to withstand whatever it was.

But then wouldn't he have warned the teachers first?

You'd think.

Actually, he'd have had to, wouldn't he? Because if he didn't, they wouldn't be braced in case one of the students really ran amok. Maybe had a psychotic break, or went postal. No, that would have been monumentally stupid.

Did you guys all see the sparks that lit up first? she asked, hoping to remind them that—hello! The rings glowed!

The chorus of "yes's" at least told her she hadn't been seeing things.

Might have been some kind of spillover from the fear-thing, Loch typed. Might work as an early warning if it happens again. . . .

If??? she typed, wishing there was a sarcasm emoticon. Because hadn't she told them? Hadn't she warned them?

And the glowing rings . . . she mentally thanked Burke for coming up with a code-way to remind the others without saying "what's with the rings?" But hey, Green Lantern effect? What was that? Did anyone else see that?

Nobody but us, Addie typed. I couldn't see the whole gym, though, too many peeps. I've never, ever heard of or seen that effect before, though.

Same here, typed Muirin.

Teacher on main chat, Burke warned. Well that was different. The teachers almost never logged on main chat, permitting the students to pretend that they weren't being eavesdropped on. They all fell "silent," as they watched MOD1, MOD4, and MOD7 try and calm some of the hysteria. Dylan was soothed and reminded that the school had a direct feed from the nearest NWS weather station and that any army of helicopter-carried commandos would show up on the radar. Fortunately, he didn't immediately think about flying "below the radar." All the students were reminded that this *was* a school full of the best magicians in the world, and although they might not be aware of them, there were "protections in place" against "perfectly mundane dangers."

There was more technobabble about "freak Magnetic Resonance Fields" and a link to some research papers in the school e-library.

Evidently this was going to be the Official Explanation. *Just like all UFOs were swamp gas,* she thought cynically.

Alles ist in Ordung, typed Loch. *Everything is in order.* Even if the German hadn't been easy to guess, it wouldn't take a genius to figure out he had come to the same conclusion about the Official Explanation as she had.

Nothing to see, move along, typed Addie. These aren't the droids you're looking for.

Peace is war, Spirit responded. I guess since no one was hurt, it's All Better now, and they'll probably have donuts at breakfast to reward us for being good and going to our rooms. That was about as dangerously close to what she *wanted* to say as she was going to go.

The fact was, it wasn't All Better, and at least now the others could see that for themselves.

Okay, no one got hurt. That didn't mean anything.

The big point was, there were only two things you *could* say about the Terror.

If it had come from outside, it had gotten past all the protections and wards on the school and the grounds. Not even the Hunt had been able to do that, and according to Kelly Langley, one of the proctors, the protections and wards had been *seriously* beefed up since then. The only way the Hunt had gotten inside the grounds had been because they'd been let inside by someone able to control the wards.

That would have been teachers and staff. Unless there were some third parties who were neither teachers nor staff, and had been able to get into the school, take down the wards, and get out again without anyone seeing them. More than that, get out and get to Radial or had some hidden form of fast transportation to get them away. Fast car? Possible, but not likely.

If, however, it had come from *inside* . . .

It meant that whoever had taken down the protections for the Hunt was still here, and hadn't given up.

And even if the Terror had come from outside, someone from inside would *still* have had to take down the protections. So, the logic came full circle. There was still someone, or several someones, in here, in the guise of one of Doctor Ambrosius's trusted people. Someone who was trying to kill them all.

There were, in fact donuts. And danishes, and bear claws, and fritters, and eclairs, and bismarks, and cinnamon buns. And pancakes and waffles. And bacon and sausage, mounds of both, which the health-conscious cooking staff never, ever served in any quantity. In short, it was a forbidden-food-fest, and Spirit immediately eyed the buffet with suspicion. What was the point here, recovery or distraction? Although Murr-cat was perhaps one of the biggest junk food fiends at Oakhurst, she was by no means the only one, and all these piled-high treats were going to distract a lot of people. And maybe send them out into the snow for the only day of no-kidding un-graded playing that they'd gotten during the so-called "break."

Ungraded, because there weren't any teachers in sight. Any-where.

The group met at their usual table; Muirin hadn't needed to be hauled out of bed by the hair, because she had gotten wind of the pastry-avalanche awaiting her. The mere sight of Muirin's plate made Spirit's eyes glaze over, and she stuck to scrambled eggs and fruit.

"If this is how we're going to get fed after mysterious at-tacks, I vote for more of them," Muirin said around a glazed donut, her eyes blissful.

"Thanks," Burke replied dryly. "I'll pass."

Spirit lowered her voice to a whisper. "The stones of Burke's ring and mine lit up last night . . . I think it was after the attack, though, because if it had been during it, I would have noticed the glow. Yours did, too. Anyone else or just us?" She had brought her ring with her, but didn't put it on. After last night she was even more reluctant to do so.

They all shook their heads.

"I didn't see anyone else. Uh, something else," Loch said, chewing his lower lip. "My stone didn't just glow. Now it has a Destiny in it."

Spirit stared at him. "What?" hissed Addie. "Let me see!"

He slid his hand into the middle of the table, and they all peered down at the ring. Sure enough, there was the image of a tiny . . . stick?

"That's not a magic wand is it?" Spirit asked dubiously.

"Get your eyes checked; it's a spear," snorted Muirin, but Burke was already looking at his ring, and without a word, slid his hand to the center of the table to join Loch's. Burke's Destiny was easier to see: a shield. The boys pulled their hands back before anyone could take notice.

"Murr-cat?" Addie asked.

"Does it matter?" Muirin replied crossly. "Big deal, it looks like everyone and his dog has a Destiny now."

"No, they don't. If the Destiny came up with the glow, it's only us. I am absolutely positive no one else had glowing rings last night," Addie retorted, her eyes narrowing.

"I don't care," Muirin began, when Spirit managed to grab hold of her ring hand.

"You may not, but we do," Spirit told her, and since Muirin couldn't pull loose without making a fuss and getting people to notice there was more going on at their table than eating, she gave in sullenly, and shoved her hand where they could see it.

And there was a Destiny in the depths of her ring, too; a bird in flight.

"A bird?" said Loch, puzzled.

Spirit peered closely at it. "A raven, I think." One of her mother's friends had been an avid bird-watcher. "It's got the right beak, anyway."

"Quoth the Raven, Nevermore," said Muirin, in tones that made it clear she wasn't even remotely happy about this. "Thanks a bunch, Blondie. Anyway, big deal, it doesn't mean anything, I knew about it before . . ." She stopped, and looked even more stubborn. And guilty.

"What do you mean, you knew about it 'before,' Muirin?" Burke asked quietly. "Before what? Before when?"

All four of them glared at her, and finally she scowled and shook her hair back. "Okay, okay, I saw it Christmas Day when we all showed our rings. And it wasn't there a couple months ago when I took it out to wear it to one of Doc A's goofy tea parties, and that was the last time I looked at it." She turned a glare of her own on Spirit. "So what about you? Does yours have an angel or something in it? I bet it's an angel, or a fairy, or a rainbow, or a unicorn."

Spirit took her ring out of her pocket and put it on the table.

Just as it had been when she had taken it out of the box this morning, the stone in it was blank and unchanged.

❧

SEVEN

The kids who actually made it down for breakfast seemed to stuff themselves, as if they had been starved all last night. That didn't make any sense to Spirit, since she hadn't seen anyone avoiding the food at the New Year's Dinner; it had been really good, actually, even if the atmosphere had been strained. Maybe there was something else going on. Could they have been—oh, drained or something, by that fear?

Or maybe some of them had been so frightened they'd gone back to their rooms and thrown up. Spirit wouldn't have blamed them.

After a huge breakfast and what could not have been a very restful night, if she had been in their shoes, Spirit would have wanted a nap. Mind, she could see why Muirin didn't— Murr-cat had gotten so much sugar and chocolate she must have been buzzing. But a lot of the kids had shoveled in heaps of hash browns, huge omelets, and mountains of bacon, ham, and sausage, and that kind of thing put Spirit to sleep. If she hadn't been so determined to use this opportunity to convince the others to get serious about the threat, she probably would have been thinking about going for the protein herself and sacrificing this rare free day in favor of sleep.

As their group gathered for Monopoly in the lounge, she couldn't help notice that the lounge was practically deserted—and so were the grounds. There were three or four die-hard winter-lovers outside—ones who'd made big inroads on the pastries and were probably on as much of a sugar-high as Muirin. They were mostly skating. There couldn't be more than a dozen people in the lounge, including Spirit and her friends.

Or maybe the missing weren't napping, just huddling in their rooms, alone or in twos or threes, still scared, maybe chattering away on the computer. Spirit didn't blame them. None of them had faced the Wild Hunt. None of them had known that the students who had supposedly run away had, in fact, been murdered by the Hunt. Oh, they were told often enough that the reason they were here was because there were people out there who wanted to kill young magicians—and some of them might have the idea that those same people were the ones who had killed their own families and left them orphans. But there was no proof of any of that, and it was one thing to hear this story out of Doctor Ambrosius but it was quite another to show up at the school dance and have something try to scare you to death.

Spirit couldn't keep her attention on the game, and for once, it seemed the others, even Addie, were having the same problem.

"I just don't get it," Loch whispered, finally. "There doesn't seem to have been a point."

They didn't have to ask what he meant. Muirin bent down over the board, her voice even lower than Loch's. "They were saying before I came down to breakfast that three kids and a teacher were missing from their rooms this morning."

"If they even got there," Spirit replied darkly. "I mean, who would know if they just went missing after the dance?"

"The chaperones and proctors, I guess," Addie said in tones of uncertainty. "But Loch's right. Nothing really *happened*. We just all saw some lights and got scared. Horribly scared out of our minds, but no one was actually hurt."

Spirit threw the dice and moved her Scottie dog at random. No one objected. "If it was a test, like Elizabeth said, it probably did exactly what it was supposed to."

"A test for *what*?" Burke asked.

"Not *what*, not exactly." Spirit was thinking out loud. "More like—a test to see what everybody's reaction would be. I mean, the lights went out, right? And aren't some of you supposed to be able to make light? So why didn't anyone?" *I sure would have if I could have,* she thought a little sourly.

"We weren't supposed to use magic at the dance," Addie objected. But it sounded as if she knew how lame that statement was the moment it was out of her mouth.

"Well, duh, the dance was pretty effectively over when the lights went out, and I'd say that was an emergency situation, wouldn't you?" Spirit retorted. "And why didn't the *teachers* do something about it? They're supposed to be really hot magicians! You'd think one of *them* could make a light!"

"So, you're thinking what was being tested was how we all responded to something no one expected?" Burke hazarded.

Spirit nodded. "I mean, think about it, whoever sent the Hunt is still out there. Or in here. But they'd want to know if *we* all thought that was the end of it. But they don't want to let *us* know what they've got. So they just whip something up to scare us, then sit back and see what we do." She was very proud of herself. For something that she was just coming up with on the fly, it sounded really good, like she'd been working it out all night.

The others exchanged glances, and for once, they weren't the condescending *"Oh, humor her,"* looks they'd been giving each other lately.

"It's what I'd do," Burke said reluctantly.

"If that's what happened, we flunked," Muirin added darkly. "Teachers and Doctor Ambrosius, too."

Nobody moved. Nobody spoke. On the one hand, Spirit couldn't help but have an "I told you so" moment. On the other hand—

On the other hand, I wish I didn't get to say "I told you so."

◆

They gave up trying to play the game and instead took over one of the TVs and DVD players in the lounge and put on something utterly mindless and outdated. A musical,

Thoroughly Modern Millie, which was pretty much typical of the stuff in the DVD library in the lounge, which was a mix of "classic cinema" that you were supposed to study and take seriously like *Citizen Kane,* stuff you saw on late night movie channels, documentaries (boring ones, not good stuff like *MythBusters),* and Arts stuff like ballet and opera. It was as if the school didn't really want kids getting together to watch something; the entertainment you could pull up out of the digital library was so much better.

Maybe that was the point of having lame lounge entertainment. It would go right along with the atmosphere of competition. You wouldn't really want kids getting together and having fun . . . they might make friends.

Each of them brooded about the situation in his or her own way. Muirin chattered cattily nonstop. Addie put in pithy comments about the movie. Loch stared out the window at the snow sculptures, not even pretending to watch. Burke stared a hole in the screen without really seeing it.

And Spirit twisted a strand of hair around and around her finger, occasionally responding to Addie and Muirin, trying to figure out if there was any way, any way at all, they could get *some* idea who had created last night's terror, and what that shadowy enemy might do next.

Breakfast had been more-or-less brunch and the dining room was still open at noon; the guys got hungry again and went and made bacon sandwiches, bringing a stack of them for everyone back to the lounge because there were still no adults in sight to object. Seeing that, Muirin dashed out and returned with another giant plate of pastries. Addie and Spirit rolled their eyes and got milk and tea. They put on another lame movie, and another. No one talked.

It was a relief to hear the summons to dinner; at least it got them out of the lounge.

They'd barely gotten their seats when Mr. Wallis came in; something about the way he moved made her think he wasn't there just to eat. A moment later, when he picked up a glass and a fork and tapped the latter against the former to get their attention, she knew she was right.

"Just to forestall any rumors," he said, once the room had quieted down, "we took Jack Croder, Susan Menners, and Judy King to the Infirmary last night. Ms. Carimar also went to the Infirmary under her own volition. After several hours in which their conditions worsened, it was determined they needed to see specialists. No one wanted to risk their health after such a shock, so they were on their way to Billings by sunrise. We took them by special rail as the fastest and safest means possible."

Of course, Spirit mused, watching Mr. Wallis through narrowed eyes, *there's no way to prove you aren't lying.* Absolutely no one had been awake this morning at dawn, not after going to bed exhausted, knowing there was no reason to set your alarm because breakfast was going to be held open.

On the other hand, she knew that she had seen at least two of the four mentioned passed out cold, and she was pretty sure if she asked around, she'd find out that all four had been laid out. So it wasn't completely insane to think that they might still be in bad shape. Ms. Carimar wasn't young, and if you had any sort of heart issues, last night's terror would have been enough to give you a heart attack.

"We'll keep all of you posted," Mr. Wallis said, wearing a look of concern that couldn't go any deeper than the first layer of his skin. With that, he sat down, and slowly the buzz of conversation got back to hushed-normal.

Hushed enough that Spirit was able to pick out some threads of conversation at other tables. At least two of the students had left e-mails for their friends.

Interesting. If only she could see what had been *in* those e-mails!

Not a chance of that, of course. It wasn't as if she was a hacker.

By common consent, they all went back to their own rooms after dinner. Too much time spent together was going to get attention they didn't want. But as soon as Spirit got to her computer, she found a message from Addie.

Gym.

She bundled on her coat, peeked out the door of her room to make sure no one was watching, and slipped out. It was already dark, and really cold. She shivered her way to the gym, did another furtive check to make sure no one was around, and slipped inside. The foyer was dimly lit, the big room itself dark except for safety lights and still decorated for the dance.

Straining her ears, she heard the faintest of whispers and

followed it. At the side of the gym proper was a kind of corridor; that was where the voices were coming from. The door, which had always been closed, and presumably locked, was slightly ajar. There was faint light at the far end of the corridor. She closed the door behind her, noticing as she did that there was tape over the dead bolt, keeping it from locking in place.

It smelled musty back here, the kind of aged-sweat-and-neglect sort of musty that made her think of her dad's old athletic gear that had been stored in a box in the attic. And there were a lot of doorless rooms along this corridor. She peeked inside one, and made out some really wrecked gymnastics equipment in the dim glow of an exit light. So this was where the old stuff went to die?

She scuttled to the end of the corridor and stuck her head into the room.

It was the furnace room for the gym. The others were sitting on metal folding chairs in a huddle in the light from a single overhead fixture. Muirin and Loch both had little netbooks and were typing furiously. Muirin was talking as she typed.

". . . all that might mean is Big Brother learned from the last time," Muirin was saying. "Vanishing into nothing and telling us they ran away didn't exactly work to hide what happened to the Tithed."

"Burke and I both got e-mails from Ms. Carimar," Addie countered. "Canceling her class, basically, and giving us options for what to take in its place."

"Doesn't that seem a little, I don't know, odd to you?" Spirit said from the door. "Here she's supposed to be half passed out, stressed to the max, and sick, and she's sending out individual course recommendations?"

"Well, no duh," said Muirin, looking up. "Hey. Grab a chair."

"Wouldn't be that hard to hack the personal e-mail accounts," Loch put in, and shoved the last empty chair toward her a little. "You wouldn't even need to hack them if you had Admin status."

Spirit pulled the chair to herself and plopped down in it. "Why are you typing?" she asked. "And where did you get those netbooks?"

"There's a WiFi hotspot here, and we're acting like we're in our rooms," Muirin said with a smirk. "Loch and I are always in chat, and it would look weird if we went missing from it. You three, on the other hand, aren't in public chat much. I'm told you are actually known to do something quaint and antiquated called *reading a book*. How very analog of you."

"I had the netbooks, they were in my luggage." Loch shrugged. "Old ones I wasn't using anymore. Father was always upgrading me to the newest model, so they were at the house, so I guess the secretary threw them in with the rest of the stuff she sent for me. At least these are useful, unlike most of the stuff that was sent."

"So you've got no jeans and t-shirts, but you've got a tailored tux and two netbooks?" Spirit hazarded.

"Four netbooks, and yes." Loch sighed. "But Murr-cat's right, even when we're studying, we're in chat, so we need to look like we're where we should be."

"Back to the subject," Spirit said firmly. "What's going on?"

"Two of the missing persons left e-mails for their friends, too," Muirin told them. "I just got sent copies."

Addie frowned. "And?"

"I don't know. I didn't know them well enough to tell if it actually *sounds* like them," Muirin replied. "It's only a couple of lines each, just that they can't take it here, and they want to get out, they can't eat or sleep, they feel like they're going to die any second, and Doctor Ambrosius wants to send them to Billings."

"Uh—if they were in the Infirmary, and never went back to their rooms, where would they have gotten a computer?" Spirit pointed out.

Muirin looked up, and Addie's eyes narrowed. "That is a good point," Addie said slowly. "And actually, why would anyone bother to have them e-mail their friends if they were sick enough to need to be sent to Billings?"

There was silence, broken only by the powerful fans of the furnace. Then Burke spoke up.

"They might not have been sick, as such, at all," he said. "Just still insanely scared, and wanting to get out of here. That would leave Doctor Ambrosius with the choice of trying to keep them here and having crazy people on his hands, or letting them go and shipping them off to shrinks. Which would get the problem out of *his* hands anyway."

"Well come look at the e-mails," Muirin said, turning her netbook around so they could all see the screen. "I can't tell if that sounds crazy *or* scared."

They all peered at the windows. Spirit pursed her lips. They were in txt-speak, or at least the two kids were, so it was hard to glean any *feeling* out of them. And the teacher's was impersonal, which you'd expect, and almost as short.

"So . . ." Spirit chewed on her lip. "You don't . . ."

Burke snorted. "Look, *something* went after everyone at the dance. That much is a fact. Our rings glowed and we don't know what that means, and *that* is a fact. You *are* right, Spirit, the Wild Hunt was sent by someone, and we don't know who that someone is, or if he's given up or not—"

Spirit got a queasy feeling. "OK, so the Tithed were more or less scared to death, right? Or killed while they were scared. Was being scared the point? Isn't there something in magic about how you terrify your victim for extra mojo?"

Addie looked thoughtful. "You might be on to something. According to everything Loch and I were able to find, yes, the Wild Hunt—and I guess whatever was behind it—more or less feed on fear and pain."

"So what they did to us at the dance—?"

Loch mussed his hair uneasily. "Different weapon, similar goal. Maybe."

"You think that would be all they want?" she asked.

All he could do was shrug. "If I were thinking all conspiracy theory, I'd think that the power gained from the fear was going to go toward taking us out."

Burke shot him a glance. "You are a *big* help."

"Forget that," Addie said steadily. "The point is that Spirit is right about one thing; there is something out there that ran an attack on us. We need to figure out who on the inside here is helping them. Once we know that, maybe we can figure out what the next move is going to be. Then we can take what we know to Doctor Ambrosius. After what we did against the Wild Hunt, he'll listen and take us seriously. Now let's see if we can figure out a place to start."

The others nodded, and Spirit would have been perfectly happy if it hadn't been for the part about taking what they knew to Doctor Ambrosius.

Because she wasn't at all sure that was a good idea.

They hadn't dared stay out too long—not only because they might be missed from their rooms, but because tomorrow it was back to classes as normal. Or rather, back to all new classes; this was the start of the second term of the year, an "Oakhurst year," which had three terms of four months each.

Spirit woke up with a sense of dread, and elected to go for a protein shake for breakfast, figuring if she needed to, she could get some yogurt or something to tide her over until lunch. She didn't think that a full stomach for her first class was going to be a very good idea.

She hurried over to the gym—to the weight room this time, the first time she had ever been in it—to join the half-dozen other students there once she had changed into the clean gym clothes in her locker. At least they were just sweatpants, a tank and sports bra, and a hoodie in Oakhurst brown . . . nothing nearly as ugly and embarrassing as the gym uniforms she'd seen pictures of.

"All right, ladies," said Mr. Wallis, prowling up and down in the front of the room like a caged panther. "This is one class where there are very clear rules. You will use the equipment I put you on, at the settings I put it on, and you will accomplish the goal I have set for you. And tomorrow, we'll do it again. There won't be any hiding behind a lucky move, and no excuses. Are we clear?"

"Yes sir," they all murmured. Although some of the more competitive types made use of this room, Spirit never had, and neither had any of the others in this class. What was more, according to the others, this was a brand-new sort of class—a conditioning class—and it was nothing that had ever been taught here at Oakhurst before. If you could call this "teaching."

Mr. Wallis picked out Spirit and Elizabeth, and put them on the two treadmills in the room. The other four he put on the fancy weight-simulation machines, contraptions that looked like a tornado had run through an archery store leaving these things in its wake. Mr. Wallis programmed in an ambitious workout for Spirit and Elizabeth, and with a sadistic grin, punched the *start* buttons. The belts hummed to life, and Spirit and Elizabeth had no choice but to start running.

Spirit soon found to her dismay that these were no ordinary treadmills. Oh no. These were state-of-the-art machines that could raise and lower their beds, and in the next five minutes she found herself struggling up a "hill" that never ended.

Then the thing went flat again, but her ordeal wasn't over.

It suddenly sped up, and she was forced into a sprint for thirty seconds. Then it slowed down. Then it sped up. A few more repetitions of that, and it turned into a hill again.

Finally, the treadmill slowed from a sprint to a jog, then a jog to a walk, and then stopped. Spirit bent over, sweating and panting. When she caught her breath and looked up again, she saw everyone else had finished their workouts, too.

"Treadmills!" Mr. Wallis barked. "You're on machines one and two. One and two, move to three and four. Three and four, move to the treadmills. Move it, ladies!"

With a deep sense of apprehension, Spirit took over one of the two designated machines. Sure enough, there was a workout already programmed into it; "all" she had to do was follow it.

"Is this usual?" Elizabeth panted, as Wallis went over to survey the students on the second set of machines.

"No, at least, not from what I know," Spirit replied. "It's something they announced for this semester after Halloween." *And I was too busy with trying to make it through my first semester and survive the Wild Hunt to think about it at the time. I wasn't even sure I'd be alive to worry about Winter Term classes.* "Everyone has it, too, you don't get a choice like you do with the other PE classes." That was new, too; almost everything else here at least gave you the illusion that you had some control over what you were taking.

"What are they trying to accomplish with this?" Elizabeth muttered, sounding as if she was talking to herself more than to Spirit.

"What do you think? You got the 'welcome to Oakhurst'

talk," Spirit replied, straining against the machine. "Those enemies out there, that war that Doctor Ambrosius keeps talking about. This is to get us ready to face it."

"Damn right it is, and don't you forget it, ladies," Mr. Wallis snapped, coming over to see what they were doing. "Put some back into it, White. There are old ladies in nursing homes that can do better than you are."

He stood over them, making occasional feints at the controls, as if he was thinking of making the program harder than it already was. Elizabeth looked in despair; Spirit just forged grimly on. Her hair was so sweat-soaked now that it was plastered to her scalp, and every time she licked her lips she tasted salt.

Mr. Wallis moved on in a regular circuit, barking at them like a drill sergeant, hammering them with insults. At least after the switch to the next set of machines, he did let them have bottles of water.

By the time they got to the showers, which Spirit sorely needed, she ached all over and felt as limp as overcooked spaghetti. She had the feeling she was really, really going to hate this class.

At least the new schedule gave her a decent amount of time for that shower.

The class following the conditioning class was the undemanding literature class—undemanding because this semester was covering books she'd already read in her homeschooling studies. She was able to just coast through that one. Mr. Kran-dal was not exactly the most inspiring teacher in the world, ei-ther—he could make *Lord of the Rings* boring—so it was a good thing she had, really. What he was doing to *Madame Bovary* should have been a crime, and she wasn't looking forward to his nitpicky tests. The one on *Silas Marner* had been . . . well, one of the questions had been "What did Silas go looking for when the baby crawled in through the open door." *I mean, come on,* Spirit thought resentfully, as Krandal droned on about Emma Bovary's dress purchases in such detail you'd have thought he was planning on wearing them himself. *It wasn't important* what *he was looking for, it was important that he left the door open so the baby could crawl inside!*

She'd gotten that question wrong, too, which only made her madder.

After that was one of the magic classes, and somehow she wasn't surprised when Ms. Groves gave them all handouts on the Wild Hunt. Which was kind of like, as her mom used to say, "closing the barn door after the horses are out." But at least it meant she could coast on this class for a little bit, too, which given that conditioning class, was probably a good thing. Maybe by the time Ms. Groves moved them on to something she didn't already know, Spirit would be used to the condition-ing class and wouldn't feel quite so baked.

At lunch, she could tell that Muirin had just gone her three rounds with Mr. Wallis by the not-quite-dry hair and Muirin's general look of weary shock. The two of them stood in line to get their food, and after a moment, Muirin finally gave her a sidelong glance. "My God. There is an eighth circle of Hell, and Mr. Wallis is in charge of it."

"Oh yeah," Spirit agreed fervently. "I don't want to think about what I'm going to feel like in the morning."

"Would you believe he knew exactly how many donuts I ate yesterday?" Muirin asked bitterly. "He was positively gloating. He threatened to load up the machine with an extra pound for every three donuts."

"I don't doubt it," Spirit replied.

"I mean, look at me!" Muirin gestured to herself dramatically, before picking up her tray and heading for "their" table. "Does this look like the body of someone who needs to worry about a couple of donuts?"

Spirit had to shake her head, because in all truth, Muirin looked like the sort of person who might need to consider packing a few extra pounds *on* rather than trying to take them off.

Addie, Burke, and Loch joined them a few minutes later; Muirin repeated her complaints about the new class.

Burke just shrugged. "Didn't seem bad to me," he said.

"Well it wouldn't, would it?" Muirin retorted resentfully. "You being the King of the Jocks and all."

"I'm so not looking forward to this," Addie replied uneasily.

"I'd like to know why they're springing it on us," said Loch. He took a bite of his sandwich thoughtfully. "Have you actually looked around at everyone here? We may not be Olympians, but we're all pretty athletic. And magic burns the fat off you pretty quickly once you start practicing it."

"Pretty athletic might not be good enough . . ." Spirit said slowly. "Not if we really *are* going to be in some kind of war soon. Maybe I was wrong about Doctor Ambrosius not taking the Hunt seriously enough. Maybe this is part of his answer. I mean . . . I don't know how you'd have a war with wizards, but any time people fight, endurance plays a big part, right?"

"Huh." Burke looked at her with new respect.

Muirin groaned. "You sure know how to suck the righteous indignation right out of something, don't you?" she said with feeling. "Curses on you, Logic Girl!"

Spirit laughed weakly. "Oh, go right ahead feeling righteously indignant," she replied. "After all, even if there *is* a good reason for it, Mr. Wallis is still a sadist."

"Amen to that," said Loch.

❋

Lunch went a long way to fully reviving her, so Spirit went on to her math class feeling less like a damp rag and more like a human being. She took her place behind the empty seat that had been Judy King's. It was with a bit of a shock and a lot of guilt that Spirit realized she couldn't even put a face to the name, only the back of a head and a severely bobbed hairdo.

Ms. Smith waited for them all to get seated, then crossed her arms over her chest and regarded the class with glittering eyes. "There is absolutely no point in trying to concentrate on mathematics today," she said, to Spirit's shock. "Believe me, I understand. What's probably making it worse for all of you is that most of the teachers don't even want you to talk about it.

They want you to act as if everything is business as usual, to go back to classes like nothing happened. But *I* don't."

She paused for effect, and raked her eyes over all of them.

"What happened New Year's Eve was a horrible shock. What caused it really doesn't matter; what matters is the effect it had on you." Ms. Smith leaned forward, and lowered her voice a little. "You all had a terrible experience. I know I did, and I'm a trained magician with . . . let's just say I have a lot of stories I could tell. Bottling your feelings up isn't healthy. In fact, it might cause problems down the road—psychological problems, like post-traumatic stress disorder, and problems with your control of magic. You need to talk about these things, and I'm here to help."

She fastened her gaze on Nadia Vaughn, who chewed her fingernail nervously. Ms. Smith didn't even call her on it. Finally, Nadia broke under the intense gaze. "It was awful," she said in a small voice. "I was so scared—it was so dark, except for those awful little sparks, and I couldn't breathe! I thought I was going to have a heart attack or something, I kept trying to say something but nothing would come out!"

Ms. Smith nodded. "I'm not sure which was worse, the dark, or those little sparks of light."

"They were like eyes!" Kylee Williamson burst out. "Like— Like the eyes of something that knows it's going to pounce on you and it's just waiting for you to be scared enough!"

That pretty much did it. Everyone but Spirit started pouring out what they'd seen, and especially what they'd felt. Ms. Smith made no attempt to soothe them; instead, she encouraged them with little nods and the occasional word. And her eyes stayed so . . . detached. Analytical. It was as if she was taking notes on everything. But why?

It was creepy. It was really, really creepy. Creepy enough that Spirit didn't want to stand out by *not* saying anything, so when Ms. Smith's eyes alighted on her, she blurted out, "I couldn't stand it! It was a nightmare!" then hid her face in her hands.

That seemed to be enough; when she peeked through her fingers, she saw Ms. Smith's attention had drifted to one of the other girls, who was in tears and on the verge of hysterics.

Well, so much for *that* class . . . .

Ms. Smith did, finally, make the effort to get them all calmed down before the class was over. And she succeeded enough that though some of the guys were flushed and chagrined-looking, and all of the girls were still wiping their eyes, they were all able to walk out and go to their next class without breaking down.

But . . . if Elizabeth had been right about it being a test, one that had been sprung on them so that no teacher could warn a favorite student in advance . . . Spirit would have been willing to bet now that Ms. Jane Smith was one of the few who had known what was going to happen in advance.

. . . maybe even the person who had done it in the first place.

EIGHT

Spirit was normally pretty indifferent about math; she didn't like it, but she didn't hate it, either. Right now, though, she would have been a whole lot happier if there'd been more equations on the worksheet on the desk in front of her, because she knew what was going to happen, as soon as Ms. Smith finished going over the last of them—

"Very good. Does anyone have any questions?" she asked. Spirit glanced at her watch covertly and wanted to groan. There was a bit more than half an hour to go in the class. Ms. Smith smiled brightly when no one raised a hand. "All right then. How are you all holding up? You know, as a fellow magician, I am here to help you with much more than just math. Mariana?"

Oh, she would *pick Mariana . . .*

"I . . . uh . . ." Mariana's thin face started to crumple, and her voice got choked up. "I can't sleep," she whispered, hiding behind her fall of dark hair. "Even when I keep a light on . . ."

Ms. Smith got a handful of tissues from a box on her desk, as if she'd prepared for this. Which she probably had. It was incongruous; Ms. Smith looked like a super-efficient secretary, with her tightly tied-back hair and her Oakhurst uniform blazer. She didn't look like a magician, and she didn't look particularly . . . empathetic. She handed the tissues to Mariana. "That's all right, I'm not at all surprised," she said soothingly. "Why don't you tell me about it? Maybe it will help."

Strangely, Spirit seemed to be the only person in the class that found this scene acutely uncomfortable, disturbing, invasive. Ms. Smith leaned over Mariana slightly, not touching her, but really getting into the girl's personal space. "Every time I start to fall asleep, I get so s-s-scared," Mariana gulped, rubbing at her eyes with the tissues and smearing her eye makeup. "It's like I can feel *it* starting all over again. And when I do fall asleep, the nightmares . . ." She faltered, and took a shuddering breath.

"Is anyone else having nightmares?" Ms. Smith asked. She looked like she was enjoying this.

"The nightmares are the worst. I keep fighting something I can't see," said Taylor Parker, in a low voice, as if he was ashamed to admit he had nightmares, but couldn't help talking. "It's—it's dark, and there's something that keeps grabbing at me and hitting me, like in blind *randori*. Only it's not practice and I'm not blindfolded and every time it hits me it slices into me so fast I don't even feel it until I look down and I'm bleeding from all these slices—"

"I'm running, I'm back at home and I'm running," sobbed Mariana. "I'm trying to get to my house, but the street keeps changing and there's something behind me, and I know if I turn around to look at it, I'm going to *die!*"

"I'm here at school in my dreams, but my brother's here, too." That was Andrew Hayes, and although his voice was steady, his face was so bleak Spirit didn't even want to look at him. Of course, just like the rest of them, Andrew's family was dead. . . . "There's this thing after him, this huge, shadowy thing, and I'm trying to get to him to save him, only I can't!"

One by one, Ms. Smith got them to tell her their nightmares. Even Spirit—though Spirit lied. She just buried her face in her hands and mumbled something about dark and evil eyes. She didn't think it would be a good idea to stand out by *not* talking.

This had been going on for days now. Only about half of the class was spent on math. The other half was Ms. Smith and her not-exactly-interrogations. This was the first time she'd grilled them about their nightmares, though, and actually, this was the first time Spirit had heard that practically everyone was having them. If it hadn't been that Spirit's mom had taught her lucid dreaming back when she was a little kid and having night terrors, *she'd* probably be having them, too. But she wondered if Burke and the others were having the same problem. *I could ask Loch. He'll tell me, even if the others don't.*

Most of the time, Ms. Smith had been asking about the night

of the dance, getting not only what everyone had experienced, but what they'd been doing and thinking *before* the lights went out. Definitely creepy . . . extracting details from the kids that Spirit was pretty sure they'd had no intention of telling any teacher. The sort of stuff you *might* put on your blog, for your friends, but not for anyone else. Certainly not for anyone *old*.

Spirit couldn't figure out how Ms. Smith was doing it. Was it magic? Or was it just that she was really, really good at getting things out of people? At least there was only five minutes more of this before class change.

Is she like this with all her classes? Spirit wondered. *Or is it just this one?* She had thought about asking Addie or Loch, but . . . no, better wait. If she started acting suspicious of Ms. Smith without any reason except that—well, on the surface, it looked as if the teacher was actually trying to *help* everyone, and they might think she was being paranoid again.

Just a few more minutes . . .

Ms. Smith handed Mariana another wad of tissues and went back to her desk. "I don't want any of you to think that we're making light of this," she said, raking her eyes over the whole class. "You've all had a nasty shock, and Dr. MacKenzie is of the opinion that this has brought up a great many things that were buried. I'm sure you're all familiar with post-traumatic stress, right?" She looked them over again, and wasn't satisfied until she'd seen each of them nod. "Dr. MacKenzie wants each of you to have at least one session with him. He wants to evaluate whether you're going to get through this on your own, or need some extra help."

Spirit repressed a groan, and she was pretty sure she heard muffled sighs and moans from some of the others, too. Another shrink . . . she'd had her fill of shrinks at the hospital. If she had her way, she'd never see another shrink again. She didn't even know what this "Dr. MacKenzie" looked like; in the months she'd been here, she'd never seen him, not even at meals or the dances. Or at least, if she had, she hadn't known who he was.

"I've got your assigned times right here," Ms. Smith said, in that tone of voice that pretty much made it clear there was no point in arguing with her. She began handing out little envelopes, and Spirit took hers with a sinking heart. From the looks on the faces of some of the others, they felt the same.

＊

From the buzz at supper, it looked like, sure enough, everyone had gotten the appointments. Some people were actually happy about it; Mariana for one. She really was in bad shape, her voice had a shrill edge that carried right across the Refectory. "Maybe he can give me something so I can sleep," she was saying, and it was true that she did look pretty awful, big dark circles under her eyes, and her eyes red from crying, lack of sleep, or both. Austin Phillips, who was at her table, smirked. "If we're going to get drugs out of this, it might not be all bad," he said, loud enough that other kids smirked or frowned or looked embarrassed, as if that was something they'd thought but hadn't said out loud.

Muirin was one of the ones who smirked. "Let's see," she

said in a quiet, mocking tone. "What drug would I like to get? Something fun, not a downer like Prozac."

"Don't joke about that," Addie said crossly, cutting her meat with a lot more energy than the ham warranted. "It's not funny."

"Why not? What put a burr up your butt?" Muirin asked.

Addie put her silverware down on the table with a clatter. "It's not funny because the Trust decided I needed to see a shrink before I came here—and he put me on so much Prozac I was a zombie, that's why!" she hissed angrily. "I didn't have two clear thoughts in a row until I got here and they took me *off* it."

Spirit started to say something sympathetic, but Muirin just shrugged. "So you should have done what I did, and either flush the pills or throw them up if it was something I didn't want to take. Seriously, Addie, lighten up. If you don't want to game the system, fine. But don't get all self-righteous about it."

Addie's jaw clenched, but she didn't retort. The rest of the meal was passed in unusual silence, and as soon as Austin got up from his table, Muirin gulped down the last of her dessert and went to join him.

Burke patted Addie's hand. "Don't worry," he said soothingly. "Doc Mac doesn't like to prescribe drugs. He's a magician, too, and he won't give out anything that interferes with magic—which is most stuff."

Addie relaxed a little. "I just worry about her, you know?" she said, looking into Burke's eyes in a way that made Spirit feel a little uncomfortable twinge of jealousy. "She doesn't think things through. What if we're all drugged up and whatever it was that hit us does it again? A lot of stuff doesn't just interfere with magic, it opens you wide up for *anything*—" She broke off. "I just don't want to see Murr-cat hurt."

"Well I saw Doc Mac for a while when I first got here, and he's okay," Burke said with confidence. "Muirin might think she can game him, but he's pretty sharp. Serve her right if he decided what she needed was more time in the exercise room as therapy."

Addie almost choked, and even Spirit and Loch found themselves grinning a little. Still, Spirit was not looking forward to her session. No matter what Burke said . . . Burke was far too inclined to think that everyone was okay until it was proven otherwise. When it came to shrinks, Spirit was going to assume that this "Doc Mac" was going to be just like all the rest. And the sooner she could get out of his office, the better she'd like it.

❦

The morning of Spirit's session with Doctor MacKenzie, she walked into the Refectory to the sound of conversational buzzing with the sort of edge to it that meant something had happened. She got cereal, yogurt, and fruit and hurried over to the usual table. Addie had been watching her, and gave her a little nod when she got close. As soon as she was sitting down, Addie leaned over and said in a low voice, "Mariana Thornton is gone."

"Gone?" Spirit paused and put her spoon back down in her bowl. "What do you mean by gone?"

Addie looked over at Loch. "She wasn't in her room this morning, her bed didn't look like it had been slept in, which meant she went some time between dinner and lights out." Loch shrugged. "So sayeth the word of Chat."

Muirin plopped down in her usual chair with a stack of buttered toast that she proceeded to load up with preserves—even though they were the "no sugar added" kind. "And so sayeth the e-mail I got before I came down, Mariana was in such bad shape after supper that she was deemed in need of getting out of here and was sent away for a nice 'rest.' Presumably in a loony bin, and presumably so decided by good old Doc MacKenzie, since she saw him yesterday." Muirin looked pensively at her toast. "Maybe I should have hysterics in front of him. Mother Dearest would have me put up in a really *plush* loony bin. You know, the kind with private rooms and 'beauty therapy' and massages. And satellite TV and chefs. No more conditioning classes, and real jelly on my toast, not mashed fruit pretending to be jelly." She bit into the slice anyway. "And I hear if you're cooperative, they reward you with chocolates."

For a moment, Spirit herself was tempted. It *would* mean getting out of here . . . but then she remembered; it wouldn't be a plush, resort-rest-home for her. She'd get dumped in one of those horrible places where they warehoused people, drugged them up like zombies, shoved them into tiny rooms with bunk beds, and locked them in at night. She swallowed hard, and drank a little milk to try and get the lump of fear out of her throat. No, there were places worse than Oakhurst.

And besides, at least here they *believed* in things like the

Hunt. Out there—she'd have no protection from it. And if she tried to tell anyone about it, they'd think she was even crazier.

"What, now you want to flip out, and play right into your stepmother's hands?" Loch asked, with a sarcastic edge to his voice. "I bet your Step would just love that. She could keep you in there forever, you know. All she has to do is pay the right shrinks to diagnose you as bipolar and a danger to yourself. You'd be locked in there and out of the old trust fund pretty darn quick."

Muirin made a sour face. "That would be funnier if it were less true," she admitted. "I have to stay alive and sane until twenty-one so I can wrestle her to the floor and take my inheritance. Stupid Trust." She sighed dramatically. "Darn it, Loch, you're right, she was looking for ways to cut me out when the Trust sent me here."

"Hey, I know these things." He shrugged. "The crap that went on with some of the guys I went to school with makes the Borgias look like the Family Channel."

"Too true. Besides, I have to stab her in the back—metaphorically of course—and take back my castle. If I don't, my robber-baron ancestors will probably show up to haunt me as a weak and cowardly branch of the family tree."

"Do *you* think she was taken away?" Spirit asked Loch. "Mariana, I mean." He actually thought about the question before he answered it, which he did just as Burke sat down.

"On the one hand, she's been pretty much falling apart since New Year's Eve," Loch pointed out. "And face it, if we end up with another attack, she'd not only be no help, she'd be a liability. So yes, I can see her getting sent away. But on the other hand, unless she's been sent to a facility that actually knows how to deal with psychologically disturbed *magicians,* sending her away from here is about the worst thing that Doctor Ambrosius could have done to her. And so far, no one has mentioned seeing the train go out, or the car going out to the airstrip. So . . ." He shrugged. "It's possible that this is another cover-up. It's not as if covering up disappearances is new around here."

"I think the official story is the most likely," Burke put in. "She was in pretty bad shape at dinner. She couldn't even eat. I don't know what the Doc said to her, but she looked like if you accidentally startled her, she'd fall to pieces right there."

"Oh, way to go, Burke." Loch rolled his eyes. "Make sure Spirit feels real good about seeing the shrink in fifteen minutes."

Burke looked startled, then sheepish. Clearly, he had forgotten this. "Oh heck Spirit, I—"

"Don't worry about it," Spirit said shortly. She got up and forced a smile. "Hey, I get out of conditioning class this way."

Muirin looked at her sourly as she walked away.

Doctor MacKenzie's office was in the same part of the main building as the Infirmary, down a long hall with stone floors. It was creepily quiet there, the lights were dim, and it was chilly. It looked like the hall of some grand hotel at the turn of the century, and she wouldn't have been at all surprised if a ghost had walked through a wall to stare at her.

If Spirit hadn't known better, she would have thought the

place was deserted. Her footsteps were the only sound in the empty hall. It was funny; when you were in the populated parts of Oakhurst, you had no idea that there were whole sections like this, where there just wasn't anyone.

The office door was solid wood, and closed, with Doctor MacKenzie's name beside it on an ornate little brass plate. The plate looked as if it had been there since Oakhurst was built; it even had the same Deco script.

She knocked on the door, hoping he had somehow forgotten her session, or that he was busy with someone else, or that he wasn't there—hoping, but really knowing that, of course, it wasn't even remotely possible that any of these things could be true. Still, you never knew. . . .

"It's open," said a deep voice with a Brooklyn accent. Reluctantly, she turned the handle and stepped inside.

The room looked pretty typical for a shrink. The same cream walls and brown carpet as the rest of the school. Oakhurst brown chair and couch, in the same "lodge look" style. Usually there was a coffee table or something like one in a shrink's office, but not here. Probably because the room was pretty small as it was. There was a wooden filing cabinet, a matching bookcase, and a tiny desk with a computer on it at the back of the room under the window, but Doctor MacKenzie was already sitting in the chair, looking at a file.

She stared at him. He looked up. She stared some more. He waited patiently for her to say something.

"You look like Lenin!" she blurted, finally. "The Russian!"

He chuckled. Somehow that made him look even more like

the Russian, with his balding head and neat little beard. "I see homeschooling pays off," he replied. "Usually the kids that actually recognize this face don't say anything. They just give me that strange, puzzled look—like a dog that hears something funny. They know I look like *someone,* but they don't know who." He waved at the couch. "Come into my parlor."

She took a seat on the couch, gingerly. It was brown suede, softer and more comfortable than it looked.

"I'm Doctor Cooper MacKenzie, you can call me Doc or Doc Mac if you like. I'm also a mage: Fire Mage, Gift of Cleansing." He tilted his head a little to one side. "And you are Spirit White, and no one knows what your ability is yet. It's there, though. The power is in you, curled up like a sleeping dragon."

"You—can see it?" she replied, startled.

"There are a few of us who can. Not many. A few more who can sense it, but not actually see it. Ambrosius for one." He raised an eyebrow. "You weren't told that."

It was a statement, not a question. She nodded.

"They like to keep people off balance here. They call it 'challenged.'" Another statement. She decided not to react to it.

"If you're a mage, why are you a therapist?" she demanded.

"Most people who become headshrinkers do so because they think there is something wrong with themselves and want to figure out how to fix it. I was no exception, though what was 'wrong' with me was magic, not neurosis." He grinned as he managed to coax a wary smile out of her. "I've gone over your file, Spirit, and I want to start out by telling you that your previous shrinks are a prime example of the truism that half the people practicing psychotherapy graduated in the bottom half of their class."

"Uh—what?" she asked, completely taken aback. It looked as if Doctor MacKenzie also liked to keep people off balance.

"What's in this file, and what they told you, was complete bullshit," he said bluntly, tapping the manila folder. "I don't know what they're turning out of college these days, but they all sound like the latest bestseller self-help book. They seemed to think you were supposed to somehow magically get over having your entire world ripped out from under you in less than a year. That's the biggest load of crap I've ever heard. *Of course* you're still not over any of it. You shouldn't be. If you were, I'd be looking for some pretty intractable problems with you and flinging around fancy terms like *severe attachment disorder*. You don't just get over that sort of loss in a few months, or even a few years." He snorted. "Sometimes I think the Victorians had the right idea. When you lost a family member back then you were *supposed* to be in full mourning, dress in nothing but black, for a whole year. *Then* you went into something they called 'half mourning' for another full year, and during those two years, you were pretty much *expected* to have emotional breakdowns, you could do it whenever you felt you needed to, and everybody would support you. Now? A month after a tragedy, maybe two, and you're expected to be all better—or down pills so you can pretend you are." He just shook his head. "Unfair doesn't even come close."

Spirit was torn between shock and wanting to hug and kiss

him. Not only was this the first time anyone had acted halfway normal around her, it was the first time any shrink had more or less given her permission to keep feeling bad. And the relief she felt was impossible to describe.

The thought fleetingly occurred to her that Doc Mac *could* be saying all this to try and trick her into trusting him. . . .

Well, if so, it was working, and right now, she didn't care. She wanted to trust him; all of her instincts were reacting as positively to him as they reacted negatively to people like Ms. Smith. She *liked* him. She had the feeling that if he had been her shrink in the hospital, she wouldn't be nearly so messed up now.

And for the first time, she felt like *talking* about it to someone, because she just knew he wasn't going to cut her off because "her hour was up." She was going to be able to vent about how bad she felt, how much she missed everyone, everything, and would give up everything to have them back again. How much she envied Muirin and Loch, because they hadn't had parents they'd miss, and Burke, because he still had his foster folks. How sometimes she wanted to punch the next person who told her it was time for her to get over it. He was going to listen for as long as it took.

So she did. She went through a lot of tissues. Doc Mac was just solid, right through it all. He didn't get all creepy and ooze sympathy and pretend empathy like Ms. Smith did; he was just there, listening, not saying much, but what he did say made her feel, not better exactly, but as if he understood.

He was a hundred times better than any of the shrinks she'd seen in the hospital.

When she finally wound down, he gave her the rest of the box of tissues and made a couple of brief notes. He talked to her a little about New Year's Eve. She told him what she'd really seen and felt. He made some more notes, then looked up. "All right, Spirit, you're good to go. I think you weathered the New Year's incident pretty well. If you have trouble concentrating, sleeping, if you're having nightmares, make an appointment. If it's urgent, come right to me, and I'll clear my schedule. We'll try a little talk therapy, maybe a week or two of meds to take the edge off and get you over the hump. Otherwise, having crying fits and being depressed is part of the grieving process, and don't let anyone try to tell you differently."

She blew her nose as he added, almost to himself: "And I wish I could get Dylan to believe that."

She hesitated a moment. Then she made up her mind. "That night . . . the night of the wreck . . . I saw something," she said. "And the crash wasn't an accident. There was something like—okay, it must have been an explosion of some kind of magic, like a flash of light, except it was dark."

"Dark, like absence of light, or dark, as if all the light was being sucked into something?" he asked, his eyes suddenly going sharp and bright.

She blinked. She'd never thought of it that way. "The light being sucked into something," she replied slowly. "So that's some kind of magic?"

He nodded, and his brows creased. "All the Schools of magic have opposites, like matter and antimatter. You probably haven't gotten that far yet. Don't get me wrong, there's nothing inherently evil about the opposite, any more than antimatter is evil. But if the usual forms of our magic are hard to control, the dark forms are even harder, because they're rooted in chaos." Doc Mac ran his hand over his balding head. "So you saw a manifestation from a magician who was either extremely powerful or just bug-out crazy. Or both. Go on."

"Something—was just there, in the middle of the road." She shuddered. "I think Dad saw it, too. It was—I'm not sure what it was. It was—I thought it was a man. A big man, but it was like the light was sucking into him, and—I don't remember exactly, just that it was evil. And I knew, I *knew* that it was after me. . . ." She started to cry again, and stifled it. "It was, wasn't it? It was after me, and it was hunting me. If it hadn't been after me, they'd still be alive. Wouldn't they?"

She couldn't help it, a sob escaped on the last word, and that set her off again, wailing softly, the guilt filling her chest and throat and choking her. She cried and cried until her eyes were all gritty and her nose was sore. Once again, Doc Mac let her cry herself out. When she got herself back under control, he sighed.

"I'm not going to blow smoke at you," he said. "Yes, I think you did see something evil. And it was there to kill you. And yes, the rest of your family died because of it. But Spirit"—he leaned over and fixed her with an intense gaze—"Spirit, that does not mean that *you* are to blame, any more than you would be to blame if you were the only survivor of a mass murderer. Whoever sent that thing, whoever did this in the first place— *that* is who is to blame. Not you." He sat back in his chair. "This is one of those 'bad things happen to good people' situations. This magician, or group of magicians—they made the choice to hurt people. You didn't hunt them down to taunt them, you didn't do anything to them; in fact, you didn't even know they existed until you came here. *They* are the bad guys. *They* are the ones who hurt people. You are innocent; the only thing you did 'wrong' was to be born, and you weren't exactly the one responsible for that. And I want you to keep repeating that to yourself until you believe it, all right?"

Spirit nodded, hesitantly. This was crazy. Here she was pouring out her secrets to someone she didn't even know—and yet Doc Mac was the first person here besides her friends she had ever felt was a real human being, and trustworthy.

And she wanted to keep right on trusting him.

He smiled a little at her nod. "Good. Now, you hop along to class. If you need me, you know where I am."

✦

". . . I didn't tell him about the Hunt or anything," Spirit concluded, as she and Loch continued to page slowly through the scrapbooks, "but I wanted to. What do you think?"

"I think he doesn't sound anything like the shrinks my dad's girlfriends all saw," Loch replied. "Which is a plus. I have an appointment with him day after tomorrow. I'll let you know what I think. Burke's sold on him. Dylan hates him, says he's a wuss."

Spirit rolled her eyes. "Anybody Dylan hates has to be all right."

Loch chuckled. "I kind of agree with you. What did Murr-cat say?"

"She was kind of pissy, but didn't actually say anything."

Loch laughed again. "Which means not only couldn't she game him, he probably read her like a book."

"Well, she wasn't rude about him. . . ." Spirit ventured.

"Which means he might have either impressed or scared her. Maybe both." Loch peered down at an old clipping. "Once I see him, and Addie does, I think we should all decide together on what we tell him."

"If anything," Spirit reminded him.

"If anything," he repeated. "Though if he's in Doctor Ambrosius's inner circle, he'll already know about the Hunt, or at least as much as we told Doctor Ambrosius."

"So? If he does, great. He wouldn't have told *me* he knows, he'd have been waiting for me to bring it up. That's how shrinks work." She frowned at her hands; they were filthy. Looking at the books together in the study carrels at the back of the stacks in the Library was a good idea, marred only by the fact that she was going to have to wait to get to her room to wash her hands.

"You're not so bad at gaming the system yourself." Loch lifted a corner of a yellowing bit of newsprint, carefully. This stuff crumbled easily.

"Practice. I wonder who made all these books, anyway?"

"Tyniger, or an assistant," Loch replied. "Could have been either. Rich guys back then did things like that." He put a marker in the pages and closed his book. "Okay, that's it. My eyes are going to cross if I have to do any more of this today."

"Mine, too," Spirit admitted. "Let's get going."

"Why do you want to tell Doc Mac about everything we've found out so badly?" Loch asked, as they headed back toward their rooms. It seemed safe enough to use one of the study carrels; no one was ever back there. Most people did all their school research electronically.

"I'm not sure," she admitted. "It just seems as if we ought to have one adult we can trust."

"Besides Doctor A.," Loch prompted.

"Uh, yeah." But she hesitated to say that . . .

And for the life of her, she couldn't figure out why.

ΠΙΠΕ

Spirit woke feeling bleary and exhausted; she'd been reading in one of the scrapbooks long after she should have been asleep. Technically she *had* been in bed, and it seemed that if you weren't on the computer or had every light in your room blazing, no one figured out you were still awake. It was pretty easy to get away with reading in bed after "lights out." She thought she might have hit something interesting, but by the time she'd gotten an inkling of it, she'd been nodding off and had to put the book away.

She was tempted to skip reading the usual school e-mail announcements once she was cleaned up and dressed. They rarely had anything interesting in them, just the usual club meetings and sports practices.

But if I don't there'll probably be something vitally important, she decided with resignation. *Or at least something that will make me look stupid for not knowing it.* She went to the desk and bumped her mouse to wake up her computer. Brushing her hair with one hand, she opened up her e-mail program with the other.

Field Trip to Billings was the subject of the first unread e-mail.

She blinked. A field trip? When did the school start having field trips?

Now, apparently.

She opened it.

A field trip to Billings will take place two weeks from today, she read. This will be to visit the Yellowstone Art Museum, and a short shopping visit for select students, a chance to socialize outside the school. Three teachers will accompany the students: Mr. Martin Bowman, Magic and Mathematics; Ms. Lindsay Holland, Art and Magic; and Mr. David Krandal, English Literature and Lore. The names of the students to go on the trip will be announced in a few days.

If there ever was an announcement of something that was obviously a reward for the perfect Oakhurst student, this was surely it. *Pigs will sing opera before my name is on that list,* she thought, deleting all the messages. She was a little angry and a little depressed at the same time—and the stupid thing was, she didn't even know why she'd *want* to go on the trip. She didn't have any money to shop with, and she didn't like art museums. Her parents had tried to get her interested in art all her life, and it hadn't worked; that had been her kid sister's thing. Spirit liked science and history museums.

Maybe it was just the idea of getting away from this place even for a day. Maybe it was the whole Tom Sawyer trick of knowing she wasn't going to get something that made her want to have it. Just another divide-and-conquer Oakhurst trick. Probably they'd make a point of dividing up kids who were friends, so one got to go and the other didn't.

Good old Oakhurst.

She deleted the e-mail. No point in having it sit there, mocking her.

Besides, this evening they were all going to get together to see what they'd found in the scrapbooks. That should keep her mind off stupid field trips.

*

"I guess I'll start," Spirit said, as they all pulled up chairs to the Monopoly board. "Most of what was in the books I've looked through so far is newspaper stories about Arthur Tyniger."

"Bleah," Muirin said, making a face. "He was probably hanging out with my robber-baron great-grandfather, figuring out how to evict widows and orphans."

"This was all stuff from the social columns," Spirit corrected her. "Lots from New York City and San Francisco newspapers. He was kind of like William Randolph Hearst, not as wealthy, but rich enough to do what he wanted, and he was considered a real catch. Most of the stories are about how he was buying up all kinds of antiquities and art for all of his mansions. English mostly. And what they called 'curiosities.' One of them was the oak, and he thought it was so important that he built the whole house around it! And guess what it was sold to him as?"

"Robin Hood's oak tree in Sherwood Forest," said Burke, with a laugh.

"The oak Bonnie Prince Charlie hid in," Addie put in.

Spirit shook her head. "He bought it as the same oak that Merlin was imprisoned in by Nimue," she told them. "*The* Merlin. Merlin the Magician. King Arthur's Merlin. He believed it, too. It was on some farm in Cornwall near Tintagel and was struck and brought down by lightning in a huge storm; that was how he was able to buy it. He had the whole thing transported by steamship to New York, then put on its own flatcar and brought here via rail."

They stared at her. "Uh . . . he was a sucker?" Burke said, finally.

"Oh I don't believe it, either," she assured them. "I mean, King Arthur's a myth. And 'The Merlin' was supposed to just be a title for a major Druid priest, so there would have been hundreds of Merlins. But I do believe there is a lot of magic in that tree, and we've seen the evidence of it."

The rest nodded. "There's probably a hundred Merlin's Oaks, too," Addie added. "It's like pieces of the True Cross, you go around collecting those from all the churches in the world and you'll have enough wood to build the Italian navy."

Muirin's eyes had lit up, and she had a strange, eager expression on her face. "Well, the runes on the trunk really *are* runes, only not the Norse kind," she said, her voice getting that lilt that meant she was excited. "They're Celtic ogham. I haven't been able to translate them yet, but they match perfectly to the ogham symbols I've found. It might not have been *the* Merlin's Oak, but it was *a* Merlin's Oak, I bet!" Spirit looked at her askance. She sounded as if she'd uncovered a cache of double chocolate chocolate-dunked brownies. "I bet it was used for human sacrifices! The Druids would do that with their sacred oaks, tie a victim to it and—"

"More likely some farmer found the tree down, didn't want to go to the work of cutting it up for firewood, knew Tyniger was in the neighborhood, and decided to make a lot of money," Loch said cynically. "Probably found a picture of an ogham inscription in some book, then burned the runes into the tree himself and got all the villagers to agree to some story that it really was Merlin's Oak if he bought them all a round at the pub."

Burke grinned and Addie chuckled. "That's a very likely story," she said. "At the turn of the century people manufactured hundreds of those sorts of things. Petrified giants, baby mermaids . . ."

"I don't know why it couldn't be a real Druid oak," Muirin replied, sullenly. "It's just as likely a story. And how do you explain the magic in it? We all felt it, the way we can't look at the oak without working really hard."

"Oh, it's almost certainly a *spell* carved into it," Loch replied. "That's how Druidic spells were cast in the first place. Written language was so sacred you weren't supposed to use it for anything but magic and prayers. For that matter, spoken language was sacred, too, and bards were also magicians. That's where the word 'enchantment' came from—you chanted at something and that worked magic. Just because some farmer carved something he found in a book into that tree, that doesn't make the inscription itself phony. If he copied something faithfully enough, it would be real magic all right. For all we know, it really *is* the sort of spell you'd find carved into a sacrificial oak."

Muirin didn't look mollified, but finally she shrugged. "There's definitely magic going on there," she repeated.

"Definitely," Loch agreed, and the rest of them nodded.

"It might have been even more powerful when it was fresh," Addie pointed out. "Probably protective. Tyniger lived to be awfully old, and his fortune managed to pass through the Great Depression pretty much intact. That's what's been in my scrapbooks. He made his fortune in the 1880s, and built mansions with it in San Francisco, Denver, New Orleans, and New York City. But instead of building a vacation home in the Catskills or the Hamptons like everyone else did, he built Oakhurst out here. He started construction around 1900 and it took ten years to finish. It was a real showplace; for the first couple of years he was bringing people here all the time by his private rail line to show it off. Then, about the time World War I started, he gradually stopped spending any time in any of his other mansions, and stopped bringing people out here. People didn't notice so much because everyone was wrapped up in the War. But the Great Influenza Epidemic in 1918 pretty much seems to have made him decide he wasn't going to bring any-one here anymore and he wasn't going to leave; he sold all the other places and lived here as a recluse. The funny thing is that one of the books has a big section of notes to him from the staff, thanking him for saving them from the Influenza; not one of them got sick. And it looks like that year is when he started making the scrapbooks. I'm no expert, but it looks as if all of the earliest ones were made in the same year, like he finally took stacks of clippings and things and made them into books."

"Huh," Burke said. "And all of them say 'Oakhurst' on the front. Not his name. It's like the house was his kid."

"The house might have been his child," Addie replied. "He never married, he never had any children at all, and he died without an heir and without a will. But he doubled his fortune in the war, and when he died in 1939 he was over eighty, and that was really old for those times."

"Then I got the oldest of the scrapbooks," said Burke. "The house was in really good shape when he died, too; the last of the scrapbooks is full of photos he took and developed himself, and it was just amazing. So if there's some spell on the tree, it explains why Tyniger devoted himself to the house and the tree took care of him," Burke said slowly. "But then what?"

"All I found in my scrapbooks were more of those photos," Loch said. "So I did some research. You had a huge estate here, from a really wealthy man, with no heir and no will. When there's that much money, the State has to be really careful how they handle everything to make sure there's no heir, because having one crop up can be really messy. It took Montana over thirty years to settle the estate, and by the time the State determined that they were getting the house, they didn't want it. It was out in the middle of nowhere, there wasn't really a concept of remote luxury spas back then, and no one wanted to buy it for a personal home, either, considering how much they'd have to spend just modernizing the wiring alone, never mind the plumbing and the heat and air. So it sat for another ten years, and then in 1979, Doctor Ambrosius came along and bought it."

"And with that oak right in the middle of it, I can see why he'd want it," Muirin said, getting back her enthusiasm. "And *maybe* the reason there isn't a *lot* of magic in the oak now is because Doctor Ambrosius drained it all to build the protections around the school!"

"Oh yeah, I bet you're right, Murr-cat!" Burke exclaimed. "That makes perfect sense!"

"That doesn't sound right," Spirit objected. "How can you drain magic out of a spell?"

"Oh, that's easy enough," Addie replied dismissively. "Any Energy Mage can do it. It's an advanced thing, but they can all do it."

Spirit stared down at the Monopoly board, reminded forcibly again that *she* didn't have any magic. . . .

Except Doc Mac said she did. It was just sleeping.

Well I wish someone would set off the alarm clock, she thought angrily. Then she bit her lip and fought the anger down. This was just one more way that Oakhurst was trying to separate her from her new friends. And she wasn't going to let it.

❖

They talked until a proctor came to shoo them out of the lounge for lights out. Two things seemed really obvious when they got done going over everything any of them had found in those scrapbooks.

First, the runes. They *had* to be pretty important. If they were protective—and they probably were—according to Loch and Addie, they would have been what Doctor Ambrosius used to "anchor" his own protections.

"The thing is," Addie said, frowning a little, "you'll have to take my word for it, but runes can actually change a little if they're used that way—if they're incorporated into something other than their original purpose. Physically change, I mean; the runes themselves will kind of get slightly rewritten to reflect the altered purpose."

Spirit didn't ask, "They can do that?" even though she wanted to, because Addie would never have said it if it wasn't true. So she asked, "How?" instead.

"Magic is a living force," Loch pointed out. "It changes. How we use it changes. So the tools we use to manipulate it have to be able to change, too. Things like runes. You can't rewrite them drastically, but you could take a protective spell that read, say, 'all that shelter under my boughs,' and by doing what we think Doctor Ambrosius did, the runes would change to read 'all that shelter within my bounds.' If he got specific about *what* he was protecting against—which would be smart—the runes would change to name those things."

"So if we translate them, we can figure out who or what Ambrosius is defending us against, and if we know that, we can figure out how we can help—" That felt better. That felt proactive. Spirit realized in that moment that she was getting very tired of always waiting for something to happen before she could act.

Burke had been very quiet all this time. When they all finally stopped talking, he spoke into the momentary silence.

"We've gotten distracted by all this," he said slowly, and waved his hand vaguely. "The runes, the history . . . even New Year's . . . it's distracted us from what's really urgent." Before any of them could ask him what he meant, he continued. "We still haven't figured out who the inside man is. Who the one trying to kill us from inside the school is." His jaw firmed. "The more I think about it, the more certain I am. There *is* someone in here, and it won't matter squat how much we figure out and how we help Doctor A. guard against what's outside, when we have someone right inside with us—"

He might have said more, but just then one of the proctors poked his head into the lounge and spotted them.

"All right, you dirty capitalists. Time to tally up your ill-gotten gains, figure out who won, and head for your rooms," he called. "Fifteen minutes to lights out."

With a sigh, Addie packed up the board that hadn't been

used all night, and they split up. Spirit only stopped long enough to tug on Burke's elbow and hold him back a moment.

"Thanks," she said, with feeling.

"For what?" he asked, looking both startled and gratified.

"For believing me. *In* me. That we're still in danger." She sighed. "I was beginning to feel as if none of you were ever going to see it."

"Maybe it's because I'm looking a little harder than the others," Burke replied, smiling down into her eyes. "Spirit—"

"Hey!"

They both jumped, instinctively separating, and both stared guiltily at the door, where the proctor was shaking his head. "Rooms. Now."

"Right," Burke said, and hurried out the door. Spirit could only stare after him a moment, wondering what he had been about to say, before she followed Addie and Muirin back to the girls' side.

❦

The names still hadn't been posted for the field trip, but a chance remark by Doc Mac had engendered—well, Spirit wasn't sure what to call it. Other than tempting fate . . .

Although she hadn't been there to hear it, evidently when one of the teachers had lamented the debacle of the New Year's Dance, he had mentioned some Scottish celebration that happened the week after New Year's that involved setting fire to a barrel of tar or a Viking ship, or both. "It'd give the kids something to get their minds off the bad experience," he'd said, and for some reason the entire faculty had taken the idea and run away with it, combining this Scottish-Viking thing with the need to take down the Winter Carnival.

So now there was going to be a big nighttime gathering featuring a bonfire with a Viking ship on top of it, a competition to take down the ice-works fast (*of course* there had to be a competition, this was Oakhurst) and what wasn't ice was to get tossed on the bonfire. The refreshments that didn't get used New Year's Eve had been thriftily saved or frozen; they were going to be served at this thing, along with grilled hot dogs and bratwurst. Muirin was already in heaven at the prospect.

Personally, Spirit thought this was a really dumb idea, not the least because it meant they were all going to have to go outside in the freezing cold, in the coldest part of the year, at night.

T he night of the thing, she went out bundled up to her eyebrows, and within moments of stepping out into the snow her toes and fingers started to freeze. The electric lights strung for the Carnival were all on, providing plenty of light.

She watched Addie and Muirin's team reducing an ice sculpture to powder snow. It was actually kind of fun to watch; the whole thing basically crumbled away like something right out of a movie. Like a vampire getting hit with sunlight, or a mummy crumbling away. She felt someone come to stand beside her, turned a little, and saw that it was Elizabeth, also bundled up.

"This is a bad idea," Elizabeth said, sounding very unhappy.

"I've seen better," Spirit said cautiously. "Somebody's going to get frostbite if they aren't careful." She glanced over at the pile of wood with a cardboard-and-wood Viking ship on top of it. "I don't know if that bonfire's a really good idea, either—"

"That's not what I meant," Elizabeth replied, then shook her head.

Spirit waited, but Elizabeth was silent. "Well, what did you mean?" she prompted, as Addie and Muirin's team moved on to the next ice sculpture, leaving a pile of tiny sandlike ice particles behind.

Elizabeth glanced around nervously. "It just seems like a bad idea. You know, like this might attract . . . something."

Spirit shivered as she felt a cold chill that had nothing to do with the weather go down her back. She looked up at the moon in a mostly clear sky. "Well," she replied, with a lightness she didn't feel, "if you're thinking it'll attract what happened at New Year's, even if the lights go out, there's no way whatever it was is going to be able to put out the moon. So we won't be in the dark and we will be able to see it."

Elizabeth gave her a dubious look. "If you say so," she replied, in a tone that said clearly she didn't believe it.

Some of the snow sculptures, like the castle, had been built on wooden scaffolding. With the packed snow evaporated by another team, Burke and several others were tearing the scaffolding down and piling it on the unlit bonfire. The thing was going to be huge. They'd probably be able to see it in Radial.

At least it would be warm.

She got a cup of hot cider from the knot of kitchen staff set-ting up the grills and the tables with food on them. They didn't look very happy, and she didn't blame them. But at least once they got the grills going, they'd have a little warm patch where they were. She wrapped her cold fingers around the cup and sipped slowly. The cider tasted . . . thin, somehow. As if some vitality had been drained out of it.

She rubbed her eyes and stared at Addie's team. There seemed to be a gray fog between her and them, and the sounds they were making as they took down another ice sculpture weren't as loud as they had been a moment before. And were the electric lights getting weaker? She rubbed her eyes again. This was weird, very weird; it was like everything was getting dimmed down.

Someone shouted; she turned, and saw a line of cloaked and hooded riders silhouetted against the night sky, just beyond the lawn of the school. There was something *wrong* about them; it wasn't just that they were wearing black, it was that the light somehow was sucked into them. She felt cold, horribly cold, staring at them.

Is this some prank from the kids in Radial? Please, let it be a prank . . .

But of course, she knew in her heart it wasn't—which was only proved a moment later when one of the Riders let out a piercing whistle and they all plunged toward the students.

Someone screamed. That made everyone turn to look.

Spirit just *knew* that the terrible, paralyzing fear was going to clamp down over them all. She even braced herself for it, getting ready to fight it, even though fighting it hadn't worked very well the last time.

But no—no, all that erupted was just plain old-fashioned panic.

People started shouting hysterically, and there was more screaming as the students scattered before the charge. As Spirit darted out of the way, something whistled over her head. A club of some kind, heavier than a bat, but swung expertly. It missed her, but not by much, and it forced her to take a tumble in order to escape the deadly hooves of another horse.

Who are they? She got no time to think about it. The Riders were turning and coming back again. There were people on the ground now, knocked down and maybe hurt. And the Riders were between them and the school buildings. There was no way to get to safety except through them.

She heard a shout of rage in a voice she recognized. Burke! She looked around for him and couldn't spot him. A moment later, something white shot through the air and hit one of the Riders in the shoulder. It couldn't have been a snowball; the missile didn't disintegrate when it hit. The Rider cursed, grabbed for his shoulder, his club dropping out of his hand. Whatever Burke was throwing was pretty solid.

Burke's famous fastball . . . It was followed by another, this time to the head. The Rider reeled—but the others charged.

But Burke's rage had infected her. Furious, she spotted a metal scaffolding pole in a pile of others and ran for it. It was just about the length of her kendo staff, if not the same weight.

She seized it and turned to face the Riders, screaming at them at the top of her lungs.

She wasn't the only one. Addie, Muirin, and Loch had taken up Burke's tactic, and now Spirit realized what it was Burke was using as a weapon.

Ice balls.

Addie was making them; Burke, Muirin, and Loch were throwing them. Murr-cat and Loch didn't have the lethal precision Burke did, but they were making up for it with volume, and aiming, not at the Riders, but at their horses.

The horses didn't like getting pelted one little bit. They fought their bits and their Riders. Spirit took advantage of this and charged, screaming like a banshee.

At least three of the horses won the fight with their Riders and bolted.

Spirit ended up beside the unlit bonfire; the remaining Riders milled around, fighting for control of their horses. Some of the other students were helping the ones on the ground; the rest responded sluggishly, as if they weren't quite sure what they should do. In that moment of uncertainty on both sides, Spirit glanced over at the bonfire and saw two things: an empty gallon of kerosene, and a fireplace lighter. Someone had been about to light the bonfire when the attack started.

Horses liked fire even less than they liked being pelted with ice balls.

Time to finish the job!

She dropped the pole, grabbed the lighter, and struggled with it for a moment, trying to get it to light. When she finally succeeded, she saw some of the wood gleaming wetly, reflecting the flame, and smelled the kerosene fumes, thick and choking. She bent down and put the flame to the kerosene-soaked wood.

The bonfire went up with a roar; she jumped back barely in time.

She took another glance at the Riders; now the horses were rearing and bucking, whinnying shrilly. That made up her mind; she seized a piece of burning two-by-four and charged them, waving the end that was on fire in front of her in wild arcs.

The Riders couldn't hold control of their mounts now. The horses had had enough. More of them peeled off, racing into the west. The leader fought his own horse for a moment, then must have decided to give up. He whistled shrilly and gave his horse its head. It galloped off after the first escapees, and the rest of the Riders followed.

Spirit dropped the burning board into the nearest snow pile, and sagged to her knees.

Mr. Bowman, Ms. Holland, and Mr. Krandal, the three teachers supposed to go on the field trip, were all hurt. Not badly, but they'd been ordered to the Infirmary along with the students who were injured. Most of those seemed to be Proctors.

Spirit sat with the others in the lounge, both hands wrapped around a big cup of hot chocolate, sipping at it. Her stomach was feeling very queasy after that confrontation. Murr-cat was on her third cup; evidently fighting didn't harm *her* appetite in the least!

Spirit watched the door, waiting for Addie to come back from the Infirmary. "There she is," she said, as Addie appeared in the doorway, a neat bandage on one hand.

Addie made her way over to them. "No one's seriously hurt, but they could have been," she said as she sat down with them. "One of the Proctors has a concussion. Those people wanted to hurt us."

Spirit nodded, and started to say something, but Addie forestalled her.

"I don't know if those Shadow Riders have anything to do with the Wild Hunt or New Year's—but I can tell you how the magic crossed the wards," she continued with venom. "I saw some of their hands. They were wearing Oakhurst rings. And since *we* were all accounted for, *they* have to be Alums!"

"Could they have just stolen the rings?" Spirit asked timidly.

"Unlikely," said Burke.

"Then we are so doomed. . . ."

ᛏᴇᴨ

Ever since the attack of those mysterious shadowed figures, there'd been a curious sense of the surreal about Oakhurst. On the one hand, almost all the physical classes had abruptly shifted into physical defense. Any time you looked outside, you'd see a teacher or staff member working on . . . something magical. Defenses, presumably. It wasn't obvious *what* was going on, but there was often some visual component, lights or vapors, or mysterious fleeting images.

On the other hand—unbelievable as it was, they were all expected to carry on as if nothing had happened. Even the ones that had been hurt. Bandages, casts on arms, and all. After her second night of nightmares, Spirit had tried to get an appointment with Doc Mac . . . but he was seeing people from six in the morning until midnight, and she just couldn't justify trying to muscle out someone who was in worse shape than she was.

And still the field trip was on. It made no sense.

Unless—maybe all this was to convince the students that no matter what happened, Oakhurst was still safe. If that was the intention . . . well, so far as Spirit was concerned, it wasn't working. And yet, as days passed, it seemed she was in the minority.

"Oh, I could really hate you this morning, Blondie," Muirin said, before Spirit even got a chance to sit down at the table. "*So* unfair. What did you do to get your seat on the train, anyway? And why didn't you tell me what it was so I could have, too?"

Spirit stared at her, brain blank. She'd spent the night fighting off nightmares of those mounted figures charging down on them; she'd clawed her way out of sleep as the alarm went off for the third time and had barely made it in time for breakfast before her first class. "What?" she replied. "Train?" She couldn't for a minute imagine what Muirin was talking about.

"Didn't you read your e-mail this morning?" Muirin asked, her green eyes dark with nameless emotion. "*You* get to go on the field trip. You, Burke, and Loch. *So* unfair!"

"I don't even want to go!" Spirit blurted, shocked. "Why should I go? Look, you can take my place, right?"

"No can do, Spirit," Burke said, sitting down with a huge bowl of oatmeal. "Designated field trippers only." He offered Muirin a smile of commiseration. "Look at it this way, are you *really* that interested in an exhibit of someone's modern horse sculptures? Not even you could convince me of that."

"It wasn't the museum," Muirin grumbled. "You know that. It was getting out of here. It was the shopping."

"Shopping?" asked Addie, with a raised eyebrow. "In Billings, Montana? After what you've been used to? You cannot seriously make me believe that *you* could be shopping for couture in Billings, Montana."

"Even Billings has mega-bookstores and mega-bookstores have magazine racks with things *other* than *National Geographic* and *Smithsonian* on them." Muirin poked at her eggs with her fork. "Stepmother won't forward my subscriptions, and there are *always* new magazines coming out that only last for a few issues. It wouldn't be so bad if we had real Internet, but I *need* my magazines without it!"

"Oh please, as if you've ever let that stop you from getting something," Addie replied with a sniff. "The only reason you haven't gotten past the firewall is because you haven't tried hard enough to find someone or some way to do it."

Muirin just gave her a sullen glare and went back to poking at her eggs.

"Well, I hate art museums, and I don't have any money," Spirit said, trying to look as irritated as Muirin was. "So I'm going to be bored with the museum and I can't do any shopping. And Billings is, what, three hours away by train? Which means that I'll have to be up *way* before dawn, and it's going to be awful. I promise you, if I could trade places with you, I would. The only good thing about this is getting out of classes for a day."

Well, except for getting Burke and *Loch all to myself. . . .*

"Oh, I bet they'll have work assignments waiting for you on the train," Addie said cheerfully. "After all, you'll have three hours there and three hours back, that's six whole hours you could be using to *achieve*. The only way you get out of class around here is if you're unconscious. Then they expect you to make it up when you revive."

Burke nodded, and for a moment Spirit wondered how they could all be so callous about the students who'd "gotten out of class" by virtue of being dead or insane, when a little movement of Burke's eyes alerted her to the fact that someone at one of the other tables behind her was listening.

Right. Everyone else seems to forget that people go crazy and die and vanish. I need to pretend that I've forgotten, too.

"There you go. I'll be stuck in a train for six hours with nothing to do but class work, then stuck at a museum. No reason for envy." Spirit shrugged. "I'll ask if we can switch anyway. Maybe they'll let you go instead."

But she already knew they wouldn't. This was exactly what the Administration seemed to want—drive a wedge between friends—and from the look on Muirin's face, they were getting it, too. Was it possible that Muirin had some reason why she'd been sure *she,* and not Spirit, was going to be going on this trip? If so, well, no wonder she was so ticked off.

She'd have to figure out some way to make it up. Maybe she could borrow some money from someone and get Muirin some candy bars.

On her first break between classes she went back to her room and checked her e-mail. Sure enough, there was the message congratulating her on being selected, along with a second, to all students, detailing who was going to go. There were about a dozen students on the list, including the new girl, Elizabeth—which made absolutely no sense, since she was having to catch up to the accelerated Oakhurst curriculum and not having an easy time of it. None of them were all that interested in art. None of them were at the top of the class.

Yes, this was definitely going to drive wedges between a lot of people.

✦

The museum opened at nine. It would take about half an hour to drive from the train depot to the museum, and three hours to get from Oakhurst to Billings. So they were all awakened at 4 A.M.

Spirit felt as if she'd barely gotten any sleep, though she'd *tried* to make an early night of it. No nightmares last night, but it felt like she'd spent most of the night waiting to hear the alarm go off. She yawned her way through breakfast, and trudged out into the dark with the others to get on the train.

There was definitely a surreal sense here. Days ago, the school had been attacked, physically attacked, and people had been hurt. Today they were going on a *field trip*. And the three teachers who were chaperoning them were still sporting the bandages from that attack, yet they acted as if they'd just had bad spills in the shower.

It was as if she was living an entirely different life from the rest of them. And yet . . . at this moment, even *she* was finding herself sucked into the illusion that everything was normal. She trudged toward the tiny station with the others, hearing the dull throb of the locomotive engine out there in the dark.

Like the train that had brought her here, this was a short, but very modern locomotive. This time it was coupled to two passenger cars instead of one. Both passenger cars had the Oakhurst logo on the side. Of course. They shuffled into single file and Spirit found herself sandwiched in between Burke and Loch. At least she could be sure of one thing; nobody on horseback was going to be able to catch them once the train was moving.

Burke took a seat next to a window; she popped into the one next to him, and Loch took one immediately behind them.

"Oh brother," Burke said, reaching for a white card sticking up out of the seat back in front of him. "It looks as if Addie was right."

Spirit checked her card. Instead of being a safety thing, it was instructions on how to use the built-in video player in the other arm of the seat back and a list of the preloaded lectures each of them were supposed to watch. But there were only three under Spirit's name, so Spirit put the card back and decided to get them on the way home. Of course, that was *all* there was to watch on the video players. And the list of available music was all from the Music Appreciation course.

"Oh man, this stuff is lame. Who loaded up this player? Good thing I brought my phone."

Phone? *Phone?* She craned her neck as the train blew its whistle and began to move out of the tiny station. No one at Oakhurst was allowed a phone. . . .

Ahead of her were four people she didn't recognize, and for a moment they looked utterly alien in their bright parkas and hoodies. Four people—who were not in Oakhurst coats and Oakhurst colors.

The train lurched into motion, and David Krandal stood up at the front of their car. He banged on the wall to get their attention.

"Those of you Oakhurst students that aren't already asleep," he said, eliciting a polite laugh, "might have noticed we have some guests from Radial with us: Brett and Juliette Weber, and Adam and Tom Phillips. They won't be with us for the field trip, but they all have business in Billings and Doctor Ambrosius offered the good people of Radial some of the extra seats on the train, in light of our new relationship with the town." He nodded at someone Spirit couldn't see. "So welcome aboard, but don't forget that if you miss the train when we head back, it's a long walk home."

Another polite laugh, and Mr. Krandal sat down again.

The train picked up speed. She was about to recline her seat for a nap when Mr. Krandal stood up again. He unlocked a door at the front of the car, and flipped a switch. Three icons lit up; a male and a female—probably for bathrooms—and a knife and fork. . . .

"It was probably early for most of you, so the kitchen is open," Krandal said. "There's box breakfasts and lunches, and we'll restock dinners for the trip back. There's only room in there for two at a time."

The four townies got up immediately and there was some

wrangling about who would get to go first. Two of them sat down, and the other two went in. The Oakhurst kids, who knew all too well what was going to be in those boxes, were in no hurry to get theirs.

The first two came back with their open boxes and looks of disappointment on their faces. They sat down and began picking through the offerings while the other two craned their necks to see. "Granola, plain yogurt, a banana, an apple, orange juice, and milk," announced one of the boys. "Not even a Pop-Tart, and no coffee. Bogus."

"I thought the Oakhats ate, like, steak and caviar and chocolate mousse for breakfast," one of the others whispered just loudly enough for Spirit to hear. She smirked. The girl of the set got up and got a box anyway, and began stirring her granola into the yogurt. Krandal ignored them. The Oakhurst kids snickered.

The train slowed down; Spirit was startled. They hadn't been under way for more than half an hour, they couldn't be anywhere near Billings yet—

"Relax," said Loch, deep in his first lesson. "We're coming up on the junction with the main line. We have to get clearance so we don't block a faster train or run up on a slower one. That's why these trips take at least three hours, and sometimes can take five."

"Five?" she echoed.

"Sometimes longer. Oh, hey, look at this—" Loch rotated his screen so Spirit could see it. He'd cued up some sort of video labeled The History of Oakhurst: From Mansion to Modern School.

"Huh, where'd you find that?" she asked.

"It's mislabled. It's under Science as Mitosis and Meiosis: The Fundamentals of Cell Division. I'm going to see if there's anything else loaded up that was mislabeled."

The train slowed to a halt and stopped. In the stillness, Spirit could hear faint echoes of music and video-game beeps from the townies' phones. The girl was txting someone as fast as her thumbs would work. After fifteen minutes the train lurched into motion again and rolled ahead in a left-hand curve. Spirit looked out Burke's window but it was too dark to see anything. She could sure tell when they got on the main line, though; things got a bit rougher and louder. So part of the quiet had been the private rail spur.

The Radial boy nearest Spirit was picking at his breakfast and making a face.

Someone behind Spirit got up. As she passed Spirit, she turned and winked before leaning over the back of the boy's seat. Spirit stared in shock. It was Muirin!

"'Smatter, Adam, not used to eating anything for breakfast that doesn't come in neon colors with marshmallow bits?" Muirin drawled.

Mr. Krandal nearly exploded out of his seat. "Muirin Shae!" he barked, looking absolutely furious. "I'm not going to ask you what you're doing here, because it's obvious you decided to stow away."

Muirin looked as innocent as she could, which was not very. Finally she shrugged. "I'm ahead on my classes, you can check for yourself. I just want to go to a bookstore. Is that so bad?"

Mr. Krandal was obviously struggling with himself. "It's too late to turn back now, which I assume you know. You sit right down there, young lady. I am going to have a conference with the other teachers about this, and we're going to call back to Oakhurst about it."

Muirin shrugged again and sat down in the empty seat beside the boy she'd called Adam. Mr. Krandal stalked down the aisle to the door at the rear of the car and through it to the second car where the other two teachers were.

"Damn, Muir, now I see why you were always jonesing for some junk food, if this is the crap they feed you," Adam said with a grin.

Muirin rolled her eyes. "You have no idea," she said. "Adam, these are my peeps, Spirit, Loch, and Burke. Guys, this is Adam Phillips. His brother Tom is the one hanging his chin on the seat back. They were the ones giving me and Seth some . . . help."

Spirit knew very well what Muirin meant by "help." Tom and Adam, who looked to be about fourteen and eighteen respectively, were the ones who had helped Muirin and Seth with smuggling contraband into Oakhurst.

"So what'd old Krandal mean by 'the new relationship with Radial'?" Muirin asked, looking at him keenly. "Last I heard, Radial thought the school was a maximum-security jail for high-dollar juvies and would've been happy to see it shut down."

"Oh that's big news." Adam smirked and Tom rolled his eyes. "Really big news. One of your Alumns made good in video games. He's the brain behind Breakthrough." At Muirin's blank look, he coughed. "Breakthrough Adventure Systems. I keep forgetting they keep you people in the Victorian ages. I'll make it short and easy for you—MMOs and console games that have pretty much taken over the marketplace. They took over about six games that failed dismally and one old favorite that *everybody* had been waiting for the update on. And they made them all into everything everybody wanted. Anyway, he decided that the best place for his new HQ was Radial, 'cause he's, like, nostalgic for good old Oakhurst."

"Yeah, right," Muirin replied sarcastically.

"Somebody has to be," Loch said.

"Anyway, this is like—like Lucas decided to move ILM out here on the same day that Sega announces they're going to put a plant here and work with him," Adam went on. "Bigger than big. Jobs, jobs, jobs, money coming into town like nobody's seen before, and every time something comes up—like the sewer plant not being able to handle all the new people—Rider just throws money at the problem and it goes away. Him and Ambrosius are all BFFs, and some people figure he's going to use Oakhurst as his game-designer-factory, 'cause you're all supposed to be super-geniuses and everything. I can tell you, though, right now, so far as most of Radial is concerned, you could take a dump in the street and they'd swear it was roses."

"Most?" Muirin probed.

"Well, you know. No matter what, there's going to be somebody who's going to hate it." Adam shrugged. "They're going to extend your rail line out to Breakthrough and start using it, 'cause the roads aren't good enough for everything he wants to bring in. They're already laying track in town. It'll probably be done in a couple of weeks."

"And what's your take on this?" Burke asked, leaning over.

Adam blinked, as if he hadn't expected Burke to speak. "It's money coming in. I graduated last year; I'm going to get a job out there and work until I get enough saved up to get the hell out of Radial. I don't care what people are saying, all that's going to happen with Breakthrough is once they get their compound put up, it's going to be us and them all over again. Anything they want, they'll bring in from outside. They'll use the train and that Oakhurst private airstrip, the bigwigs'll live in California, the code-monkeys'll come from Oakhurst or outside, they'll put housing up out on the Oakhurst land and the money's going to dry up as soon as the construction's over. Don't care, 'cause by then, I'll be gone." His brother Tom nodded in agreement.

"Yeah." The girl—Juliette?—piped up. "Like my gramma says it was like back in the day when it was a mansion. She never saw anything of Crazy Tyniger or the people he brought to it. 'Cause, like, rich dudes don't mix with the po' folks unless there's something they want out of 'em." The girl shot Muirin a sly look, as if she expected the dig to hurt. Muirin didn't even notice. "Gramma says it was almost better when that biker gang took the place over in the Seventies, 'cause at least they came into town and bought beer and groceries."

Biker gang? That's new . . .

Of course—if it *had* been in the Seventies, it would have been after Tyniger was dead and the estate was tied up. Spirit filed that away for further investigation later.

"That's why so many kids run off," the last townie said. He looked like the girl; they both were brown-haired and had the same square face and deep-set eyes. "There's, like, nothing for us in Radial. Best thing you can do is hitch a ride out and disappear. No matter how bad it gets out there, at least it ain't Radial."

So kids are vanishing out of Radial, too! No wonder the Radial cops don't care. They've gotten into the habit of deciding a kid that disappears is a kid who ran away, and that's the end. Spirit was willing to bet just about anything that those missing kids hadn't "run off," they'd been taken by the Hunt.

She was going to ask Adam some questions herself, but that was when Mr. Krandal came back with the other two teachers.

Adam and Juliette became very interested in their phones, and Tom's head vanished back over the seat. Mr. Krandal crooked his finger at Muirin. "Come with me, young lady," he said, frowning. "We have some things to discuss."

Muirin got up and followed them back into the other car.

"What do you think they're going to do with her?" Spirit whispered to Burke.

He shook his head.

They were back about fifteen minutes later, and Spirit relaxed a little. Muirin looked exactly like someone who had gotten away with murder, even though she had her eyes cast down penitently and had her mouth in a very slight frown. Spirit could tell, though, that she figured she had won this one, just by her eyes.

Her eyes were very smug indeed.

Mr. Krandal pointed at the seat she'd been in, and she hesitated. "Can I please have a breakfast box, Mr. Krandal?" she asked quietly. "I didn't eat before I left."

"Get one, get back here and sit down. And study those extra assignments," Krandal growled, and went back up to the front of the car and took his own seat.

Adam glanced back at them. Muirin winked. Adam grinned and gave her a thumbs-up. She got a breakfast box and busied herself with it.

Spirit went back to the video player and cued up the mislabeled segment.

By the time it was finished, she wasn't sleepy anymore, so after a glance back at Muirin, who was studiously watching her own videos, she plunged into her lessons. Might as well get them over with. Mr. Krandal interrupted her when she'd finished the second by advising them all to get lunch. The Radial kids groaned at the sight of the healthy sandwiches, broccoli and dip, and fruit. She ate hers with both eyes on the screen, and figured out why there were only three lessons here. . . .

Nothing about magic, of course. They would have known there would be people from Radial on the train, so whatever was on there had to be perfectly ordinary.

She finished the last lesson as the train slowed again; a glance out the window showed that there was light out there now, and they were pulling into suburbs.

Great. A million questions I want answered, things stalking us, and now . . . I go spend a day looking at artsy horse statues. . . .

✦

The museum was just as boring as Spirit had feared. The horse statues were very artsy. The docent waxed eloquent about the deep meanings embodied by the horse statues. Spirit took notes. Loch took notes. Most of the rest of the students looked bored and pretended to take notes. Burke had wandered off to look at something else. Muirin said, "You'll loan me your notes, right?" then vanished into the gift shop. When they all caught up with her she looked very smug indeed.

The same Oakhurst cars that had picked them up at the train station showed up to get them at the entrance to the museum. Elizabeth attached herself to their group, which Spirit really didn't mind, although Muirin rolled her eyes a little. Once they were all inside the thing, which was an SUV with an Oakhurst crest in Oakhurst colors that was big enough to need its own ZIP code, Mr. Krandal turned around to look at the five of them in the back.

"Here," he said brusquely, handing Elizabeth, Loch, Burke, and Spirit sealed envelopes in Oakhurst gold. "Obviously you can't get a snack or shop without money." He looked pointedly at Muirin, who had *not* gotten an envelope. He turned back too quickly to realize she wasn't looking disappointed, she was smirking.

Spirit opened her envelope. There was fifty dollars in tens in it. She blinked. Her parents hadn't ever given her very much money at one time, but she knew she had to be in the minority there, because plenty of kids her age had jobs after school. This was probably like the change after paying for coffee to Muirin and Loch.

"Remember, you can't get anything Oakhurst doesn't approve of," Krandal said without turning around. "No Victoria's Secret. No violent video games."

"Yes, Mr. Krandal," Spirit said. Muirin elbowed her and whispered, "Ladies' Room." Spirit nodded. Was there anything she could buy for fifty dollars that might be useful against whatever it was that was after them all? A gun? There were guns at the school, and knives, and even real swords. This was all so crazy. . . .

Maybe she should just . . . try not to worry about it. After all, the teachers *were* all being proactive now, and presumably they had a lot more experience at this than the kids did. And this business of Breakthrough coming to Radial . . . Doctor Ambrosius was certainly happy to see them. Maybe this was a kind of cover for the Alumns to come back and join Doctor Ambrosius! Despite the fact that those Shadows were Alumns . . .

But no, Doctor Ambrosius surely wouldn't be that easily fooled.

She worried about that all the way to the mall. The cars

dropped them all off, with orders to meet at the entrance where they'd been left at three. Ms. Holland stayed with them; the other two teachers drove off with the cars.

Seeing as it was Ms. Holland who was with them, Spirit worried that she and Muirin wouldn't be able to get rid of her, but the teacher immediately latched on to Loch. Muirin grabbed Spirit's arm and babbled something about the Ladies' Room and hustled her off.

Of course they didn't go that far, since there was absolutely no one following them. Instead, Muirin virtually hauled her into a hole-in-the-wall computer store.

A computer store?

The guy behind the counter was somehow geeky and gothy at the same time. He absolutely lit up to see two girls coming into his otherwise empty shop. He opened his mouth—

Muirin cut him off. "I'm Desdemona. Have you got my thumb drives?"

The guy closed his mouth and went all wistful. "Yeah, I do. Here you go." He shoved over six sealed packages of tiny thumb drives marked down to ninety-nine cents. Muirin picked one up and looked at it critically. She looked up and beamed.

"Brilliant!" she said. "I can't tell they were ever opened!"

The guy flushed and looked pleased. "I get a lot of practice." Muirin pulled out a charge card and shoved it across the counter at him. Spirit was staggered at the number he rang up, but Muirin didn't bat an eye. "I don't suppose I could have your number?" he asked.

Spirit expected Murr-cat's usual scathing response, but for once Muirin surprised her. "You are totally my type, but Oakhurst is practically a convent," she said apologetically. "That's why I needed you to get my stuff this way."

The guy sighed. "Well, you've got to graduate some time, right? And I'll probably still be here when you do."

Muirin smiled at him sweetly, and took the bag with the drives in it. She left the store, Spirit following.

"What—" Spirit said.

Muirin shoved the bag at her. "These are yours until we get back to the school. If anyone asks, you got them to back up your class work in case that thing at New Year's really was an EMP and the next one will blow out the computers. Okay?"

"Uh, okay, but—"

"Seth and Adam were my contacts to this guy, they knew him from gaming. This is six months' worth of downloads so I don't go mental listening to Oakhurst-approved music." She rolled her eyes. "And so I can see a movie that isn't PG-13. Don't worry, these are special. If you don't have the unlock code they look like two-gig drives with nothing on them. If you do, it opens up the hidden storage."

Spirit was impressed. "Wow, you know a lot—"

Muirin shook her head. "Not me. It was all Seth. Now let's go get some magazines. I wasn't kidding about that, and they're going to expect me to figure out how to use my own money anyway."

They ran into Loch and Burke at the bookstore. It was one of those really big ones with places to sit and read, and on a weekday afternoon there was no one in here and only one person at the register. They took over the chairs in the Hobby section.

"What was with Ms. Holland?" Spirit wanted to know.

"Yeah, did she come on to you?" Muirin made a kissy-face. "Oh teacher, teacher!"

"Cut it out Murr-cat," Loch said with annoyance. "It wasn't like that. She was trying to convince me to pull a runner. She told me she had a lawyer friend who would go to my trustee for me and get him to petition for a new guardian. She said her lawyer friend would convince my trustee that Doctor Ambrosius just wants to get his hands on my money."

"Say what?" Muirin looked at him as if she didn't quite understand the words coming out of his mouth. "What did you tell her?"

"I told her I didn't think I would be any safer away from Oakhurst," Loch replied, and shook his head. "She said I had no idea what was going on, and that anyone who stayed was going to come face-to-face with an evil I could never imagine."

"Well, gee, that was helpful," Muirin said sarcastically. "I don't suppose she could have been more specific?"

Loch shrugged. "No, she just spent about ten minutes trying to convince me that staying at Oakhurst was a fate worse than death, then literally threw her hands up in the air, said, 'Fine,' and stomped off."

"She must have gone after me," Burke said. "She cornered

me in the Food Court and gave me the same story. Well, except for the part about the lawyers and the trustees; she said she'd get me a bus ticket back to my foster parents and convince them that Oakhurst was some kind of weird cult compound so they'd keep me with them. I pretty much said the same as you."

Muirin looked from Loch to Burke and back again. "You both just had a chance to get out of here practically shoved in your faces, and you turned it down," she said incredulously. "*Why?*"

Burke scratched his chin. "You want the logical reason or the illogical reason?" he asked.

"Logic first," Muirin said. "Convince me."

"We know there's someone inside Oakhurst that's helping the Shadow Knights."

"Shadow Knights?" Spirit interrupted. Burke blushed.

"That's—just what I call them. Stupid, I know, it sounds like a bad fantasy movie or a video game."

"No, it fits, go on," she urged, smiling at him. Burke blushed a little more.

"Okay, so, we know there's someone at Oakhurst working with the Shadow Knights, and we don't know who it is. We just know there's a good chance it's a teacher, and so far, *who* are the people that have managed to get in the way?"

Muirin chewed her lip. "Us."

"So what's the best way to get us out of the way? Break us up. Separate us." Burke nodded as Muirin hissed a little. "You know, the whole bundle of sticks routine. So *maybe* Ms. Holland knows what's going on and is trying to help us out. And *maybe* she's the inside man, or one of them. So okay, we've been warned and it isn't Spirit being paranoid. We're better off sticking where we know the territory and can maybe put up a bunker somehow."

Muirin pondered that for a while. "Okay. So what's the not-logical reason?"

Burke gazed earnestly at her. "Because you're all my friends. And I don't bail on my friends."

"What he said," said Loch.

ELEVEⅡ

The cars came to pick them all up; when they got to the train, a third and fourth railcar had been added. One was a sleek metal thing with no windows and a big double door. It didn't look like a baggage car, more like something meant to hold a lot of cargo. And behind that was one of those container cars stacked two high. There were people loading the cargo car when they arrived, but it looked as if they had just started—and they were packing it tight.

The townies were already there, waiting; Mr. Krandal unlocked the doors to the passenger cars; he went into the rear car, and they all settled into their seats, but the train showed no signs of moving as the light faded.

The townies stirred restlessly, and Spirit was beginning to feel hungry. That was when Mr. Krandal came into their car from the rear car.

He rubbed his hand unconsciously over his bald spot. "As you can see, we're taking this opportunity to get in some supplies for the school, and in addition, a generous Alumnus is getting us some new equipment we're sure you'll appreciate. However, since this is causing something of a delay in leaving, I've unlocked a game feed to your seat consoles, and . . ." A pizza delivery van pulled up to the platform. ". . . ah, there we are, right on time. We have some hot food for you."

There were cheers at that, and a tall stack of pizza boxes was unloaded into each car. There was a little grumbling from the townies to discover that most of the toppings were "healthy"—a lot of veggies were involved, including shredded broccoli and "pepperoni" made of tofu. But there wasn't *too* much complaining. Everyone was very hungry. These were gourmet pizzas, not stuff from a chain, delivered so hot the cheese was still bubbling. Spirit overheard Adam saying with awe that he'd heard one of these pies cost more than he made in two days at his job. That couldn't be true, but it impressed the townies. There was contented silence, broken only when someone got up to get another slice. Then there was more silence as people put on headsets and plugged into the promised video game.

Out of curiosity, Spirit called it up, and was unsurprised to see that it was from Breakthrough. The game didn't interest her; it was a futuristic combat game, and you were fighting what looked like alien Nazis in powered armor, big spherical flying things with tentacles and energy beams, and robotic wolves and eagles. It allowed several players to form a team and either take on things in the game or fight one another. You could be either some kind of soldier, or people in black bodysuits with all kinds of powers. Soldiers could only fight the Nazis or the people in the black bodysuits; people in black bodysuits could only fight the Nazis or the soldiers. Or both could team up to fight the Nazis. Interestingly, a lot of the powers involved magic that seemed to work exactly like the magic being taught at Oakhurst. It was *very* pretty, very fast moving, and as far as she could tell, very inventive, but she wasn't in the mood to fight anything. Judging by the antics of most of the others, though, it was immediately popular with everyone playing.

The car was warm, the seat was comfortable, and Loch, Burke, and even Muirin were deep in the game. Elizabeth wasn't playing, but she was staring at the screen, watching the others. With a mental shrug, Spirit pulled out one of her carefully considered purchases—a book—and pulled out her iPod, glad that she'd loaded it with music *she* liked, not the Music Appreciation stuff.

It was nearly 8 P.M. by the time the train lurched into motion. Spirit looked up when it did, but the others didn't notice. She pulled up the game briefly to see what had them so immersed, but couldn't tell which little figure was which person and shut it off again.

They had to detour to a siding halfway to Oakhurst to let an express freight go by and that delayed them further. By the time they got to the school, it was almost midnight and Spirit was too tired to think. The others were even more tired than she was, and they all shuffled like zombies into the tiny train station, where there were four more teachers waiting to check their purchases. The three chaperones didn't stop at the station, and she was pretty sure they'd gone straight to their own quarters. She waited with the others while her purchases were examined for contraband—she half expected someone to say something about all the thumb drives, but no one did; they didn't even give more than a cursory look inside the little white plastic bag from the computer store. She was really glad when they sent her off to the main building.

Muirin tailed her all the way to her room, chattering about nothing; as soon as they were out of sight of teachers and proctors, she held out her hand and Spirit passed her the white bag. Muirin blew her a kiss, and dashed off with it. Spirit got into her room and dumped her purchases on the bed.

A red sweater, some candy, a lipstick, two books, and a magazine. Everything but the magazine had been on sale, but she'd always been used to shopping carefully. Before.

She frowned and picked up yet another thumb drive. She hadn't bought *this*. And it wasn't anything like the thumb drives Muirin had bought. For one thing, this wasn't in a blister pack. For another, it was in a brushed-metal case, not plastic. There was a little logo and a single word across the bottom just above the indicator light. IRONKEY.

Maybe it was already in the bag at the computer store. But she'd handed the whole bag to Muirin. *It must have fallen out.* If so, it was too late to return it, and there was no way to tell them she had it. Well, she was too tired to look at it now. She tossed it in a drawer and went to bed.

She woke to someone banging on her door; blearily she opened her eyes and saw it was just two minutes before her alarm was going to go off. "What?" she yelled, fighting her way out of the blankets.

Kelly opened the door and stuck her head in. "Special Assembly before class, in the Auditorium," the Proctor said, and closed the door again.

Special Assembly?

She dressed with a little more care than usual—this might be a kind of inspection, and she didn't want to take the chance on failing it; that left her a little behind, and the others must have already gotten breakfast, because there wasn't any sign of them in the Refectory. She ate in a hurry—everyone else was bolting their food, so she figured that was a sign she'd better, too. The cold air hit her like a hammer as she went outside and hurried toward the Auditorium. And it was dark. She couldn't help but think that if there was going to be an ambush by the bad guys, this would be a good time for it; either while they were all in the open, scuttling to the Auditorium, or even better, once they were all *in* the Auditorium.

When she got there, she got another surprise; no "free seating" this time, they all had assigned seats in alphabetical order. A proctor consulted a list and sent her to hers just as Doctor Ambrosius came out on the stage, and the house lights dimmed.

"Ladies and gentlemen," he said, casting his gaze around the room. "Some of you are already aware of our generous Alumnus donor, although you don't yet know what he is giving us. I won't spoil his surprise, but I will tell you this. After the incursion of those unwelcome visitors last week, Oakhurst put out a call for help, and the generous Oakhurst family has responded. We will be receiving both visitors and new residents today; I would like you to be on your best behavior and prove to them that the quality of Oakhurst students has not diminished over the years." He cleared his throat, and scanned the audience again. "We will be playing host to students who graduated and went on to greatness, experts in protection and defense both arcane and—well, given the level of technology involved, I could not in good conscience call it *mundane,* so let us just say arcane and physical." He smiled, grimly. "And let those who oppose Oakhurst beware."

Well, everyone was surely awake by now. Spirit found herself sitting bolt upright in her seat.

"Now, if I may, let me introduce our benefactors: the CEOs of Breakthrough Adventure Systems and graduates of Oakhurst, Mr. Mark Rider and Master Theodore Rider. The microphone is yours, Mark."

Astonished applause broke out across the room as two men in suits so perfectly tailored to them that they looked like second skins strode across the stage and took over the microphone that Doctor Ambrosius had relinquished. One was older than the other by at least a decade, dark-haired and powerful, though he could not by any stretch of the imagination be called handsome; he was the one who took over the mic. The other was blond, tall, and catlike; the way he moved gave Spirit the impression that he never stirred an inch without planning every step in advance.

"Good morning, fellow dwellers in the halls of Oakhurst," the older man said genially. He had a deep, gravelly voice. "I'll be sure and make this short enough so that you don't get bored, and stretch it out long enough that you get to skip your first classes."

There was a scattering of laughs. Spirit frowned a little as she watched and listened. The man reminded her of something or someone—but what, or who? He spoke without any "ums" or hesitations, however, so he was obviously used to speaking for an audience.

"I'm Mark Rider. Some of you may already know Breakthrough, or at least, know our products. Thanks to Oakhurst, when Teddy and I graduated from here, we had everything we needed to make ourselves into as big a success as we wanted—and we dreamed big." Rider nodded a little at the murmur of appreciation. "We were grateful. So today we're bringing that success back to the people that gave it to us. Now, what the outside world will know is this: Breakthrough is moving its HQ to Radial and entering into an historic partnership with Oakhurst Academy. We'll be building and installing a brand-new, state-of-the-art computer facility here, and Oakhurst will be adding game design courses to the curriculum. Those of you with free time will be invited to become beta testers for Breakthrough, and for any of you who want a job with us after you graduate Oakhurst, or after you graduate from college, it will be there waiting for you."

There was an outburst of wild applause at that, and Spirit

could hear people whispering excitedly to each other. Mark Rider held up his hand. His class ring glinted brightly.

"Of course, that's just what the ordinary world will see. But—as we all know—Oakhurst transcends the ordinary world. The first skirmishes of the war we've anticipated for so long, the war that Doctor Ambrosius trained us for, have broken out. Here. The enemy has come to the place where the next generation of magicians is trained and hardened. Obviously, his plan is to kill our future." Rider's face lost that professional smile. "We aren't going to let him. And we've come back to Oakhurst to make sure that *our side* wins this thing. Our first order of business is to make sure that Oakhurst Academy is safer than the Vice President's 'undisclosed location.'"

There was a nervous laugh. Rider put his smile back on again. "This is not our first rodeo, kids. Breakthrough has security on its campus that would make the Secret Service bleed with envy, and we're going to duplicate it here. We'll be putting in new protections, and we've designed a whole new set of computer games to help train you—the world's first Magic Simulator. The time is at hand; and when the enemy shows up for the first real battle, Oakhurst *will* be ready!"

More cheering.

"Of course this means that your classes will be changing; some will be dropped, others added. For the time being, we'll keep up your academic and career classes—my hope is that we won't have to change to full combat training for you, that we Alumni will be able to handle things and keep you safe, and this will all be over in time for me to welcome the next generation of Oakhurst graduates to my Developer Teams." He grinned. His teeth were extremely white; somehow they looked like wolf teeth. "So now I'll introduce to you some of my staff and family who will be the ones implementing that change. First, my lovely wife, Madison Lane-Rider, who will be replacing Ms. Lindsay Holland."

He made a little beckoning gesture as Spirit blinked in surprise at the abrupt announcement that Ms. Holland was—gone. A supermodel-beautiful red-haired woman in a tailored suit moved across the stage in a catwalk strut, giving a professional smile to the audience, and ended up at Mark Rider's side. She didn't take Mark's hand, nor did they kiss, which Spirit had half expected. She took a pose with all her weight on one foot, one hand on one hip, the other relaxed at her side.

"My brother Teddy, of course, who will be directing the new computer-training courses."

Teddy Rider gave a little wave; he was as blond as Mark was dark, and had the most penetrating blue eyes Spirit had ever seen. He seemed to be looking through the students for someone.

"Anastus Leontivich Ovcharenko, who will be directing some of the new defense courses and supervising the installation of new defenses here at Oakhurst." Another blond, this one *very* Russian looking, stalked like a prowling tiger across the stage to join the others. Spirit was startled to see he was wearing body armor under his suit jacket, and was openly carrying some sort of large firearm in a shoulder holster. "Anastus has been head of Breakthrough's security division for the last year. He'll be joined by Mia Singleton and Zachary York, who will be taking over the defenses here once the new installations are complete, as well as assisting him with martial arts and other classes. Ms. Singleton and Mr. York should be arriving this afternoon." Mark Rider paused significantly; Doctor Ambrosius signaled what was expected by beginning the applause.

When it died down again, Rider leaned over the podium. "Make no mistake about this, kids. This is going to be a war, and it might last longer than we hope. We're not sure if it will break out into the open or not, but even if it doesn't, when it's over, the world is likely to be a very different place, because this *will* spill out into the world. But we're going to keep you all safe until you have the strength and the skill to stand with us. And we aren't the only ones who will be doing so. There are more of us out there than any of you guess, and we aren't going to let you down. As they can free themselves up, the rest of the Oakhurst family will be coming here to answer the call to arms. But for right now? When we're done, only an idiot would try attacking this place." He grinned. "So you can turn the watch over to us. And when you're ready, we are *all* going to kick some serious ass!"

The room exploded in applause.

⁎

When they filed out, the area next to the gym was already swarming with a construction crew. Spirit had no idea how they were actually going to build anything in the middle of winter, but by midafternoon she had her answer. They'd erected a giant inflatable building over the site, a construction that was presumably going to make it possible to lay and cure a foundation. She'd seen similar buildings used for Indian casinos; they were easy enough to keep warm inside. There was already a separate generator out there, and Spirit heard a rumor that it was actually a hydrogen fuel cell able to supply enough power for all of Radial.

By evening, the school had already taken on a different tone. It was subtle, but obvious. Students who'd been looking over their shoulders ever since the New Year's Dance were beginning to relax and go back to normal—well, Oakhurst normal, which meant that people were already scheming on how to get into the game design classes or some of the specialized "defense" classes. Just before sunset, the Russian, Anastus Ovcharenko, had been seen supervising the setup of what could only be a shooting range. The Refectory buzzed, and for the first time in weeks, Muirin, Burke, Loch, and Addie looked at ease.

Spirit, however, was *not* at ease. Nothing about this felt right, starting with the way Ms. Holland had just been erased from Oakhurst without a murmur—right after she'd tried to warn Loch and Burke.

They moved from the Refectory out to the lounge, and Addie set up the Monopoly board as usual. Spirit was determined to wake them out of this complacent state. "So Loch found this video on the system in the train," she began, "and one of the townies was saying—"

"Whoa, Spirit, give it a rest," Loch interrupted. "We don't have to worry now. The cavalry's here."

"The—what?" she managed, staring at him. "Are you nuts? After what Ms. Holland said to you, and then she just gets *replaced*? Doesn't that seem the least little bit fishy to you?"

Loch shrugged. "And Ms. Holland could have been the insider, trying to peel me and Burke off from the herd and Rider's crew figured her out. Or she could have just quietly snapped, and what she told me and Burke was just part of her delusion, and they sent her away. Don't read too much into this. Anyway, the point is, there are *adults* here now who actually believe that the war came to us. Adults, not kids, and they've got a lot of real-world power, just for a start."

Muirin nodded sagely. "Mark Rider is worth billions. I'll bet an imported Belgian truffle that as soon as she gets wind of this, Step is going to turn up here to cruise his younger brother. Enough money can buy us just about anything, including an army of security guards if we need them. And have you *seen* their auras? If they glowed any more you'd have to put a dimmer switch on them. That means magic power, baby, and lots of it."

"So, Mr. Rider was right, even if he did have to grandstand about it," Loch continued. "We can relax and let them take over. We can go right back to just worrying about school stuff. And it's about time."

She tried not to splutter. "And doesn't it seem awful convenient that they turn up within days of those Shadow Knights? Shadow Knights wearing Oakhurst rings? Hello! Anybody?"

227

Muirin sneered just the littlest bit. "Shadow Knights? Where did you get *that* from, some bad fantasy novel?"

"Come on, Murr-cat," Burke said. "Keep your claws for people who deserve to get scratched."

Loch shook his head. "Of course they turned up within days, Spirit. Doctor A. said he'd called them. You're confusing cause and effect. The attack was the cause, having them turn up was the effect. And so what if the bad guys were wearing rings? Heck, they could have stolen them, made them, or just used an illusion to throw us off and put us at each others' throats."

"But!" Spirit began, and Addie made a lip-zipping motion.

"Relax. You've been keyed up for so long you're probably having an adrenaline crash," Muirin said shrewdly. "I bet it's got to hurt, not being the boss anymore, too. Let it go. You don't have to be in charge now, and it's not going to hurt you to give the boss-hat to someone with real experience."

"But I wasn't—but I didn't—" Spirit stammered, taken aback.

Muirin just raised a knowing eyebrow at her. *I know you enjoyed bossing us around, and being the Special One who saw there was danger before anyone else did, but you can't be the Special One forever.* That was what that look said. She flushed.

Suddenly she didn't have any taste for Monopoly.

The others weren't paying that much attention to the set anyway. Burke and Loch were quickly deep in a discussion of whether or not Burke would make a better game designer, developer, or programmer. "After all, it's not like I've got a pile of money waiting for me when I turn eighteen," Burke said with a shrug. "And with any luck, Doctor A. and the Riders will clear this war out before we graduate. So I'll need a job, you know? Might as well be something I like."

Muirin laughed. "Maybe I actually *can* scrape Step off onto Teddy Rider; when she's stalking her prey she always forgets I even exist."

They all seemed to have forgotten everything they'd learned; Spirit could hardly believe it. Didn't they want to find out what was really going on? Didn't they want to *know* who the insider was, instead of just guessing? And what about the "other" Oakhurst, the one where people who *didn't* have magic went? Because, supposedly, they were all Legacies, right? And she knew darn good and well that her parents hadn't had the least little bit of magic. If they had, life would have been a lot different. Maybe they'd have hidden it from their friends, but their own kids, kids who might have some of that magic themselves? No way. So where was this "other," this "shadow" Oakhurst?

And if it didn't exist—well that would mean that they'd all been lied to. They weren't Legacies. They'd been found some other way. And what did *that* mean?

But the others acted as if the last several months had never happened, as if Oakhurst was going to go back to normal. Loch argued with Burke about taking shooting classes. And Muirin was asking Addie if she thought that the Russian was worth making a pass at!

Spirit wanted to jump up and start screaming, just to get them to stop.

And then she noticed that they were all wearing their rings, which glinted brightly with the colors of their School of Magic. In fact, as she looked around, she realized *everyone* in the lounge had taken to wearing their rings.

Except her.

It was horrible. There she sat, with the conversation going on around, over, under, and past her. It was as if she wasn't even there.

Finally she made an excuse and went back to her room.

She lay down on her bed and stared at the ceiling, feeling desperately that something horrible was going to happen, and knowing there was nothing she could do to prevent it. It was like being in a nightmare, where you ran from one person to another, screaming at them that something awful was going on, and they acted as if you were nothing more than an annoying fly. Except this was *real*.

Was she wrong? Everyone else seemed so *sure*. The adults were here, the "cavalry," and it was true, they had resources and abilities the kids could only dream of having. Money, skills, experience—and magic, lots of it. Spirit didn't even have a spark of magic. Was this just her wanting to hang on to the moment when *she'd* been important, when *she'd* been the one figuring things out? Loch had been the first one to say it on Christmas Day. She should have known he wouldn't be the last.

But . . .

Ever since the week before Christmas, she'd been the one warning everyone that it wasn't over, and look, she was right, it not only wasn't over, here were a bunch of adults saying that stuff was just beginning. She'd been proved right. This was the ultimate "I told you so." Shouldn't the arrival of the "cavalry" make her happy? Hadn't she wished more than once that she could feel safe again? And now, she should be able to feel safe, right? Not only were these people setting up magical defenses, they were setting up physical ones, expensive ones that probably not even Oakhurst could have paid for. The Riders had come *flying* back to Oakhurst when Doctor Ambrosius called. It wasn't easy, out there in the big world, to just shut your business down and move it elsewhere. They'd sacrificed a *lot*. Shouldn't she just shut up and be grateful?

She should. Her head said she should. But her insides were seething with revolt, telling her there was something so wrong about all of this that there was not one bit of it that could be right.

And no one would believe her.

Not even Burke. Not even Loch.

Her head ached with the effort of not crying; finally she got up and splashed some cold water on her face. She glanced at the clock, and couldn't believe it was only eight. It felt as if she had been lying there for hours. No way she was going to be able to get to sleep, not this early. She thought, briefly, about trying to see if Doc Mac was available. She still trusted him—and maybe he could tell her if she was just being paranoid, if she was just trying to hang on to her teeny little bit of fame, manage to reassure her—

But it was really too late at night for something that wasn't an emergency. Besides, he was probably meeting with the new people. It sounded like Mark Rider was the kind of guy who wanted the psychological profiles of everyone around him. . . .

Might as well fire up the computer. She still had class work to do, even if the classes she was doing it for were going to be canceled in the next couple days and replaced with—what? More martial arts? Magic classes she could do nothing in?

Maybe I can learn to shoot a gun and be cannon fodder.

She plopped down in her seat, successfully kept herself from opening up the school chatroom, and got her after-class assignments. Math problems and an essay, oh joy. Resolutely she did her assignments, and reached into the drawer for a thumb drive to save them until she could get time on a printer. For all she knew, there *would* be an EMP or a power outage or an undervolt, and she'd lose everything she'd just done.

Her hand fell on something smooth and cooler than the thumb drive she was looking for. She pulled it out.

It was the mysterious "Ironkey" drive she'd found in her bag.

She hesitated a moment, then shrugged, and plugged it into the USB port. The worst that would happen would be that it would infect her computer and the school net. Bitterly, she decided that wouldn't be so bad . . . it would give Mark Rider and his computer geeks another chance to save the day. And the best? There might be something interesting on it. Something to take her mind off this mess.

Her computer registered and recognized the device. She clicked on the book-shaped icon.

A window opened. Words appeared.

Are you alone? Y/N

OK, that was weird. Y, she typed.

What is your name?

Spirit White.

Correct answer. Who was Mr. BunBun?

Spirit blinked. She hadn't thought of that in *years*. When she was five, for some unknown reason the stores had run short of stuffed rabbits at Easter, and her parents had gotten her a pink stuffed plush dog instead. She'd called it Mr. BunBun and for three years she couldn't be separated from it.

How did a program on a flash drive know that?

Muirin. This had to be some kind of prank of Muirin's. She didn't remember telling Muirin about Mr. BunBun, but obviously she had. And Oakhurst did have killer computer labs. Even if Muirin couldn't write a program like this, she could find someone to do it for her.

Might as well see what happens. . . .

My stuffed dog, she typed.

Correct answer. Welcome, Spirit White.

A new window opened, full of text. She began to read it, slowly.

Instructions. Instructions—supposedly—on how to use a code package in a file on this key to do what, so far, none of the school hackers had ever been able to. Get past the firewalls undetectably, and reach outside the intranet and onto the Internet. Into the world.

Muirin couldn't have done this. If she knew how, she'd do it herself. If she meant to share it with Spirit, she'd have bragged about it. Spirit's mouth went dry, and she sat back in her chair, staring at the screen. If this worked, she could talk to anyone—do research—get advice.

But then the temporary euphoria abruptly vanished. Who would she talk to? She was all alone. She didn't know anyone. She wasn't like Muirin, who had contacts everywhere and knew how to make more. Everyone she knew, everyone she cared about, was right here.

And if it was a trap—would it be a trap laid by the Oakhurst insider? Ms. Holland could have planted this in her bag. What would happen if it *was* a trap? Could you use a computer program to do magic? Would it bring a Shadow Knight straight to her? Or had whoever put this in her bag figured she *did* have friends outside the school, and intended to use her to find them?

She stared at the screen for a good minute before finally unplugging the drive and throwing it back in the drawer.

It was no use. She was alone, afraid, and without allies. She got undressed, went back to bed, turned off the lights, and cried herself to sleep.

✶

TWELVE

Spirit woke up with a start—with someone's hand clamped over her mouth. She froze. Her body couldn't seem to move even though her brain wanted her to leap out of bed and—

"Don't scream," came a hissing whisper. "It's just me, Elizabeth."

The hand came away, and before she could get a good breath to let out a shriek, the light over her bed clicked on. It *was* Elizabeth, looking pinched and anxious. Spirit struggled up into a sitting position and rubbed her eyes, still sore and sticky from crying. "Elizabeth, what are you doing in my room?" she asked angrily. What was wrong with her? "It's after hours. You're going to get us both in trouble."

The girl shrank away a little and sat down on the floor beside the bed, breathing shakily. "I had to talk to you," she said.

"You're the only one that doesn't seem all sucked in by the Breakthrough people."

She was actually wringing her hands. Spirit had never seen anyone wring their hands before. It looked strange. "I'm not buying into it," she said, cautiously. "You were there when the Shadow Knights turned up, and they were wearing Oakhurst rings. A week later, these guys are here—but you can't just pack up and ship building crews and tons of stuff in a week, so I don't buy that they came running when Doctor Ambrosius called last week. From what one of the Radial kids said, it sounds like they've been in Radial for weeks, setting up this move. So . . . maybe Doctor Ambrosius called them a couple months ago, and it's just strange timing that they turned up now, but . . . I don't like it. It just seems all wrong."

Elizabeth was shivering, but looked up sharply. "The Shadow Knights! You know what they're called!" she exclaimed, her eyes darkening.

Spirit blinked, startled. "Uh, what? Burke just made up that name. . . ."

"But it's the right name for them! The Shadow Knights—they're the ancient enemies of the Knights of the Grail!" Elizabeth clutched Spirit's arm; her hands were freezing. "It all goes back to Arthur!"

"Arthur?" It took Spirit a moment for her brain to come up with the right association. "You mean *King* Arthur? Camelot? Excalibur? Merlin?"

"Yes!" Elizabeth had her arm in a death grip. "Listen, it's all deeper, all larger than you think. It's not just Oakhurst, and it's not just now, this is a war that's been going on for centuries, and now it's getting near the end—"

And then, the words just poured out of her, as if they had been kept behind a dam all this time. More words than Spirit had heard Elizabeth speak in the entire time she'd been here. As Spirit listened, caught in a kind of bemused numbness, Elizabeth spun a story so wild that it belonged in a book, not real life. Spirit's friends had been calling her paranoid for weeks, but even though she was dead certain they were all in danger and smack in the middle of some horrible conspiracy, even *she* hadn't come up with anything this crazy. And Elizabeth wasn't exactly making it easy to follow her story.

Finally, when Elizabeth ran out of air, Spirit tried to get it all sorted out so it was more or less coherent. "So . . . all this is about King Arthur and the rest of those mythical people. First, there are these Shadow Knights. And they're serving Mordred. Mordred has been reincarnated, or else he never died, you're not sure which. But some of the Shadow Knights are people who served him, or were his allies before, and they *are* all reincarnated over and over. And Mordred wants the usual Evil Overlord stuff, and the Shadow Knights are going to help him get it. Right?"

Elizabeth nodded and opened her mouth to start again. Spirit held up her hand. "Whoa. Wait. I'm still trying to get this straight."

Elizabeth nodded, and watched her expectantly.

"But the Shadow Knights have never been able to defeat the Grail Knights, who were the ones that served Arthur and

Merlin. And the Grail Knights haven't been able to defeat the Shadow Knights, either. Which is why they all keep getting reborn."

The girl nodded. "And Arthur, too. Arthur is reborn." She faltered. "Merlin and Mordred, I am not sure. I am not part of their story, so I do not know these things, I only know what I have been a part of myself—"

Wow, now she's even starting to talk . . . odd. Like someone who's not really from around here . . . as in a zillion years ago not from around here.

"Wait! I'm still—Okay, so now we talk about Oakhurst. Some of the Oakhurst people are Shadow Knights. Some are Grail Knights." She paused, trying not to think about how absurd this all sounded. "Some aren't anything, except magicians. And you can't tell which is which."

"It is all part of the curse that fell upon Britain when Mordred betrayed Arthur and sold himself to the Dark," Elizabeth said earnestly. "Everyone involved in any way with Arthur's kingdom is doomed to be reborn over and over until either the Shadow or the Grail triumphs. One must destroy the other. But I do not recognize any of the people here at Oakhurst, because I did not know them in the past."

"So why doesn't anyone remember all this?" she wanted to know.

"The Shadow Knights do, but only once they turn to the Dark. Their master, Mordred, wakes their memories. I do not know about the Grail Knights." She looked as if she knew that part of the story sounded pretty weak. "Possibly Merlin wakes theirs as well. But when they are reborn, they have no memories of their past lives."

"But—I don't get it, if they're reborn over and over and fight the war over and over, why hasn't anyone noticed until now?" Spirit shook her arm a little, and Elizabeth finally noticed she was holding on to it and let go.

"Because until the spirit in the Tree was freed, they had no leader and no direction," the girl said simply. "Their conflicts were random, skirmishes rather than battles, and since none of them recalled their pasts, they did not even know why they fought with each other. That Tree is the one here in the Entry Hall. That is why we are all here, because of the Tree."

"And the spirit was freed when lightning hit it and killed it?" Spirit replied.

Elizabeth shrugged. "I do not know, but that is a good notion. I'm not part of that story. I know I keep telling you that, but all I can tell you is what I know—I was just a tiny part of the original story. I never met Arthur, or Lancelot—I only ever knew a few on the side of the Grail or the Shadow."

"Wait—you—"

"I am a Reincarnate," Elizabeth said quietly, but with conviction. "I am—was—Yseult of Cornwall. Iseult the Fair. Isolde."

"Wait, what—*Tristan and Isolde*, that Isolde?" Spirit's jaw dropped a little. This was getting crazier by the minute.

Elizabeth nodded.

"Prove it," Spirit demanded.

Elizabeth looked off somewhere over Spirit's shoulder, her

eyes unfocused. *"Ol an tekter a wylys ny yl taves den yn bys y leuerel bynytha. A frut de ha floures tek menestrouthy ha can whek fenten bryght. Avel arhans ha pedyr streyth vras defry ov resek a-dyworty worte myres may tho whans,"* she said.

Well, it *sounded* like another language, and not gibberish. And it sure didn't sound like any language Spirit knew. She had a smattering of Spanish, some French—Oakhurst insisted you learn Latin and Greek, so she was getting those now—it wasn't any of those. And it didn't sound like anything she'd ever heard people speak, like Italian, German, Japanese, or Russian.

"I mean, that's all I can do," Elizabeth said apologetically. "I can speak Cornish, old Cornish, and no one's been able to do that in hundreds of years. I speak what we now call Irish-Celtic. I could tell you where to find landmarks in Cornwall and Ireland. But things that I knew are probably not even two stones on top of each other now. The ruins at Tintagel aren't even from my . . . lifetime." She shrugged helplessly. "I know this sounds mad. You look at me and see an American, a sixteen-year-old girl, but I have been Yseult—known I was Yseult—nearly the whole of my life. I thought *I* was crazy when I first started getting my dreams, except I finally figured out they weren't dreams after all. They were memories. That's when I started seeing the Shadow Knights, too. I think they were looking for me." She shuddered. "I—Yseult, I, we're the same person, don't you see? There *is* no Elizabeth Walker. There's only Yseult of Cornwall, and I wasn't on either side originally, and if the Shadow Knights can get me to choose them—that's more power for them. Plus my Gift. I can see things, past and future, and that would be really useful to them. I think that's how I ended up waking my own memories, because I saw my parents dead, and I was trying to find out how they died and warn them, but . . . I got all this other stuff instead."

Spirit licked dry lips. "So . . . Breakthrough . . . Mark Rider, all of them . . ."

"I don't know," Elizabeth said, sounding desperate. "I know *some* of them are Shadow Knights. I think Mark Rider is, but that's only because—well, I don't have any proof. Maybe I think he is only because he's one of those guys you know would run over you then sue you because you ruined their tires. And you don't have to be a Reincarnate to become a Shadow Knight; they'll recruit anyone who's a magician, so even if he *is* a Shadow Knight, he might not be a Reincarnate. Reincarnates are the most powerful, but anyone who is a sorcerer is useful. So Mark Rider could be a new recruit, he could be a Reincarnate, I could be completely mistaken about him. I mean, the only way I can find out for sure is to get close to them, and if I do, and it's someone I recognize and a Shadow Knight, then that person will recognize me, too, and then they'll know I'm more than just someone with a Gift." She looked up at Spirit, shivering again. "If they do that, I'm dead. Either they'll kill me because they can't get me to join them, or they'll—well, it won't be *me* anymore, so I might as well be dead."

Suddenly, she raised her head. "There's someone coming. I can't be found here."

She was on her feet faster than Spirit would have believed,

had the door to the room open and was out into the hall before Spirit could react.

Spirit jumped out of bed and ran after her. She paused in the hall, trying to remember which way Elizabeth's room was. Before she could remember, she heard footsteps and a flashlight shone in her face.

"Spirit, what are you doing out here?" Kelly Langley demanded.

"I thought I heard something." Lame, but it was the only thing she could think of. "Like someone dropped something out here."

Kelly panned her flashlight around the hallway, which was, of course, empty and clean. "You were having a nightmare or something," Kelly said firmly. "Go back to bed. Now."

There wasn't exactly a choice. Spirit nodded, and went back into her room. She thought about trying an e-mail to Elizabeth, but . . . well, probably not a good idea. Besides, Kelly was probably waiting outside the door to make sure her light went out. With a sigh, she got back into bed and turned it off.

Fat chance getting any more sleep tonight.

❦

Merlin. And Arthur." Burke shook his head. "It sounds like a bad fantasy movie."

"Or a manga, or an animé, they've got plots that screwy," Muirin said. "Ha. Park Place, Addie. Pay up. Seriously, Liz needs to market herself to Japan, they'd eat that kind of thing up with a spoon."

"I know but . . ." Spirit had woken up this morning with the conviction that, as utterly unbelievable as it had all sounded, that was exactly the reason why it must be true. If Elizabeth had been making something up, she surely would have gone for a story that was a lot more plausible.

"Look, Spirit, if it makes you feel any better, how about if I go find her?" Burke asked. "I'll go get her right now, we can talk to her, and we'll—" he paused. "Not interrogate her, but if she really made all this stuff up, unless she's psycho, we can probably point out enough holes to make her admit it."

"It's already got more holes than Swiss cheese," Muirin muttered.

"No, I'll go," Addie said, getting up. "I'm almost out of Monopoly Money anyway, what with Moneybags Muirin there owning every property on the board that I land on. If she's in her room, you couldn't go there anyway, Burke. I'll try there first."

But Addie came back only five minutes later, and she had a very strange look on her face.

"What?" Spirit demanded.

"She's gone." Addie shook her head. "I mean, completely. The name tag is gone from her door, the room's been cleaned out. And there wasn't any announcement or anything—"

"Well, there's your proof she was delusional, Spirit," Muirin said, tossing her hair over her shoulder. "I bet Kelly caught her wandering the hall looking for Excalibur, sent her to Doc Mac, and he shipped her away. I mean, think about it. Mark Rider said we're under attack, and the last thing you want here is

243

someone damaged like that. She wouldn't be safe here, and who knows what she'd do if she decided she didn't like the protections? And there wasn't an announcement because—well, who'd care? It's not like she had any friends."

Spirit was more than a little shocked by Muirin's callousness, but . . . if Muir was right, then . . . well, Muir was right. Poor Elizabeth *was* safer somewhere else, and Oakhurst was safer without her. But . . .

If Muirin was wrong . . . had the Shadow Knights found Elizabeth, just as she had feared they would? Was everything she had said, crazy as it sounded, actually true?

❧

The next day, all classes were canceled while the new schedules were made up—but that didn't mean they were free. In fact, they were even *less* free. Divided into groups—and, of course, none of the five of them was in the same group—they were tested in every way possible. A battery of physical tests— not just physical fitness: Their reflexes were tested and timed, their proficiency in anything like a martial art underwent the scrutiny of Anastus Ovcharenko and his two underlings—were interspersed with academic tests. By the time the day was over, Spirit was too tired even to think, and she wasn't the only one. The Refectory that night was extremely quiet, people dully shoving food into their mouths as if they were too tired to taste it. Even Muirin was too tired to complain.

"I'm going straight to bed," she announced as she got up from the table. "Thank God there's no homework."

Burke, who was sporting a fine crop of bruises as well as looking as if he had packed a hundred pounds up a mountain, nodded. "Me, too. Just check your e-mail; Mr. Krandal told me they'd send our new scheds after supper."

"No argument here," Addie groaned. "I just hope there's hot water with everyone wanting baths."

Spirit and Loch just nodded; she was so exhausted she found it hard to concentrate on even the simplest of things. It took her two tries to get at her e-mail, and she must have stared at the screen for fifteen minutes before she figured out which e-mail was the right one.

She was unsurprised to see that music and art classes had been canceled "until further notice." They'd been replaced with new language courses and new literature courses. Celtic, Norse, Japanese, Chinese, and Russian had joined Latin, Greek, Spanish, French, and German. The new "literature" classes were all folklore, intensive studies in mythology—of course, this was Oakhurst, so "myth" wasn't so "mythical." Celtic, French, German, and Italian had already been on the list, now there were Ancient Egyptian, Ancient Roman, Ancient Greek, Ancient Persian . . . the list was enormous, and the notes said it didn't matter if you were the only one that wanted to study a particular culture, you would be accommodated.

Everyone was taking marksmanship, which was going to cover every possible weapon you could shoot.

Oh, that'll make Loch happy. Not.

Everyone was taking something called *Systema*. Since Ovcharenko was teaching it, it was probably a martial art.

Spirit's morning "conditioning" class remained; her Art class was now a class in Celtic language, her Music class was now her choice of mythologies. She picked one at random, sent the e-mail back, and went to see if there was hot water. She almost fell asleep in the tub, and when she did drop into bed, she was out without a chance to even think about anything.

✦

It seemed very strange to see Madison Lane-Rider standing where Ms. Holland should have been. Up close she was even more impressive than she'd been on the stage. A long fall of thick red hair so perfectly smooth and shining it looked like it was Photoshopped dropped to just below her shoulders and was parted on the side. Her pale skin looked Photoshopped, too. With that hair and skin, Spirit would have expected green eyes—but no, she had eyes of a very strange gray color.

She wasn't wearing the Oakhurst uniform, and today she wasn't even in Oakhurst brown or gold. She wore a slim skirt and bulky sweater in shades of dark emerald, a carved jade pendant, and jade bangles. Spirit got the feeling Madison Lane-Rider was deliberately showing that she wasn't to be slotted into some preset place on the "team." And Spirit also got the feeling that between the outfit and the jewelry, what Ms. Lane-Rider was wearing could probably have paid for the White's old house.

Evidently, Spirit had ticked off "Nordic folklore," because that was what Ms. Lane-Rider began to lecture on.

"Death," she said, when everyone had settled. "Death is

omnipresent in Nordic lore. There is probably not a single culture that celebrates death or elevates it to such a level of importance as the Norse. Other cultures have the cult of heroic self-sacrifice to save others, to be sure, and the Japanese have, or had, the *Kamikaze* of sorts, but only the Norse placed so much emphasis on 'dying well' regardless of what was won or lost—"

Dylan raised his hand. She acknowledged him with a raised eyebrow.

"What about Klingons?" he asked, eliciting a laugh.

"Very good. Writers have to start with something, and it is quite clear that the Klingon *attitude* is Nordic, though their catchphrase of 'It is a good day to die' is Native American. Now, the question we must answer as magicians, is: 'What does this mean to us, and how can we use it?'"

Spirit listened, and took copious notes, even though she didn't agree morally with an awful lot of what Ms. Lane-Rider had to say. Or maybe more to the point, Ms. Lane-Rider lectured from a completely amoral point of view, and Spirit could not have been more opposed. She could tell that Muirin was just drinking all of this in, though, and that worried her. When the class was over, Ms. Lane-Rider even stopped by Muirin's desk to talk to her about something, which worried Spirit even more. She couldn't wait, though; her next class was that *Systema* thing, and she was pretty sure Anastus Ovcharenko was not going to cut anyone any slack.

He didn't. And *Systema* proved to be a martial art, but it wasn't like anything that had been taught at Oakhurst before this. As Mr. Ovcharenko explained it, it was all about control-ling the joints of the opponent, since this was where you got the most gain for the least force. He talked for about ten min-utes, then said abruptly: "Bah! Enough of talking. Now we spar."

And instead of exercises or *kata,* that was exactly what they did. He broke them into teams of two—and he seemed to have a pretty good idea of who the bullies in the class were, because he paired them off against each other and the glint in his eye said that this wasn't an accident. After he'd let the pairs match off against each other for a while, he stopped them, and dem-onstrated some moves, drilled them, then set them to sparring again. But he wasn't looking for "the right counter." In fact, when Dylan repeated the same strike three times, he inter-rupted, shouting *"Nyet! Svinya!* This is not tournament! *Systema* is to be flexible, reactive, and never, never to set up pattern! Now, again! This time being to think!"

Up close, he was a surprise. He couldn't have been much older than twenty; very blond with brilliant blue eyes, almost too handsome to be real. But he had very cold eyes, and Spirit got the feeling that almost everything he did was a carefully calculated act—a *Systema* of behavior, designed to fool every-one around him until he decided to take out a weak spot.

All through dinner, all that Muirin could talk about was Madison Lane-Rider, and it was driving Spirit crazy. It was as if Muirin had discovered a long-lost older sister. Not that

Spirit was jealous—but because her instincts were screaming at her not to trust the woman.

"Muirin," she finally snapped, "you're acting like you and this woman you didn't even know existed two days ago are BFFs! I mean, we don't know anything about these people, and *she* could be one of the Shadow Knights for all we know!"

Muirin looked offended. "I'm not stupid! All I'm trying to do is get information out of her! Can I help it if she's the first person I've ever met here who knows the difference between Donatella Versace and her brother? It's the first time in months that I've had an intelligent conversation that *wasn't* about conspiracies, disappearances, or people trying to kill us!" Her voice took on the tiniest edge of something like hysteria. "I *just* want to have a normal conversation like a normal person and enjoy some normal things in this lunatic farm!"

"Whoa, Murr-cat," Burke said soothingly. "Spirit didn't mean you were being stupid. Did you, Spirit?"

Spirit shook her head, although she was pretty sure that Muirin was lying. These people were exactly the sort that Muirin wanted to be around and be like—rich, connected, and fashionable. Muirin might not betray their secrets consciously, but subconsciously she was likely to give a lot more away than she realized.

"Anyway, I *did* find out something and I was getting to that," Muirin continued resentfully. "You know how I said there's some kind of Skull and Bones thing going on here? Well, I got Madison to admit to being one!" She tossed her head with a look of triumph. "She told me that the strength of your magic isn't the only way you can stand out here. She said there's what she called an 'inner circle' of exceptional students. She said the Gatekeepers pick these people because they've 'embraced their potential to accomplish great things.'"

"And I'm the Keymaster," Addie drawled, which made Loch crack up while Spirit and Burke were completely lost. "Never mind. So, what else did she tell you? Secret handshake? Password? Do they all have little tramp-stamp tattoos? This isn't quite on the same level as Elizabeth's Sekrit K-niggits of Arthur, but she could just be feeding you a line, Murr-cat."

"Ha! That's where you're wrong, and I can prove it!" Muirin retorted triumphantly. "They all wear badges. It's the Oakhurst coat of arms, and they do it as a pin or a tie tack or cuff links—"

"Muirin, we all get those pins in the second year," Burke interrupted.

"We get *a* pin; it's not the same," she replied. "The regular pins, the snake is gold. The Gatekeepers, the snake is *black*." She settled back to finish off the last bites of her dessert with a satisfied air.

"Huh . . . ," Loch said thoughtfully. "Madison Lane-Rider *was* wearing one of those and I thought it was kind of strange because, well, think about it, I've never seen anything other than gold and brown on anything from Oakhurst."

Right, so everyone wears a little name tag that says HELLO, MY NAME IS EVIL? *Spirit thought.* It can't be that easy. And you don't have a shred of proof that these Gatekeepers are the same as the Shadow Knights, either!

"You don't . . . could they be the Shadow Knights?" she asked tentatively.

"Oh, get real, Spirit! They're the ones that came pounding up like the cavalry," Muirin snapped. "They're *just* as likely to be the Grail Knights, if you're going to buy into Elizabeth's fantasy. Which I *don't*. Just because the snake on their badge is black, that doesn't mean a thing; and since when would bad guys advertise who they were with a nice handy sign?"

Since that pretty much echoed Spirit's own thoughts on the matter, she looked down at her plate.

"No, if this is like Skull and Bones, then that means whoever is in it is going to be *really* influential," Muirin continued, a bit of gloating in her tone. "Once they get the Shadow Knights or whatever you want to call them taken care of, that's where I want to be. I mean, have you seen what Madison wears? Not to mention the kinds of people Mark Rider gets to party with—"

Muirin went on and on in the same vein; Spirit stopped paying attention. This was making no sense at all. Granted, Muirin had been the last one to believe her about the continuing threat, and was still the most shrill skeptic among them, but within hours she seemed to have cast aside all thought of the very real danger they were in because Madison Lane-Rider had spent time talking to her. Now Muirin was acting like the most important thing was the kinds of social contacts she could make with the Breakthrough people, and completely ignoring the fact that the Breakthrough people were training them as if they were going to be on the front lines any second now. And they *had* been openly attacked.

What was *wrong* with Muirin? First being completely cold about Elizabeth, and now this?

She glanced over at Addie. Addie could usually be counted on to rein Muirin in, but Addie was just sitting there with a little frown on her face, twisting her ring on her finger.

Burke—

For the first time since they'd sat down, she really looked at him. Burke looked completely exhausted. There were more bruises on him, and now that she was really paying attention, he had the expression of someone who was on his last legs, but couldn't see an end to the tunnel. Despair, that was it. And as Muirin chattered on, he finally held up a hand and stopped her.

"I just spent the entire day either getting beat up, or trying to wrap my brain around stuff I am never in a million years going to get," he said, his voice a little rough, like he was holding back his emotions. "Mostly beat up. Almost all my classes now are actually martial arts, and the ones that aren't are things I am *not* good at. And you know what? I'm going to admit it. I'm beat. We got lucky before, when we didn't know any better, and the people who called the Hunt thought there was no possible opposition. Now we know better, and they do, too, whoever they are, and I think I just realized I've hit the end and there's no more rope." He sighed—it was almost a moan—and rubbed his eyes. "I can't do this anymore. I keep thinking about you guys getting hurt—or worse than that. I can't. I'm not a superhero. There's going to be trouble here, and I think we need to leave it to the people who are already trained to handle it."

Spirit sat up in alarm. "You're not going to tell Rider about the Wild Hunt!" she exclaimed. "You're not going to tell him it was us who stopped them!"

"No. I'm just going to go to Doctor Ambrosius and tell him I want to leave Oakhurst. If he wants, he can send me wherever they sent the others. But I just can't take any more of this." He looked as if he was about to cry for a minute. "I'm—just a guy. Just a dumb jock with a little magic. . . ."

"I think we need to tell Doctor Ambrosius that it wasn't just an accident that we stopped the Hunt," Addie said firmly. "I think we should tell him about the files marked *Tithed,* about what we've seen written on the Oak, about what Elizabeth told Spirit. All of it. We're just kids, this isn't what we should be doing."

"But Addie—" Spirit began.

"Enough, Spirit." Addie's expression hardened. "Look, I understand that figuring all this out is partly your way of handling that your family is gone. I get that. I get that since your magic hasn't bubbled up yet, this is your way of feeling effective. But it's gone way beyond what we can do now. We need to stop, let someone else take over, and do what they tell us to do."

She looked around at the others; all of them were nodding, even Loch. Her heart sank. Could they be right? Could she be trying to keep them involved in solving the problem, rather than turning it over to more competent people, just because she couldn't bear to come to terms with her family's death?

I need to talk to Doc Mac, she thought—but then she'd have to tell *him* everything. Could she trust him? She tried to remember. Did he wear one of the pins with the black snake on it?

And did that black snake even mean anything? Was Muirin right about that, too?

"Look," she said desperately. "There *is* something we need to keep looking at! They keep telling us we're all Legacies here, right? No one just pulled in off the street to go to Oakhurst. One or both of our parents *had* to be Oakhurst grads, even though they never told us about it. Which could make sense since Oakhurst is kind of secret, and for all we know, the other kids' parents told them, and ours were just keeping things back."

Addie nodded, but there was a look of faint impatience on her face. "Yes. So?"

"And have you seen anyone around here who *didn't* have magic?" *Other than me.*

They all shook their heads.

"I know for a fact my parents didn't have a smidge of magic. And they weren't hooked up like the Riders are." She ran her hands through her hair nervously. "OK, maybe they chose to give up the magic and the perks, like being in a witness protection program so they could just bail." *Like Burke wants to,* she thought, and a shadow of guilt passed over Burke's face, confirming her thought. "And maybe the kids that didn't get Tithed to the Hunt but actually do leave are doing that. But we're *orphans,* and underage, and we can't just leave and get jobs or inherit anything without a guardian and not everybody has Trust

Funds to do that. So our parents being Oakhurst grads and us not knowing that, and—well, everything—it only makes sense if there's another Oakhurst somewhere. One where no one has magic, or at least, no one uses it, ever." She turned to Muirin. "Remember what Madison Lane-Rider told you about magic not being the only way you get noticed? So if you wanted, you could get all hooked up and get rich and all that without having and using magic at this other place. But unless it exists none of this makes sense—"

"Spirit, you're starting to sound like Elizabeth," Burke said, quietly. "Come to the point, will you?"

Now even Burke . . .

"We need to find out if there are any kids here who aren't Legacies. We need to find out if there's anyone here who is *not* an orphan—"

Muirin raised her hand. "Duh. Me."

"Your stepmother doesn't count," Addie and Loch chorused. They looked at each other. Loch shrugged. "She doesn't," Addie continued. "She doesn't want you, she's been trying to dump you anywhere but with her, and besides, she doesn't control your money, your Trust does."

"And the third thing is—" Spirit rubbed her aching temples. "We need to find out if any of the Alumns have kids, if the kids are magicians, and if so, why they aren't here."

"And what will all this prove?" Muirin demanded.

"If we find out that we've been lied to about any of that, which is, like, pretty basic and important—what else did they lie to us about?" Spirit replied, feeling a horrible headache coming on. "I mean look, maybe it means what happened to our parents wasn't—"

"What? You're trying to say that what happened to our parents was murder, is that it?" Addie said, her tone icy. "And then what? If we've been lied to, maybe it was *Oakhurst* that killed them, or someone inside Oakhurst? More Shadow Knights? More conspiracy?"

"And how would a few people do all that anyway?" Loch added. "Because it couldn't be more than a few, or *someone* would talk. Cops were investigating the hotel fire—don't you think they'd have noticed arson? And how would you control a fire so it didn't kill me, too?" Now he was twisting his ring, and shrugged. "Spirit, you have *got* to get a grip. If all our parents were killed by magic, there would be some trace of it. Face it, what we do isn't exactly subtle, people would see things. If it was done by some other means, there would be evidence."

But you didn't see what I saw, she thought, starting to shiver.

"You're confusing cause and effect," Burke said, wearily, but in a tone that still sounded patronizing. "Or something like that. Most people our age have parents that are alive. People our parents' ages generally don't die, and when they do, it's going to be something unusual. We're just the ones in the minority who lost our parents, so of course how we lost them is unusual. So we're orphans *and* we have magic, *and* our parents went to school here, so this is where we got sent by their wills. It's no different than if we were all Native American and we got sent back to the rez when we were orphaned, even though we didn't know we were Native American because our folks kept it secret from us."

"Parents do that, Spirit, keep secrets from you," Loch told her. "I don't care how wonderful you thought they were, or how open, I know for a fact they were keeping secrets from you. The proof is that they never told you about Oakhurst. They might have been doing so because they were trying to protect you, or because they were ashamed of not having magic or ashamed that they *did,* or a million other reasons."

"I'll say it again, Spirit. Get a grip. It's all coincidence." Burke rubbed his head. "Seriously. Keep this up—"

"And they're going to send you to the Shadow Oakhurst Loony Bin and you and Lizzie can trade hallucinations and be BFFs," Muirin said, with a nasty glint in her eye. "Maybe she'll decide you were her mother, the Queen of Ireland. Or her rival, Isolde of the Fair Hands, would *that* be nice to be confined with?"

"Muirin, chill," Addie said warningly.

Spirit felt her eyes starting to burn as she held back tears. She didn't get it. Was it just that they really *were* all burned out and wanted someone else to take over? Was she really the paranoid one? Was she delusional?

She got up and left them abruptly, scrubbing her sleeve across her eyes as soon as she was out of sight. The tears came anyway, and she had to grope her way the last few steps to her room. Once inside she leaned against the door, feeling physically sick from her emotions. Anger, betrayal, despair . . . mostly despair. And abandonment. Maybe that was the worst. She sat on the edge of the bed and cried for a while. And that made her feel even more abandoned. Part of her had thought—hoped—that Addie or Muirin at least would come after her. That Burke or Loch would try. Hoped for a knock on the locked door. But nothing came. Not even the sound of a whisper or footsteps in the hall outside.

So maybe you're the one who's crazy, here, a little voice whispered in her mind.

If only she could talk to someone outside this place . . . one of her Mom or Dad's friends, or something . . . but there was no getting past that firewall.

Was there?

The thumb drive!

She went to the desk and dug it out, and this time she went ahead and followed the instructions.

The instructions didn't open a browser. They sent her straight to what looked like a chatroom. There was one other user in it, someone called QUERCUS.

After a moment, a long moment, she hesitantly typed *hi.*

Hello Spirit, QUERCUS replied. I am glad you found the way out.

A shiver ran up her back, quickly quelled when she looked at the screen and realized the software had already put *Spirit* as her user name.

Who are you? she asked. The next logical question.

A friend. I want to help you.

Yeah, right. She glared at the screen.

I know about feeling alone, QUERCUS typed when she didn't respond.

Why did you send me this software? she asked, instead of responding directly.

To give you hope in the dark times.

Well, that wasn't exactly helpful. And—how did she know she was actually outside the school firewall? All she had was this chatroom.

Why should I trust you?

Open a new window, bring up your browser.

She did so.

Now go to one of your old favorite Web sites.

Well. Okay. How about CanHazCheeseburger? She opened a browser, typed it in, expecting to get nothing, as usual, and—

"... shoot ...," she whispered. There it was. And it wasn't cached, either, the time/day stamps on the posts proved that.

As long as this chatroom is up and open, you can get onto the Internet. When you close it and take off the thumb drive, that will automatically close the link to outside. Magic.

She stared at the LOLcats. Stared at the chatroom.

If only this didn't feel so much like a trap. ...

THIRTEEN

For three days, Spirit avoided the others. It wasn't difficult; they were all being worked like dogs. It was incredible; she'd thought Oakhurst was hard before . . . well, now she knew what "hard" really was. She'd never worked so hard physically in her life, although at least now there was so much supervision over their training that there was no chance for cheap shots from any of the others. Anastus Ovcharenko was sadistic, but he spread it across all of them, so nobody got singled out as the favorite and nobody got singled out as the goat. His two assistants were absolutely indifferent. "Cruel but fair" was what kept coming to mind. The course work was tough, but at least she was spared the courses geared for specific Schools of Magic, since she didn't have one. That gave her a precious free period to study and work on the other ones. The time she used to spend with the others, well . . . there was QUERCUS. By the time the day was over, her brain was so numb and her body so tired that QUERCUS was about all she had energy for. Not that he was much help.

Yet she couldn't keep out of that chatroom; she still couldn't make up her mind if it was some kind of trap or if he really was there to help her somehow.

What about these Breakthrough people? What do you know about them? she asked.

You should trust your own instincts.

She sighed. Thanks, Yoda, she typed. She had decided there was no point in holding back with him, because what did she have to lose?

He didn't respond to that. She wondered if he was some sort of robot program, but even she knew there weren't any "fake" AIs this sophisticated. And if somebody'd written one, why waste it on her?

So just what am I supposed to do, here? she asked. My friends bailed on me, I don't have any magic, I don't know what's going on—

He actually interrupted her. You are at the center of a war. The beginning of the war was in the time of King Arthur.

There was a long pause; she waited.

The situation is complex. While the followers of Mordred, the ones called the Shadow Knights, are completely in the service of Darkness, blame for the war is not entirely on their side. Partly they chose Darkness, but partly they were driven to it. Partly, Mordred himself was driven to it.

All right, she typed cautiously. So?

So now the past is past. For centuries, Mordred himself was power-less. While some few of the Shadow Knights and Arthur's folk were reborn, it was only a handful, and the conflicts between them were limited to mere duels. Now Mordred has come into his power again. The Shadow Knights are reborn, awakened to their true nature, and more are being recruited. Only Arthur's followers, the Grail Knights, can effectively oppose them. The war itself has been reborn, and the time for confrontation is at hand. Yet, if one side does not defeat the other this time, the cycle will continue to be repeated, down the long years.

She was startled. This was—in clearer words—exactly what Elizabeth had told her! And QUERCUS had told her this without any prompting. She felt a cold lump in her stomach and a chill running up her spine. *Okay, so he's saying the same thing. But that doesn't make it true.* Facts, though . . .

Doctor Ambrosius *and* the Breakthrough people were talk-ing about a war. There *were* Shadow Knights, and they'd actu-ally been killing people, or trying to. People had gotten badly hurt at the bonfire. People had been Tithed to the Wild Hunt. And people were missing. Gone? Or—dead? Okay, this expla-nation sounded crazy, but was there a better one?

Her practical side came to the rescue. *Well, plain old regular human greed. There doesn't have to be a Mordred around for people to be evil.* There were wars all over the world for the same reason. This one just happened to involve magic. Which she didn't have. And she really didn't want to become "Disposable Extra Number 23."

So assuming this is true, she typed, what am I supposed to do? I don't even have any magic! I just want to keep my head down—

He interrupted her again. Ignorance and powerlessness is your greatest defense.

Well, that made no sense at all. QUERCUS was back to cryptic mode. She sighed, gave up, and went to bed.

As for avoiding the others, all she had to do was to change her habits—sit somewhere else at breakfast, lunch, and dinner. It helped that all pretense of formal dining had gone right by the wayside; everything was cafeteria-style lines now, and the linens and china had been put away "for the duration." That might have been the only good thing about the new regime. Everything else—if people had been thinking that having the Breakthrough people more or less in charge was going to make things easier, they must have had a sad awakening.

Oakhurst was now being run like a military academy. The *really* athletic kids, the ones with warlike Schools and Gifts, had to get up before dawn. The few glimpses she got of Burke made her feel sorry for him, when she could get past the feeling of being betrayed. He really looked haggard. Actually, all of the ones being singled out as "warriors" looked haggard; he wasn't alone in that.

Strangely, Spirit saw more of Muirin than she saw of anyone else; usually glimpses of Muirin and Madison acting like BFFs outside of class, though inside, Madison didn't cut her any slack. On the afternoon of Spirit's third day of "exile"—as she thought of it—she even saw Muirin being driven somewhere in some sort of sports car with *Mark Rider* at the wheel. That was so astonishing that for a moment she thought it was an hallucination. But . . . no. Word later had it that Mark Rider had driven Muirin into Radial at Madison's request for some unspecified appointment. Appointment? For what?

Probably a dentist. Oakhurst doesn't have a dentist, she finally decided. *Serves her right for eating all that sugar.*

There was no doubt she wasn't the only person who found it odd that Muirin was so friendly with the Riders. She caught sight of a lot of funny looks from some of the other kids when Muirin came back, this time driven by Madison. It was right after supper, so a lot of people were free, and some of them had taken to hanging out in the Entry Hall instead of the lounges. Ms. Corby didn't like that, but there wasn't anything she could do about it. To avoid her *former* friends, Spirit was there, too, covertly studying the Tree.

The sports car came roaring up to the front entrance, and Muirin got out. She leaned over and said something to Madison, then closed the door and waved. The sports car roared off again, and Muirin came sailing through the front door like she owned the school.

Little murmurs followed her, but nothing Spirit could catch.

And for a dose of something definitely on the dubious side, Anastus Ovcharenko seemed to like to hang around Muirin. Okay, maybe he was a lot younger than Mark Rider or even Madison, but still he was twenty or older. It just felt wrong to Spirit. It made her wonder all over again . . . how much of what Elizabeth had said was a fantasy and how much had been the truth? Because if Anastus actually was a Reincarnate. . . .

No, that was crazy. He was Russian, and for all she knew, twenty-something guys in Russia dated teenage girls all the time.

She wasn't going to say *anything* to Muirin; Ovcharenko had this dangerous vibe that made Spirit really queasy. Like you wouldn't want to be there if he actually got mad at you.

Finally, on the evening of the fifth day, Loch ambushed her as she left the Refectory. "Spirit . . . we're sorry we got you upset. We want to apologize. Okay?" he said awkwardly, as people detoured around them.

"All of you, or just you?" she replied, crossing her arms over her chest. She wasn't going to give on this one. As he twisted his hand over his watchband, nervously, she noticed that he wasn't wearing his ring anymore.

"All of us . . . except Muirin." He shrugged. "You know Muirin. She likes to needle people."

"Yeah." Spirit watched him warily, trying to figure out if he meant it.

"We'd really like it if you'd hook back up with us," he faltered. "I—uh—please? You were the first friend I had here." He gave her a big puppy-dog look. She couldn't help it; she folded.

"All right," she said, but made it grudging. Let him know he—they—weren't getting this one for free. She followed him back to the lounge. Burke greeted her with enthusiasm, Addie with her usual friendly reserve, and Muirin as if she hadn't gone crying back to her room five days ago.

Muirin was sporting new (non-Oakhurst-Dress-Code-approved!) jewelry: earrings and a bracelet. The earrings were two little black snakes that coiled against her earlobes; the bracelet was another black snake with its tail in its mouth. Muirin saw Spirit looking, and thrust out her hand. "The Worm Ouroboros," she said, with a giggle. "The big snake that coils around the world. Madison and Mark gave them to me. Enameled silver. Oh, and here, this is for you—"

She reached under the table and pulled out a bottle of perfume. "They gave this to me, but once I had it on, it turned too sweet." Gingerly, Spirit took it. The bottle said "Bulgari," and it looked expensive. "I figure it would suit you."

Nice. "Too sweet." But that was probably as close to an apology as Muirin was going to get, so Spirit took it. The perfume *was* nice, it smelled like roses. Yeah, very much not Muirin.

"I'm sorry, Spirit," Burke said quietly. "For the other night."

Addie nodded. "Me, too."

"Okay," Spirit replied, and slowly sat down. They started their usual desultory game of Monopoly, and that was when she noticed the only one still wearing the Oakhurst ring was Muirin. "So . . . how are things, under our new overlords?" she asked, trying to sound light.

Muirin made a face. *"Awful,* but Mark and Madison are pretty cool. They're helping me get stuff in here, so that's good. This might be Stalag Oakhurst, but chocolate helps everything."

The Riders are helping her with her smuggling ring? Uh, what?

"I haven't changed my mind about leaving," Burke replied, shoulders sagging. "I have an appointment with Doctor Ambrosius in two days. I can't do this. I just can't."

Spirit's heart sank as Addie nodded sympathetically. She'd been thinking about telling them about QUERCUS—but with Muirin all cozy with the Riders, and Burke wanting to leave, it looked like she was the only one wanting to find out the truth anymore.

Except . . . Loch gave her a significant look. And when Addie cut the game short, because Muirin had pretty much cleaned her out, she lingered behind with Loch to clean up their area.

"Tonight. The basement," he whispered. With a thrill and a little lift to her heart, she nodded.

❧

You're right about one thing, Spirit. We've got to figure out if there's a place where the Legacies with no magic go," Loch said, as they went through more of the old boxes. "I don't think it's safe for Burke to go back to his family, and for another . . ." He stopped, and shook his head. "Your sister, Phoenix, didn't have any magic, did she?"

"No, and believe me, she'd have been showing it off if she did," Spirit replied, with a lump in her throat.

"So there has to be another Oakhurst. And we have to find it. If we find it, maybe we can get ourselves transferred to it or something. Heck . . ." he hesitated. "Maybe you were lied to at the hospital; maybe Oakhurst told them to lie. Maybe Phoenix is still alive, and *there,* and Oakhurst didn't want you to know about it because, oh, I don't know, because they didn't want you thinking and worrying about her or something."

Her heart contracted—hard!—at that thought. She pushed the idea away. She didn't want any false hopes right now.

"I don't think so," she said, around the painful lump in her chest. "I think he would have told me—" She stopped, both hands buried deeply in a box of old papers, just about to blurt out the secret of QUERCUS. She stopped herself before she did.

Before Loch could ask her who she meant, she quickly changed the subject. "I can't believe they're still having a February Dance," she said. "I mean, that's crazy! Look what happened the last two times we had some kind of thing like that! It's like asking for another attack!"

Loch shrugged. "They could be sending the Shadow Knights a message. I'm pretty sure it's all to make us think things are normal. They're probably laying traps. Breakthrough seems to do psychological things like that. Like, the way they changed the classes—okay, it's like a military academy, and they're telling us we're getting *ready* for the war, but they're also telling us that it's okay, they're protecting us and some things can still be the way they were."

"Which they aren't!" she exclaimed, throttling down the edge of hysteria in her voice as best as she could. She sat back on her heels. "Nothing is normal—"

"Tell me about it. Even for Oakhurst. Even this thing. They want us to go as couples. Girls are supposed to ask guys." He laughed bitterly. "If I went as half of a couple, I wouldn't want to go with a girl anyway."

She turned to look at him, blinking. "You—what?" Then what he actually meant dawned on her. "You're *gay?*"

He nodded, and flushed. "And there's somebody I really like, a lot, but—can you imagine what would happen if I came out? *Here?*"

She grimaced, and he slumped. "Uh . . . yeah. This place isn't exactly—open." Suddenly she remembered something Loch had said to her a few weeks ago and barely kept from gasping out loud. "*. . . he said since I cared so much about them and so little about him there was no reason for him to go on anymore . . .*" Loch's friend David at Carnarvon Academy. The one who'd killed himself in front of Loch. He'd been bullied—*Loch* had been bullied—because they were gay. . . .

She thought hard, and the only reference to *anyone* being gay here she could remember had come from her History courses, where they were always referred to as "ho-mo-SEX-u-als." *Yeah, nothing but Rainbow Pride here,* she thought bitterly. She gave Loch a sympathetic smile. "Dylan would probably prank you—if you were *lucky.* As lousy as things are now, it wouldn't take much to make your life complete misery."

"Besides, I've got no idea if he likes me back, not like that. And I don't want to screw things up. I just thought . . . I like you, Spirit. I just don't *like* you."

She smiled again, and it was more real this time. "Friends are harder to get than boyfriends. I like you, too, Loch. That won't change," she promised.

Loch's answering smile was beautiful. He dusted off his

hands and stood up. "That's it. We've been through absolutely everything. If there's something about another Oakhurst, it's not down here."

❧

They all got together for lunch the next day; Burke sported a bandaged wrist. He didn't comment on it, and Spirit didn't ask, but even under the bandages it looked swollen. "I've got to get out of here," he said numbly. "I just—"

They all looked up as David Krandal and Ms. Corby came into the Refectory and headed straight for their table. Burke's back was to the door, and he didn't notice they were staring at anything until Mr. Krandal was right there.

"Mr. Hallows, Doctor Ambrosius would like to see you immediately," Ms. Corby said, just as Burke looked up.

Burke went flush, then a little pale. Ms. Corby didn't say anything else. She gestured toward the door, so he got up quickly and followed her out, with Mr. Krandal following both of them.

As soon as they cleared the door, the room began to buzz with speculation.

The others exchanged looks, and even Muirin was unusually sober. "That can't be good," Addie said, slowly. "And I don't think it's because he punched someone or something."

Spirit nodded, a feeling of dread coming over her. "I—I think something is really wrong. I think maybe we should go wait for him."

Addie nodded, and they all got up, even Muirin leaving her dessert half-eaten, and headed for the Entry Hall.

It was a good thing they did, too; just as they got there, they saw the doors to Doctor Ambrosius's office open, and Burke stumbled out. "I'm very sorry, Burke," Doctor A. was saying. "Very sorry indeed."

The door closed behind him, and they all converged on him. Before any of them could ask what was wrong, he looked up at them with a dazed expression. "It's—my mom and dad. They're—they're *dead*."

"What?" exclaimed Loch, going white.

"How?" demanded Addie at the same time.

"House fire," Burke said. He was as white as paper. "There was just barely enough to identify. He won't let me go. He won't even let me go to the funeral. I—" He stopped, and stood there looking like a touch would shatter him.

"Burke, that can't have been a coincidence!" Spirit exclaimed before she could stop herself.

He turned on her with a face like a mask. "I'm sick of all this conspiracy crap!" he said, his voice cracking. "For God's sake!" He shoved out a hand at her. "You can just leave me the hell alone while you're all involved in that. And—just leave me alone!"

He pushed his way through them and ran toward the dorm rooms. "Go after him!" Spirit said, shoving Loch a little. "Go! Go talk to him!"

Loch shook his head. "Leave him alone, Spirit. He's hurting. Let it go."

"But he trusts you, and besides, you're another guy, he'll listen to you!" she exclaimed. Addie nodded, backing her up. But Loch shook his head stubbornly.

"You don't understand. Just leave him alone," he repeated, and walked off in the direction of the classrooms.

"I thought 'you don't understand' was supposed to be the girl's line," Muirin said, but even the gibe didn't have her usual force behind it.

☙

I still think we should take all this to Doctor Ambrosius," Addie said stubbornly. "I think we should ask him about our parents, and find out about this other Oakhurst. He *has* to know where it is. Maybe he could send Burke there . . ." Her voice trailed off. "I don't know . . . maybe he'd start to feel better there and want to come back."

Burke hadn't been at dinner last night, and he hadn't shown up at breakfast or lunch. Loch wasn't talking much. Muirin said if Loch wasn't going to talk to Burke, *she* would—since she had a break after lunch—and headed resolutely toward the boys' side. Spirit still felt his rejection like a blow to the gut. She felt muddled, and was having a hard time thinking.

"I don't—" she began, then gave up under Addie's gaze. "Oh, all right. I sure don't want to ask the Riders . . ."

Addie got up and gestured to Spirit imperiously. "He has open office hours today. We'll never have a better chance. Come on."

For the second time in two days, Spirit found herself right

outside Doctor Ambrosius's door. They could hear him in there.

". . . and sign here," Ms. Corby was saying.

"Indeed. Jam tarts. We must start serving more jam tarts, Ms. Corby. The children will love them. Little rewards for good behavior. Like pretzels."

". . . and here."

"Pity about the cricket pitch. But the lawn was just too torn up."

"We've ordered the special equipment. It should be arriving in two weeks."

"Lovely. And don't forget the Dance."

Addie and Spirit exchanged startled glances, but neither spoke. It wasn't just that Doctor Ambrosius was rambling, it was that his *voice* even sounded vague. Addie gestured to Spirit, and the two of them slipped away, pausing in the door of the lounge. "What was that all about?" Spirit asked, wide-eyed.

Addie looked back in the direction of the headmaster's office. "He's always had times of being a little . . . you know . . . *absentminded*. But I've never heard him like that before." She sucked on her lower lip. "I think he's had a stroke or something. He's losing it, or maybe already lost it. I bet that's why he called the Riders—he must have realized he was in trouble, and called them while he still could."

Spirit felt that all-too-familiar sinking feeling of despair. She hadn't really *trusted* Dr. Ambrosius, but now she realized she'd counted on him more than she'd known. "Now what?" she asked, helplessly.

"I don't know," Addie replied. "Just . . . let's keep this between us and Loch for now. Okay?"

"Because Burke doesn't want to hear about it—" Spirit said tentatively.

"And because Muirin's too close to the Riders, and . . ." Addie bit her lip apprehensively, "And if Elizabeth's story was even partly right . . . some of the Breakthrough people *are* Shadow Knights. Whether or not there's mythical King Arthur stuff mixed up in there, the fact is, we do have enemies, we know some of them are from here, and infiltration is always the best way to get things done. Doctor Ambrosius seemed perfectly all right until the Breakthrough people got here. So . . . maybe it isn't a stroke or something. Maybe *they* did it to him. If that's true, the last thing we want Muirin to know is that *we* know Dr. Ambrosius has gone senile."

B urke wasn't at dinner—again. "He wouldn't even come to the door of his room," Muirin said, nodding her head at the empty chair. "He just said none of us understood and to leave him alone." She looked for a moment as if she was going to make one of her catty remarks, then shrugged. "He's probably right. If Step died in a fire, I'd throw a party."

"He needs—I don't know, something I guess he figures he can't get from any of us." Loch sighed.

"Well *I* need some fun. Getting all emo isn't going to help Burke. I've got a date," Muirin announced.

"A date? You call watching a movie in the lounge with a guy a date?" Addie asked, amused.

"*Au contraire, ma fond,* this is a real date. Going out to a movie in Radial." Muirin rolled her eyes a bit. "Okay, so it's not bright lights, big city. But it's off the campus. Madison's dropping us off and picking us up. This was her idea."

So now she's aiding and abetting dates? Spirit thought. This was getting stranger all the time. *Tell me it's not Ovcharenko . . . because I think that might be illegal.*

"Who with?" Addie asked, eyes narrowed, probably echoing Spirit's last thought.

"Dylan Williams." She made a face as all three of them stared at her as if she was crazy. "What? He's okay. Besides, I think he's on the short list for the Gatekeepers, and I know I am."

Spirit felt completely appalled. Muirin wasn't even *considering* that these Gatekeepers—or some of them anyway—might just be the Shadow Knights *who had tried to kill them.* Okay, maybe not them, specifically, but they'd certainly been trying to kill other students. And succeeding!

"Anyway, I have to get ready. Let me know if Captain Emo comes out of his room, maybe he'll listen to one of us. If nothing else, I'm going to tell him he needs to see Doc Mac. That's just sense." Muirin got up, gave them all a twiddle of her fingers, and bounced out of the room.

"Lounge," Addie said. Spirit and Loch nodded.

When they got there, the first thing that Loch asked was: "Did you talk to Doctor A.?" The looks on their faces must have given everything away, because his own face fell and he said, "Oh hell. That bad?"

"Worse," Addie replied. "We eavesdropped. Ms. Corby was in there with him, getting him to sign papers, and he was talking about jam tarts and cricket pitches. As in, senile, demented, Alzheimer's, or a stroke."

"He was just rambling about absolutely nothing," Spirit added. "It sounded like Ms. Corby was just in there to get his signature and wasn't even bothering to listen to him."

"Great. Just great." Loch rubbed his forehead. "So effectively Rider and Company are in charge?"

"That would be our guess," Addie told him. "We need to talk to someone. Right now, the only ones I can think of would be Doc Mac and Lily Groves."

"Ugh," Loch replied. "Both bad choices. Groves . . . she's got a poker face I can't read, and she's been here since the beginning and she's more than good enough a magician to have been the one to call the Wild Hunt. I can't tell if she's in favor of Breakthrough or against them. Doc Mac—I don't trust shrinks. And since Muirin thinks Burke ought to be talking to him, I'm not sure where that places him. Maybe he's another recruiter for the Breakthrough people and their Gatekeepers."

All Spirit could think of was QUERCUS telling her to trust her instincts. It wasn't as if they had anything else to go on right now.

"Doc Mac," she said, finally. "I'll go—he already said to come talk to him whenever I needed to."

The other two nodded; Loch reluctantly, Addie with reserve.

"Good thing I have that free period every day," she said with a grimace. "I'll set it up for that. And don't tell Muirin."

"Not a chance," Loch replied quickly. He shook his head. "Muirin and Dylan. If I didn't know better, I'd say she was mind controlled."

Maybe she is, Spirit thought as they broke up. *I can't think of any other reason.*

◆

Spirit," Doc Mac greeted her, gesturing at the chair as she hesitated in the doorway. "Still having nightmares? Or do you want to know how you can talk Burke into coming here? Don't worry about that, he already is."

Spirit took the chair. "Actually . . . I guess I'll come straight to the point. Doctor Ambrosius told me that the reason we're all here is because we're Legacies—that our parents graduated from Oakhurst, so when our parents died, part of the deal was that we got to come to Oakhurst until we were eighteen. That's because we have magic. Nobody comes here who doesn't, and if I hadn't had magic, I wouldn't be here."

Doc Mac nodded.

What Doc Mac didn't know (she hoped) was that Spirit had a wireless microphone in her pocket, courtesy of Loch, who'd bought it from a spy store in Billings, slipping away by cab and returning before anyone got suspicious. Muirin, it seemed, wasn't the only one with a charge card that Oakhurst didn't know about. Loch's purchases at that store had been tiny things, all easily concealed; his shopping bag of books and magazines had been nothing more than the cover for what he had really been after.

"That's what I've been told myself," Doc Mac said. "I've only been here for about five years, and of course, I'm *not* a Legacy."

"Well . . . see, that's kind of the logic hole I've run up against," Spirit told him. "If I'm a Legacy, then my parents had to go to Oakhurst. Same for Loch, we were both told that when we got here. The problem is, my parents didn't *have* magic. Believe me, they were not the types to keep that sort of thing secret. Dad especially." She rolled her eyes a little, even though the memory made her tear up. "If there was any way to pull a prank on us, he'd do it, and if he'd had magic he would have used it. Mom . . . she would have, too. The same way she showed us she had a gun just in case, and showed us she knew how to use it. . . ."

Doc Mac looked at her warily. "So—you're saying?"

"That either they didn't go to Oakhurst, and Doctor Ambrosius was lying, or they did, but it wasn't *this* Oakhurst—that there's another Oakhurst for the people that don't have magic." She didn't add that this would be really strange if it was so. "In fact, there has to be, doesn't there? Not every kid that's a Legacy has magic. My sister didn't— So Burke really needs to be allowed to go there before he snaps. And—I'd like to go there, too. I'm not cut out for this and even though you keep saying I have magic, if I do, it's obviously completely useless for what's coming."

Doc Mac cleared his throat, and when he spoke, he sounded troubled. "Spirit, if there *is* another Oakhurst, I've never heard about it. Never. I'm sorry, but that's all I can tell you. If that was what you were counting on to help you and Burke, well . . ." He stopped and shook his head. "This is all there is, Spirit. I can't account for the fact that your parents never showed any signs of magic, but sometimes the very people you think would have no secrets at all are the ones that harbor the most."

"But—do you think the people from Breakthrough might know about it?" she asked, feeling desperation clutching at her throat. "I mean, they'd have to, they'd have to protect both schools, right?"

"I'm not part of the Inner Circle, or whatever they call themselves, probably because I didn't go to Oakhurst myself," Doc Mac replied with a wry twist to his mouth. "But trust me, they've dropped everything to come here, and they aren't dividing their time and attention three ways. Only two. Mark Rider has already effectively moved *his* part of the Breakthrough headquarters here; they're only waiting on building construction. There is no second Oakhurst, I'm sorry. You and Burke are going to have to cope with the fact that you are here to stay—or at least, until you graduate."

Spirit somehow managed to make coherent conversation until her hour was up. He let her out, and let another student in. She headed for the lounge, where Addie and Loch had been listening to her session.

"I recorded this," Loch said. "I want Burke to hear it."

Spirit nodded, and combed her fingers through her hair distractedly. "I'm not sure what this means."

"If our parents went to Oakhurst, they had to be magicians. But if they *were* magicians, there is no damn reason why they should be dead," Addie said angrily. "Yours—car wreck—*every* School teaches ways you could keep yourself and your family safe in a situation like that. Mine, plane crash. Same thing there. Loch—"

"My mother died in a riding accident when I was a kid. Maybe *she* was the Legacy and not Father. But if she wasn't, I can't think of any School that wouldn't have some way to get out of a fire," Loch said bluntly. "I mean, *I* got out, and I didn't even know I *had* magic! Now I do, and I know it wasn't just dumb luck and *parkour,* but *parkour* and magic that did it."

"So we have three sets of supposed Legacy parents who could not possibly be dead if they really were magicians," said Addie, and Spirit realized Addie—calm, quiet, *gentle* Addie—was more furious than Spirit had ever imagined she could be. "And there's no mirror-Oakhurst for ordinary people to go to. Which means—"

"We were lied to. We aren't Legacies at all." Spirit bit her lip. "So . . . how did we end up here?"

"We're here because Oakhurst is *looking* for kids with magic, and is somehow diddling with records to get themselves named our wards," Loch said immediately. "In a lot of states that wouldn't even be a problem. They're an institution with no black marks against them, orphans are a drain on the state. Most states would be happy to turn us over, no questions asked."

"Even those of us with *money*," Addie said, her eyes flashing dangerously. "Because our Trusts have to put us somewhere. Why not here?"

"Please don't call me a 'conspiracy theory nut' again," Spirit begged. "But . . . is it possible that *because* we have magic, that's why our families . . . died? Like . . . whatever sent the Hunt is trying to kill us off, and got our families, but not us?" That horrifying figure on the road loomed up again in her memory.

"Or maybe it's our magic that saves us. I know it was in my case," Loch said thoughtfully. "Given what we know now . . . that's not all that crazy, Spirit."

"My turn to sound like a nut bar," Addie said, slowly. "We know there's someone here trying to kill off the students. What if that same person is the one that found us in the first place, tried to kill us *then*, and got our families instead? Because our families didn't have magic to protect them?"

Vindication should have been sweet. Spirit realized vindication meant having to tell her only friends their families had been murdered because of what they were. Vindication wasn't sweet. It hurt.

"That's not nutty, Addie," Spirit replied, wrapping a twist of her hair around and around her finger nervously. "Take that a step further. What if that person already knew, because they've done it so many times already, that they couldn't kill *us* at a distance, so they killed our families, knowing we'd be brought *here*, where it would be easy to get us?"

"Argh," Addie replied, knuckling her temples. "I wish that didn't sound so logical! It fits what we know too well!"

"And why didn't Doctor Ambrosius tell us the truth about our families in the first place?" Loch frowned. "Because he *had* to know it. And I don't think he's the type to spare our feelings, either. Hell, if anything, he'd use the guilt. You know: 'Your families died because Dark Powers were trying to get to you, now you have to train to become the Great and Powerful Oz and avenge them!'"

Both Addie and Spirit nodded. "That does sound more like his speed," Addie agreed.

Then they all looked at each other. "He might not know . . . ," Spirit said, slowly.

It was Loch who addressed the elephant in the room. "Or he might be the one behind it."

If that was true, Spirit thought they'd better be praying Doctor Ambrosius really had gone senile.

FOURTEEN

One of the mandatory new classes was horseback riding. But not just any old trail riding, the way the old class had been—this was endurance riding. It was something like a human marathon—assuming the humans were running, not on streets and roads, but on unimproved land, through any kind of weather, and over marked obstacles known as hazards that were parts of a course as extreme as the terrain allowed. In Montana, even this flatter part of it, that could be very extreme indeed. It even required a special lightweight saddle with a breastplate that kept the saddle from sliding backward when the horse was scrambling up steep inclines. In competition—because to Spirit's astonishment, this was actually a *sport*—the races were fifty and one hundred miles long. They weren't doing that—yet. They were doing shorter distances, the kind of riding called "competitive trail riding," which sounded so . . . well, nice. "Oh, let's get on the horse and ride a trail and see who gets there first!"

Wrong.

These were ten-mile rides. They all started together. Beforehand, they had to kit up the horse as if they were going to end up making camp at the other end, which meant *everything* for the camp and the horse had to be on the horse. The more stuff you thought you needed, the more the horse had to carry . . . and so on. And what the horse had to go over, under, and through meant that at any moment you might be trotting, off the horse and walking, or helping the horse to get over something. Or swimming—though this was winter, so the water they'd had to cross was all frozen right now. What the point of this was (aside from, to make you feel as if you had been beaten from head to toe at the end of the ride) Spirit didn't know.

She, who had never ridden until she got here, had at least discovered that she had what the new riding instructor, Mia Singleton, said was "a natural seat." That at least meant she could stay on the horse and manage to get in rhythm with it so she didn't get pounded to death. It didn't mean that she had any idea of how to handle this huge thing, and she always had the feeling that the horses she got took one look at her and started snickering about how they were going to make her miserable.

At least Addie was in her class, and Loch. Loch was good enough, but Addie had ridden all her life; she'd stick to Spirit like a burr and make sure the horse didn't run off with her, or stop and not move at all.

"What's the point of all this?" she asked Addie in despair, as she fumbled with all the gear that was supposed to go on the monster. "Do they really think we're going to be charging at the Dark Lord on horses, and when we're done, camp on the battlefield?"

"We might have to run for it, and there aren't exactly a lot of cars at Oakhurst," Addie pointed out somberly. "At least this way we've got a chance of getting away and surviving to get to a rally point."

"Oh. Um," Spirit replied, shivering with both cold and apprehension. Apprehension, because she had the feeling that if it ever did come to that—she'd die.

"Don't worry, Spirit," Addie told her. "If it comes to that, I'll be right with you."

They didn't have any chance to say anything more, since Ms. Singleton showed up and started her inspections. When everyone had everything loaded to her satisfaction, she whistled shrilly as the sign to mount up, opened the stable doors, and waited for them to line up at the "start."

Ms. Singleton didn't talk much, and generally in as few words as possible. Skinny, tough, hair cut short—if she'd had tattoos, she would have looked like a girl gangbanger. But on the rare occasions she did open her mouth, out came perfect English with a cultured accent. Spirit had never seen her outside of the gym or the barn. She couldn't help but wonder what it was that Ms. Singleton did for Breakthrough. It was obvious why she was here, though; like the others, she had an Oakhurst ring. Horses would do *anything* for her—though truth to tell it seemed more a matter of control than because they wanted to. From what Spirit knew at this point, this was one of the things Earth Mages did—Animal Control, rather than Animal Speech. Coercion rather than cooperation. That seemed to fit Ms. Singleton.

When the kids were lined up—eight of them, including Spirit and Addie—Ms. Singleton whistled again, circling her hand above her head three times and pointing down the trail. They all dug heels into their horses' flanks and started. Most with more success than Spirit, whose horse snorted and stood there, until Addie came alongside, leaned over and gave him a sharp smack on his butt. Then he lunged forward.

This wasn't a horse she'd had before, and he settled quickly into a very hard trot. Fortunately that "natural seat" thing came in to save her. When he figured out he wasn't going to bounce her off, he snorted and eased into something a little less bone-jarring. By that time they were at least a mile from the school. The others were all several hundred feet ahead of her. Loch turned to see where she was, and pulled his horse to a complete stop, waiting for them.

"Smack him, Spirit!" Addie called over her shoulder. "Or—wait, this is Pendleton I'm on. I'll fix your mount for you. Pendleton does hate laggards."

Addie wheeled around and came in behind Spirit. Her brown horse (they were all brown, Addie called them by different color names—bay, chestnut, whatever—but they were all brown to Spirit) laid his ears back, and Spirit could have sworn he looked gleeful. He rolled his eyes, snaked out his head, and before Spirit could react, all she could see was a set of big yellow teeth heading straight for her horse's butt.

They connected.

Her horse squealed and lurched forward into a gallop. Pendleton kept pace with him, and whenever he threatened to slow down, those teeth headed for him again. When they caught up to the rest, Addie somehow managed to steer her horse away far enough that he couldn't bite Spirit's, but kept him within "threat" distance. Loch joined them, so that he and Addie bracketed Spirit's horse. Now the only direction he could go was forward. He put his ears back. He was not happy. Well, neither was Spirit; she was already sore, her nose was freezing off, and they weren't even halfway done yet.

Now they were about two miles from Oakhurst, and outside the "safe" area. Oakhurst was just a dark smear on the horizon. And ahead of them was the first hazard, a big, deep gully with steep, crumbling sides and ice at the bottom. A broad swath of it was marked out with a pair of red flags; that was where they were *supposed* to cross and they got marked down if they didn't. Given the competitive spirit at Oakhurst it was a bet that if anyone cheated, three others would tell on him.

But before they reached the gully, a distant whine of motors and plumes of snow to the right warned Spirit—and everyone else—that they weren't alone out here.

Oh hell, it's Saturday . . .

Which meant no school for the kids in Radial.

Sure enough, as the small horde of snowmobiles headed in

their direction, it looked like all the drivers were teenagers. The horses were going to hate this.

Whooping and shrieking, the Radial kids buzzed the horses, circling them and forcing them to crowd together, bucking and shying. Spirit's horse backed into Addie's, who didn't snap at him this time. Addie was holding him steady, but his eyes showed whites all around, and he was trampling the snow in tight little steps. Spirit's horse bounced stiff-legged; she tried to hold him in and soothe him at the same time, and it wasn't working—

And that was when the sky suddenly darkened. Out of nowhere, huge black clouds just boiled up and covered the entire sky. The kids on the snowmobiles started looking around, startled. The horses all went rigid.

A sound like thunder came out of the gully. Except it wasn't thunder. It was the hooves of more horses, twenty or thirty, that came boiling up the steep slope out of the gully as easily as if it was level ground. There were riders on those horses, in gray hooded parkas with gray scarves over their faces. *They* circled the Oakhurst kids and the snowmobiles both, and as soon as the circle was complete, a wall of wailing wind and snow sprang up behind them, cutting them all off from the rest of the world.

And then they turned their powers loose inside that confined space.

Spirit was caught in a maelstrom of screaming horses, screaming kids, wind, ice, fire, and shadow. The earth under them shook and heaved. She saw things—when she could see at all!—that couldn't possibly be there. Horses bucked, bit, kicked. Snowmobiles careened into the horses. One kid in Oakhurst colors got plucked off his horse before her eyes and thrown about twenty feet into the air; she didn't see where he landed. She was battered, cut by flying shards of ice as sharp as razor blades, and all she could think of to do was to get as far down on her horse's neck as she could and cling for dear life while he reared and bucked and screamed. If the others were getting their powers to work, *she* couldn't tell. She was crying and screaming with terror herself; she felt blood running down her face from a cut over one eye, and something hit her in the back hard enough to knock all the breath out of her. She started to feel herself falling, hung on tighter. Something smacked her in the head and she saw stars.

This is it, she thought, in a single moment of fear-sharpened clarity. *This is where I die—*

Then . . . it stopped.

The wind dropped to nothing. Her horse, exhausted, stopped bucking and stood there trembling. She looked up.

The circle of gray-clad riders was still there, watching them under a cloud-laden sky that looked like a blizzard was about to cut loose any second. Then, as one, they turned away, rode down into the gully again—

And disappeared.

Spirit looked wildly around her. All the snowmobiles were stopped, turned over, one was wrecked with its driver still in it, and from the way he was lying . . .

Oh my God—he's dead. . . .

People were lying all around, bleeding, with arms and legs going in directions that they shouldn't, screaming, moaning. The kid who Spirit had seen thrown into the air wasn't moving, either. She spotted Addie, still miraculously ahorse, with a black eye. She looked frantically for Loch, and saw him on the ground, curled in a ball with both his hands over the back of his neck. She jumped down out of the saddle and ran to him.

"Loch? Loch!" As she went down on her knees next to him, she was suddenly afraid to touch him. "How are you hurt? Where? How badly!"

He moaned, and rolled over onto his back. His eyes were unfocused, and one of his pupils was bigger than the other. "Head," he said. "Hurts. Dizzy."

"I'm going for help!" Addie called, and dug her heels abruptly into her horse's flanks, sending him in a gallop toward the blur on the horizon that was the school.

"Don't pass out," Spirit urged Loch. "I'll be back." She began methodically checking on the others.

She might not have magic, but at least she had first aid.

* * *

My God," Muirin said, her eyes wide and her face blank with disbelief. "One townie dead, three of us . . ." For once she had nothing snide, catty, or amusing to say. "I—I've got nothing."

"Stitches, concussions, broken bones . . ." Burke shook his head. "I should have been there."

Loch blinked at them all groggily; he'd been concussed and

had a cracked collarbone. Spirit had eleven stitches in the cut across her forehead and another fifteen in one across her scalp that she hadn't even felt till they got back to Oakhurst, and *they'd* gotten off lucky. Addie was in a sling: a torsion fracture of her left arm. As for the rest, aside from the four dead, there were broken arms and legs, concussions, and lacerations enough to fill the tiny Radial emergency room twice over. But, of course, only the townies had gone there, in a fleet of vans supplied by Mark Rider and the town's two ambulances. All the Oakhurst kids had come straight to the Oakhurst Infirmary. It wouldn't do to have the townies see Earth Mages healing people by magic.

Besides their own Mages, Mark also seemed to have his own group of three people that could just do that—plus Madison, who made four.

Now most of the injured were resting and recovering in their own rooms. Spirit's cuts were half healed already. She had no idea what story Mark had told the townies about what had happened—but she *had* seen Ms. Singleton going from one stretcher to another, briefly putting her hand on the occupant's head, muttering something. She had no doubt that Mark's story had replaced whatever the kids themselves had seen. She had a guess that animals weren't the only things Ms. Singleton could control.

"If that's what a mage-battle is like," Loch said thickly, "we are seriously outclassed. I couldn't even get myself organized before the horse threw me, and all I could do was try and protect myself."

"Well, I was about as much use as a beach ball," Spirit replied, wincing a little as the cut on her head pulled and hurt. It would be fully healed by morning, but with so many injured, the Healing Mages had been forced to ration their power. "How do you fight stuff like that?"

"I should have been there," Burke muttered again, looking guilty and worried.

Muirin fiddled with her ring and with the snake-bracelet on her wrist. "All right, there's an elephant in the room, and I'm going to talk about it," she said. "The Gatekeepers. Mark Rider's group. Would joining them be so bad? I mean, I know Dylan's being scouted for it and you guys don't like him, but if the alternative is what just happened? Come on! At least they know what they're doing!"

"We can't choose a side until we know what's going on," Burke insisted stubbornly. "Muirin, I know you don't want to hear it, but so far . . . well, we don't know anything about them, except that they're rich and Oakhurst Alumns. But we *do* know that the people who attacked Spirit and Loch and Addie were Oakhurst Alumns, too."

"So the Gatekeepers are also the Shadow Knights?" She rolled her eyes. "Oh come on!"

"The point is not that they are, or that *only some* of them might be, but that we don't know!" Burke said earnestly. "Do you see the difference?"

"Yeah. I guess," Muirin replied.

"I need to go lay down," Loch said, looking a little green. "They said I was going to feel sick and dizzy for a while and . . .

I'm feeling sick and dizzy." He got up and wobbled out, Burke going with him to give him an arm.

"Me, too," Addie replied.

"Too sick for chocolate?" Muirin asked, looking oddly hopeful, then crestfallen when Addie nodded. "Spirit?"

Spirit had the oddest feeling that Muirin was . . . lonely. Maybe she was all BFF with Madison, but maybe that was just on the surface. "I'd rather just hang out with you," she said. "'Cause right now, you know, I want to hang with a friend."

Muirin lit up like a Christmas tree. She immediately tried to cover it, but not that successfully. "Let's get Addie to her room then."

The two of them helped Addie get into bed, and Spirit got her a glass of water and some pills she said were for pain. "I'll be glad when this is healed tomorrow," she said, as she tried without much result to find a position that didn't hurt. They turned out her light and left her to try and sleep.

"Penny for your thoughts," Muirin said as they headed for her room.

"Worth that much? *Schadenfreude,*" Spirit replied. "The kids from Radial. I know I should feel sorry for them, but *they* showed up and tried to spook our horses. They kind of got what they deserved. Well, not the one that died," she amended, "but . . . you know."

Muirin blinked at her. "Spirit White, I thought I knew you! You have a dark side!" She opened the door and waited for Spirit to go in.

"Everybody does," Spirit said, shrugging. "I just don't show mine that often. It's still there. You just . . . I don't know, you have to know it's there, and not so much fight it, as . . . learn from it. About it. I guess. I sound like a moron, don't I?"

"Nah," Muirin replied. "Well, a little hippie-dippy with a side of Doc Mac, but that's not *bad*." She flipped on the light and, a moment later, placed a small gold box in Spirit's hands with a triumphant flourish. Even closed, it smelled of chocolate. *I bet this didn't come from Radial,* Spirit thought.

When she looked around the room, it was obvious Madison had been "helping" with the smuggling more than a little. There were new items of clothing in Muirin's closet that stood out because they weren't in Oakhurst colors. There was a stack of CDs next to the computer that hadn't been there before, and Spirit had no doubt that if Muirin hadn't been so careful about getting rid of the evidence, the little box of chocolate truffles would represent only the tip of the pyramid of junk food she'd been getting in. Briefly, for the millionth time, Spirit wondered how on earth Muirin managed to eat all that and still look good.

She started to pick up some papers off the bed, when she realized she was holding the picture of the runes on the oak . . . and a lot, a *lot* of notes.

"Aren't these the oak-runes?" she exclaimed. "Did you finish the translation?"

"Oh, yeah," Muirin replied dismissively. "But it doesn't mean anything. I asked Anastus and Madison, and they said so. Anastus thinks it's fake, like those Viking runes up in Minnesota."

Spirit was horrified, but she grabbed her reaction with both hands and held it down so it wouldn't show on her face. Muirin was finally acting like her old self for the first time in . . . well, since New Year's Eve. "Muir—look, I know I sound like I'm beating the same dead horse, but this is the second time we've been physically attacked by people wearing Oakhurst class rings. And this time . . . people died. Me, Loch, and Addie were hurt. We know there's someone on the opposition team here, and there's the chance it's the same at Breakthrough." Then she decided to use a low blow. "Besides . . . Anastus? Isn't it kind of creepy, an old guy like him hanging around you? Eww Lolita creepy? He could be saying that just to throw all of us off. Or even just to get you to concentrate on him, you know what I mean?"

Muirin started to protest, then grimaced a little. "Well . . . maybe it *is* kind of creepy . . ." A brief expression of guilt passed over her face, and she thrust the handful of paper at Spirit. "Here, you might as well have them. Anastus wanted them but . . . yeah, that's creepy, why would he want something he said was worthless, unless it's like some weird souvenir or something."

Spirit took the papers. And though it required every bit of her willpower, she stayed in Muirin's room right up until lights out, listening to her talk about fashion and the latest from her stepmother (who seemed to belong to the Boy Toy of the Month Club) as if there weren't four dead kids in the county morgue, three of them people they knew. And it actually occurred to her, as Muirin nattered on about Vivienne Westwood, that *this* might be Muirin's way of dealing with just that. To pretend it hadn't happened, and hide it behind a wall of trivialities.

When she had to leave, it seemed to her that Muirin had been grateful for the company. Maybe it was harder to cope with all this when there was no one to chatter at. . . .

But right at the door of her room, a shadow detached itself from the wall. She gasped and started to scream—

—and stopped herself just in time. "Burke!" she whispered harshly. "What are you doing here? You'll get in trouble!"

"I had to talk to you," he whispered back. "Spirit, I—I don't know anything anymore, except that you guys are my family now. I can't bail on you again. Especially not you. You're—I should have been there. I should have been with you to protect you. I know you aren't a fighter—"

"No, I'm not," she said, and then, felt something strange, like anger, but not like anger, ignite inside her. "I'm not. But I will be."

He stared at her. Then slowly, a faint smile passed over his face. "I think you will. And I'll help. Good night, Spirit."

He faded into the darkness.

She slipped into her room.

As soon as she closed the door and got into bed, she began to go through Muirin's notes. There were an awful lot of notes for something that was only a few runes long . . . but Muirin had been as meticulous in her research as she was with her design and sewing, hunting down alternate meanings, considering, then rejecting, things that eventually didn't seem to match.

Finally, near the end, Spirit read the conclusion Muirin had come to. It was written as if she were writing a letter, and Spirit wondered if Muirin had planned to give her the papers all along.

Okay. So this is the only thing it can be. And it's right out of Lizzie's goofy story, but nothing else matches. It kind of goes like this: "Interfering stranger (foreigner, you-who-would-meddle kind of thing) Beware! Touch not (do not disturb) the Sacred (or Shunned) Oak sealed (closed, locked up) by the Druid (priest, magician) Merlinus (whatever, dude). Herein is imprisoned (confined, enclosed, banished) the son of the Great Bear (it says Arturus), Medraut (that's Mordred), Kin-slayer, Parricide, and Most Accursed. Turn your back, and flee." Which, of course, is insane. Mordred wasn't the one that was shut up in the oak, or the cave, or whatever—that was MER-LIN, duh—and anyway, it's all myth. Some farmer probably carved this into the oak figuring to make money off that old man, just like we thought.

Spirit stared at the words, because they were suddenly making horrible sense. QUERCUS and Elizabeth said the Shadow Knights were leaderless until Mordred was freed. And *when* had that happened? When the Oak got struck by lightning? No, that couldn't be it—could it? If it had been recently, when Doctor Ambrosius started Oakhurst, then what had done it? Who had turned Mordred loose? She pondered those words: *"Stranger beware, touch not the shunned oak."* Could someone have freed

297

Mordred *after* the house was built? Maybe when it was lying empty and abandoned?

Crazy as it sounded, it all seemed to be adding up. Elizabeth's story was true after all. They really were caught in a war between Mordred and Arthur, and it wouldn't end until one or the other was truly gone, forever.

But . . . she couldn't take this to the others. Not yet. Not until she had more proof.

❧

Spirit woke up the next day with that odd feeling of determination burning. Maybe it was because she'd been so helpless out there during the attack; maybe it was because Burke had acted like she alone needed protecting when Addie and Loch had been just as helpless.

Whatever the reason, she waded into her martial arts and shooting classes with dogged persistence. If she didn't have magic, well . . . there were always things that didn't need magic.

And she decided to befriend Muirin all over again. All this time, she'd thought Muirin was the way she was because she really didn't need any of them and was only hanging with them because she thought they were entertaining. Now Spirit was beginning to think it was because Muirin didn't fit anywhere else. And maybe if Spirit started acting like a real friend . . .

Well, she'd see.

So at breakfast, before Muirin could start in on her usual snide stuff, Spirit asked her a question. "Hey Murr-cat. You've been here the longest of us, right?"

Muirin looked up from her fruit-laden oatmeal. "Huh. Yeah, why?"

"Was there a point when things started getting weird?" she asked.

"Like, weird like now, weird?" Muirin thought, then shook her head. "It's always been that way." She took a furtive look around to make sure there was no one within earshot, and leaned over the table a little to whisper. "The thing is, nobody actually noticed the weird stuff—the Tithing—until you and Loch showed up. We all just bought the story that sometimes kids ran."

Spirit nodded, as the other three leaned in to listen. Muirin flushed a little, enjoying the attention. "Can you think of anything else besides that?"

"Not really," she admitted. "Well, aside from the fact that it was pretty funky to be going to a school for magicians." She made a face. "You know, I've been to a *lot* of boarding schools, and I'll tell you the truth, Oakhurst isn't the only one that's this competitive. So that didn't seem all that strange to me."

She looked at Loch, who nodded agreement. Addie just shrugged. "I only went to the one, and it had very strict rules about fair play, ethics, all that sort of thing."

"So—" Spirit frowned. "You're saying the weird stuff was happening, but you only noticed it because Loch and I did?"

"Sometimes it takes an outsider's eye, Spirit," Burke finally said. "We were all . . . used to it, I guess. . . ." His voice trailed off uncertainly.

"Nuh-*uh*!" Muirin shook her head emphatically. "Addie and

I were kind of used to the competition. And it just seemed logical to me, and probably to Addie, that some kids would pull a runner from this stalag. But Burke, face it, you're, like, the most conformist guy I ever met, and you'd believe *anything* a teacher told you. It'd never occur to you that a teacher would lie."

Burke flushed, but didn't deny it.

Muirin screwed up her mouth in concentration. "So okay . . . you know what? I think the reason all this is happening now is that Spirit and Loch said, like, whoa, what's going on, and we noticed, and we all started poking around, and maybe that was like hitting the beehive. Which I don't think is a bad thing because . . . well I'm beginning to think that once whoever it is figured out that Step would be *really happy* if I disappeared and wouldn't go looking too hard for me, I'd have been on the Tithing list."

Spirit nodded soberly. After a moment, so did Addie, Loch, and Burke.

After breakfast, Spirit followed Muirin out. "Hey, got a sec before class?" she asked before Muirin could get out of earshot.

Muirin stopped and looked at her curiously. "A couple, why?"

She took a deep breath. "Okay. So whatever magic I have might as well not be there. But there has *got* to be something a non-magic person can do when there's Combat magic flying around. I mean, not every magician even *has* anything that's good in combat. So I need to know how that stuff works, and if you, you know, know anything I could actually *do* the next time. 'Cause I am *not* going to stand around like a moron a second time."

"You're asking *me*?" Muirin replied, looking stunned.

"Why not? You're a really good magician, and you're smart, and I bet you've already thought of some of this." Spirit waited for her answer.

It came as a slow smile. "You're right. I have. And I'll help you out. We'll hook up after lunch."

Am I getting through to Muirin at last? I sure hope so. . . .

❋

Things had been quiet for three days.

There was actually a funeral—well, a memorial service—for the three kids who'd been killed. No one in Radial knew about that—or about the deaths of Oakhurst kids in the first place. Spirit had used her QUERCUS connection to get the online version of the Radial newspaper, and found out that the one townie that had been killed had been officially reported as a "snowmobile accident while joyriding." The article basically said the townies had been trying to jump the gully. Well, now Spirit had a pretty good idea of what Ms. Singleton'd been doing to the townies before the emergency crews took them back to Radial.

Muirin was as good as her word. She was teaching Spirit all about Combat magic. And it turned out there were things that could interfere with it.

"A bullet through the head is pretty effective," Muirin had said dryly. "'Cause, you know, it's hard to control your powers when your brain's been blown out." But then she'd gone on to school Spirit in other options.

Muirin wasn't the only one Spirit had gone to about this. It had occurred to Spirit that this would be a good way to test Ms. Groves, one of the magic teachers. If what *she* said matched what *Muirin* said, then that was a good test at least of whether or not Ms. Groves was giving people misinformation. Plus she might get some angles from Groves that Muirin hadn't thought of.

Even though Ms. Groves was . . . scary.

Ms. Groves looked at her with an expression that made Spirit think she was about to get reamed out. "And why would you want to know something like that?"

"Because I don't want to be known as First Casualty," Spirit replied.

Ms. Groves had smiled. Actually smiled. It was, as expected, a scary smile.

"Very good, Miss White," the teacher replied, and rubbed her hands a little. "It pleases me to see you applying yourself at last. When you next get on your computer, you will find you have been given access to a number of new files. Study them. There will be a test in the morning."

Spirit thanked her, but sighed inwardly. *Of course. There's always a test in the morning.*

FÍFŤEEⴖ

The Oakhurst Alumns had descended in force now, and were doing their level best to make things look scarier and at the same time more secure. They were sending one big message, that was for sure. "It's all right that people have died, we're here to protect you now, so you can go back to your dances and your classes."

Except, of course, that half the classes had been canceled in favor of things that were all defense oriented . . . so the message for Spirit was decidedly mixed. Maybe the others weren't that bright . . . or maybe they were just so desperate to have things back to normal they'd grasp at anything to hang on to that illusion.

Most of the new arrivals were Breakthrough employees; the few who weren't seemed to be friends of the Breakthrough employees. *All* of them had the little Oakhurst pin or tie tack or cuff links with the black serpent on it. Now that had a perfectly reasonable explanation, of course; the Gatekeepers would naturally have kept in touch with each other to a greater extent than ordinary Oakhurst grads. Mark Rider probably kept tabs on all of them and had them all in his address book. When Doctor Ambrosius called him for help, all he had to do was have his secretary work his phone tree.

Still, you'd think there'd be at least one or two without the black snake . . . and one or two who didn't make her skin crawl. But they all seemed to be out of the same mold—oh, not in the way that they looked, because they ranged from geeky nerds with thick black-rimmed glasses and rumpled clothing, through people who looked like career soldiers, to people like Mark Rider and Madison Lane-Rider—but in the intensity of how they looked at you. As if they were sizing you up, all the time.

And most of them were actually *living* here. The building crew already had dorm-trailers and they brought in more for most of the Alumns. The rest were in guest rooms in the same wing that housed the Infirmary and Doc Mac's office. Mr. and Mrs. Rider were the only ones who weren't physically at Oakhurst. From what Spirit heard through Muirin, there wasn't a motel in Radial that suited their lifestyle so they were living out of two enormous and blindingly luxurious bus-sized RVs, one serving as their office complex (complete with high-speed wireless), the other (which had a hot tub!) as their "apartment." The four geeks had taken over all of the old storage rooms in the gym and had filled them full of computers—and other things that looked sort of computer-ish, but which no one was allowed to look at too closely. The six army guys were out doing things on the grounds. They assured everyone that whatever they were doing would absolutely ignore anyone who belonged here at Oakhurst. And even though most of them carried at least sidearms, it was magic stuff they were doing out there.

With all of these people here, Spirit expected something big and magical, but in fact . . . the siege began quietly.

All the Gatekeepers-slash-Breakthrough employees began mingling with the students in the lounges after supper—or popping up and offering to help with something, generally in classes or training. *Okay*, Spirit thought, *that kind of makes sense. We're all living together here, so they're just being friendly. Right?* But she kept a very sharp eye on them anyway, and she started to notice how they'd ooze up to kids who were sticking loosely together. Then a couple of them would get one of the lot aside for something. A couple of rounds of that, and the kids who'd been as much friends as you could be here started keeping their distance from the others, and if anything, spending time with the Breakthrough people. (Which was kind of more *eww* because even the youngest of the Breakthrough people was over drinking age.)

Spirit waited, and sure enough, one night a couple of them moved in on Burke.

Except when they were getting together specifically for games or when Spirit was going out of her way to hook up with Muirin under the twin guises of "teach me about fashion" and "teach me about Combat magic," Murr-cat was mostly still hanging out with Madison Lane-Rider. Burke, however, was sticking with the group while still radiating body language that said "I'm not sure I'm completely comfortable here." Maybe that was why they zeroed in on him.

It was a couple of the military types, which really should not have been a surprise. Burke looked kind of like them, with his athletic build, his short hair, and his quiet and polite manner. She caught them talking to him casually between classes, murmuring earnestly. Then that night, they intercepted him at the door of the lounge, and pulled him off to the side.

She knew Burke pretty well by now, and it seemed to her that he didn't like what he was hearing but was too cautious to show it. Much. As an experiment, she got up and headed in the direction of the kitchen for a juice. One of the geek-girls just happened to turn up at the open fridge just as she was reaching in.

"Hi, you're Spirit, right? I'm Mandy." The girl pushed her glasses up on her nose and got the same sort of ginseng tea that Spirit had chosen. "This place make you as crazy as it did me when I was going here?"

Spirit might not have noticed before she'd gotten her series of fashion info-dumps from Muirin, but now . . . she tried not to frown as she cataloged Mandy's outfit and realized that it could not have possibly been more precisely put together to appeal to the "old" Spirit. No-name, unpretentious sneakers, no-name jeans, a muted t-shirt with a worn Lord of the Rings eagle graphic in earth tones layered over a comfy sweater . . . Mandy was dressed *exactly* the way Spirit used to.

"Mostly I'm scared," Spirit said hesitantly. "I mean, they

keep telling me I have magic, but so far it's not showing, and . . ." She shrugged. "I don't know how to fight. That attack when we were out riding . . ." She teared up, and didn't try to stop it. "People *died*. I was just lucky it wasn't *me*."

"Don't worry about fighting. That's what the meat-shields are for," Mandy said with a little snort. "As for the magic, late-bloomers tend to get the more interesting Schools anyway. Early gets flashy; late gets the good stuff. Your peeps giving you a hard time for not having anything yet?"

"Yeah," Spirit lied, to see what Mandy would say.

"Figures. Trust Fund set. Used to getting everything handed to 'em; you can bet they're thinking once they're graduated, you'll make a great maid. They have to put up with you 'cause Oakhurst is all about making us equal, and probably you've got something they can use, but boy, does that ever change once you're out." Mandy leaned against the door frame and drank her tea. "Not like Mark. He made his own way and his own money. He's one of us."

I'll just bet, Spirit thought.

"Have you thought about what you *are* going to do when you graduate?" Mandy continued.

"Don't you mean, 'if I get out of this alive'?" Spirit countered, allowing herself to sound bitter. "'Cause that isn't looking good from where I sit."

Mandy waved her hand carelessly. "Stick with my bunch when the fireworks start, they don't dare let us die, we're too important. No, seriously, you need to start thinking about things like that. You don't want to end up in fast food. Breakthrough's got scholarships for Oakhurst grads who don't have Trusts to fall back on. Who else do you think would be willing to hire a Bachelor of Arts in—oh—Languages, Mythology, and Literature? At Breakthrough, we don't call that degree 'useless,' we call that a researcher. Archaeology, oh man, you bet, there is an outstanding scholarship for anyone willing to go all the way to a Ph.D. in Archaeology. But, of course, anyone who got these scholarships would have to be a *magician,* and there aren't a lot of those around."

"Huh," Spirit said. "I didn't know . . ."

"Go ahead and use those so-called friends of yours, because God knows they'll use you. But when Breakthrough comes through before graduation recruiting, sign up for the college sponsorship program. Hell, if your foreign languages are good enough, they'll send you overseas to college. Always wanted to go overseas? Want to attend Oxford? Glasgow University? The Sorbonne? University of Vienna? Study in Rome?" Her eyes glittered behind her glasses. "They've sent people all over."

It made Spirit a little sick and a lot angry to realize how much Breakthrough knew about her. They'd obviously picked out the right person with the right offer to tempt her. Before she'd come here she'd never been outside of Indiana—she would have *killed* for a full scholarship to study abroad. And when she'd first gotten here, it would have worked, too. But the more Mandy bad-mouthed *her friends,* the angrier Spirit got.

But she was smart enough not to show it. Instead, she nodded, and continued to look scared and timid, and finally Mandy seemed to think she'd done her job and let her go. Spirit wasn't sure whether to head back to where she'd left the others, and hesitated just inside the door, trying to see if anyone was still there. It was pretty obvious from the body language in the room that the Gatekeepers were having the effect they wanted. Those who were still sitting together were doing so warily, and the lounge was emptying.

She was about to go further into the room when Loch passed her, hands shoved in his pockets. "Train station. Now," he muttered under his breath as he passed, paying no outward attention to her. She waited just long enough for him to get well into the boys' dorm, then headed quickly for her own room to snatch up her coat and slip out the door. There was plenty of time before lights out, and even now, no one restricted movement on campus. Officially, anyway.

As always, the winter cold nearly took her breath away. But now there was the added hazard of having to avoid the military guys. She scouted carefully. Tonight there were only two of them on the school grounds: one guarding the stable and one the gym. But just to be sure, she tried to keep as much in the shadows as possible as she sprinted for the tiny rail station.

She reached it and ducked inside. "Hey?" she whispered into the darkness.

"We're all here," Burke said, in normal tones. "You're the last one. Well, except for Murr-cat . . ." His voice trailed off.

"I passed her a note, but she was pretty wrapped up in Ovcharenko," Addie said sadly into the darkness. "I don't—"

But then the sound of light footsteps running toward them made them all fall silent and hold their breaths. Spirit felt someone grab her and stifled a squeak as arms went around her. "If it's anyone other than Muirin, pretend like we're making out," Burke breathed into her ear. "That's the plan." He turned her so that she was facing into his chest, and put both his arms around her.

Her heart thudded and she felt a little dizzy. She had to lock her knees to keep her legs from trembling.

Nice plan—

"Guys?" Muirin said from the doorway.

Burke didn't let go of Spirit for a good long moment. "We're all here," Addie replied. "Glad you could make it."

"Are you?" came the uncertain reply.

"Yes!" Spirit said firmly, before anyone else could speak—and so that it wouldn't sound as if they were hesitant. The others chimed in just as firmly.

"Okay then . . . 'cause I think if you aren't sitting down, you'd better. Or, wait." Spirit heard the shuffling of feet as Muirin worked her way along a wall. "Yeah, here, I thought I remembered right. There's a closet here under the platform, sometimes people use it for making out. Let's all get in there so I can make a light. Follow my voice."

Now Burke let Spirit go, but kept a firm grip on her gloved hand as he led her toward Muirin. They all crowded into the closet, which was low-ceilinged, but bigger than Spirit would have thought. The door closed, and Muirin muttered something. Spirit winced away as a ball of light that was *way* too bright after the darkness of the station flared up in Muirin's hand. The room was about six by ten and completely empty.

"So?" Burke said, once they were settled.

Muirin looked away from him uneasily. "Uh . . . I'm not sure where to start," she said, finally, and sighed. "Okay, look. I've been hanging out with Anastus, not Dylan. I mean, come on, he's Russian, he's hot, and it's a kick to be with an older guy, okay? So I knew that tonight was going to be 'recruit the kids' night for the Breakthrough peeps."

"And you didn't—" Loch began, then shrugged. "Yeah, no point in warning us, it's not like we could have done anything about it."

"Well . . . something happened today with Anastus." She swallowed. "He met me after dinner and we went out in his car, but all we did was sit in the driveway with the heat on while he drank. My God, I thought Step could put it away!" she added, aghast. "I mean, straight vodka, right out of the bottle, like it was soda!"

"He's Russian," Loch said, as if that explained everything.

"What*ever*! Anyway, I think he was trying to get me drunk, but he was so mad he didn't notice when I just kept passing the bottle back to him, and pretty soon . . . he was talking. A lot." Her voice took on an edge. "So that's when I found out I'm second string to Madison so far as he's concerned. I heard *all* about Madison and how bad he wants to get into her pants. And how since I'm her *sestra,* which I guess means sister, I'll do until he gets a shot at her."

There was awkward silence for a moment. "Well," Addie said judiciously, "that's not the sort of thing I want to hear out of a guy, but—"

"That's not why I'm here," Muirin interrupted. "Okay, that was bad enough, because I don't like being *anyone's* substitute mama, but then he started telling me about his family. Only I mean Family, with a capital "F." He's *Bratva*."

"Holy crap," Loch swore. "*Russkaya Mafiya*. Maf. Russian Mafia. Now a whole lot of stuff starts to make sense."

"Yeah," Muirin said bitterly. "He told me all about his connections. His father is supposed to be pretty big stuff; specializes in murder-for-hire and he's a high-dollar smuggler. Which is how Dr. Ambrosius met him and then met Anastus, and Dr. Ambrosius persuaded the old man to let Anastus come to Oakhurst."

There was a shocked silence when Muirin stopped talking. "You mean—" Addie said in a small voice.

"Yes, I do. I don't know that Ambrosius ever used him as a contract killer, but he's been using him to get stuff into the country he wouldn't be able to get legally."

"Like?" Addie prompted.

"Magical stuff that also happens to be stolen artifacts."

"Okay," Loch said warily. "Well . . . I can kind of see the need, but that's dancing really close to the fire. Look, you do *not* have friends in the Russian Mafia. You have people you've killed, people you haven't killed yet, clients you might have to kill, superiors whose job you are gunning for, and your thug-puppets." He paused. "My father ran an international financing cartel—Spearhead Venture Partners—and even though we weren't close, there was just no way I couldn't absorb a bunch of this stuff just from being around. He'd always get his security firm to investigate potential partners, and if there was even a hint of *Bratva* about them, he'd back off."

Muirin nodded. "So Anastus kept talking when I stayed quiet. He told me that when he was sixteen, he took on two of his father's jobs to prove to his father that he was worthy of being the old man's heir. And he does the same for Mark Rider, contract killing, except these days he usually has his thugs kill people, he doesn't do it himself." Muirin swallowed hard. She looked very white, even in the dim light from the glowing ball in her hand. "And you know, I could *almost* have gone, 'Okay, he's kind of a vigilante, he's just taking out people like the Shadow Knights, right?' Except—he's not. At least, not for Mark Rider. He got *really* drunk. He told me who some of those people were—some of his victims." She stopped, and shrank into herself. "Burke . . . I am so sorry . . ."

Burke's head came up, but he looked bewildered. "Huh? What?"

"Your foster parents," she whispered, staring down at her hands. "It wasn't an accident, Burke. He killed your foster family and burned the house down around them to cover it up, so you'd have nowhere to go."

It took all four of them to hold Burke down. But it was Spirit's shoulder he cried into when he finally broke.

⁂

Spirit stared into the darkness of her room for a very, very long time that night. It was more vindication for her, but— yeah. It was vindication she'd really rather not have had. This was the hard evidence that the Shadow Knights and the Gate-keepers were one and the same. Maybe not *all* of them, but certainly Mark Rider and his core group. Even Muirin agreed. Spirit had been vindicated.

But Burke . . .

Poor Burke.

She was pretty sure he wasn't going to run off and do any-thing stupid now, although if they hadn't restrained him, in those first few moments he probably would have. The big ques-tion now was, what were they going to do about all of this? They were in the middle of enemy territory. The enemy didn't yet know that *they* knew, and the longer they kept that a secret, the better off they'd be, but . . .

Then she remembered what QUERCUS had said. *Ignorance and powerlessness is your greatest defense.* And *now* that made sense. The longer they looked stupid and weak, the more likely it was that they'd be left alone.

She got up, plugged in the Ironkey, and logged on her com-puter, touch-typing in the dark. QUERCUS? she typed into the chatroom.

I am here.

She wondered about that. She wondered how he could *al-ways* be there. But then . . . maybe he knew her hours, or guessed them, and slept when she was in class. Or more likely, he was more than one person.

What you said about ignorance and powerlessness—

Yes. The more ordinary you appear, the safer you are. And they must never think you have somewhere to run to, or they will look for that haven and destroy it.

But I actually don't have anywhere to run to, she replied, feeling a lump of fear in her gut and tears burning her eyes.

Then QUERCUS replied with something utterly unexpected.

Yet.

She bit back a gasp.

Be careful. Be very careful. And Spirit, you have a weapon that they will see as a weakness. Do not hesitate to use it.

A weapon? she typed. What weapon?

Kindness.

Okay, that sort of made sense. Because the Shadow Knights were trying to divide people up, but you couldn't *do* that if the people you were trying to divide them from kept doing nice things for them. Shoot, it had even worked with Muirin!

And it wouldn't look like she was doing anything at all, not to them. Just being all touchy-feely-hippie-kid. Not a threat, not even close.

I can do that, she typed back, and closed the window. With all of Mark Rider's geeks living here now, she was even more paranoid about not chatting too long to QUERCUS. She figured five or ten minutes was all right, but not more.

She slipped back into bed, wishing she had some idea of what might come so she could be ready for it.

The next day was a grueling one, so hard Spirit really couldn't do anything but spare a thought now and again for Burke. If anyone here knew how he felt, she did. When they finally all met up at dinner, though, he looked a lot different than she had thought he would. She'd thought he would be broken up, but he wasn't. He didn't look angry, either, which she'd been afraid of; she didn't want him running off and challenging Anastus or something equally suicidal. She slipped her hand into his under the cover of the table and gave it a squeeze; he squeezed back, glanced over at her, and gave her the faintest of smiles, then let go. It took her a while to figure out what he reminded her of; finally she did. He was like a marathon runner at the beginning of the race—no idea of what was ahead of him, only knowing it was going to be incredibly hard, but determined to get across that finish line.

It was Muirin who looked absolutely miserable. She poked at her food until Burke finally spoke into the silence.

"Murr-cat. *It'll be okay*. I promise."

She looked up, hope warring with guilt in her eyes. She was about to say something when—

The power went out.

All of it. Lights, emergency lights, everything. They were in the Refectory with the curtains drawn, and it had been an overcast day, so by evening it was as dark outside as it suddenly was inside.

Within moments of losing the light, the crushing fear descended.

People started screaming; you could hear them all over the

room, jumping up, chairs going over, even tables. People stumbled toward the exit, or tried to, fell, tripped over other people and furniture. It was a good thing their table was against the wall, but even so, someone shrieking like a banshee blundered into the back of Spirit's chair, flailed wildly and smacked the side of her head, then stumbled away again.

Spirit fought the fear back and grabbed first Burke's hand, then Addie's on the other side of her. "Hold hands!" she managed to choke out, over the fear and the noise. *"Grab hands!"*

She couldn't have told when she knew, but she did, the moment that Addie on one side and Loch on the other managed to get hold of Muirin's hands, completing the circle. *We need to break this somehow,* she thought, dimly, through terror that screamed at her to run, run anywhere. People *were* running; she could hear them stampeding into the dark, out into the hall, screams receding as they made it past the Refectory door. And beyond? She thought she heard doors slamming. Were they running outside?

Desperately, she started chanting the first thing she could think of.

Multiplication tables. Neat, orderly, logical. Always the same.

"One times one is one," she shouted hoarsely. *"One times two is two. One times three is three. One times four is four."*

The others caught on pretty quickly to what she was doing and, raggedly, their voices joined hers as the dining room emptied, the screaming was all somewhere distant, and the terror tried to force their hands apart.

They got as far as the *twelve times* when suddenly, with no more warning than when it had descended, the fear vanished.

In the next moment, the lights came back up.

And there they were, sitting around the table, blinking in the light like a bunch of spiritualists interrupted at a séance. Around them the room was a wreck: tables overturned, chairs flung all over, food and dishes on the floor and broken. There were two people here besides them, and both were huddled in far corners, weeping and shaking, curled in fetal positions.

Doc Mac charged into the Refectory a moment later, hair wild, eyes wilder. He spotted them, and barked out, "Stay here! Don't move until another teacher or one of the Breakthrough people comes!" and dashed out again.

They looked at each other, then at their shattered classmates in the corners. Spirit shrugged, got up, and went over to one of them. Addie joined her a moment later, and they tried to get Sharon Hastings to uncurl. Loch and Burke went to the other—Noreen Templeton. Muirin stayed where she was, paper white, eyes dilated, shaking.

Truth to tell, Spirit wasn't far from that, herself.

Finally Lily Groves showed up, grim-faced and angry. By that time the friends had managed to get Sharon and Noreen over to the table; for lack of anything better, since they were shaking like leaves, Spirit had gotten a couple of the tablecloths that weren't too splattered and wrapped them around their shoulders. Addie was getting them—and Muirin—to drink some hot tea so loaded with sugar it was practically syrup.

"Nothing fixes things like a nice cup of hot tea," she was saying firmly, as Ms. Groves shoved open the Refectory doors.

"That's seven," she said into a handheld radio she was carrying. "Hastings, Spears, Templeton, White, Lake, Hallows, and Shae."

The radio cracked. "Roger that. Get them to their rooms. We're still searching."

Addie was already getting Noreen to her feet. Spirit did the same for Sharon, then Muirin. "We heard, Ms. Groves," Burke said as he took Sharon's elbow, then put his arm around her. "You don't mind if Loch and I take them to their rooms—"

"Go, go, go—" Ms. Groves said impatiently. "Rules are temporarily suspended. In fact, if you all want to huddle in the *same* room, I authorize it, just as long as we know where you are. Do you?"

They looked at each other. "Yes, please," said Muirin in a small voice.

"Mine's closest," said Addie.

"All seven going to Lake's room," Ms. Groves barked into her radio as they passed her.

It took a lot longer than Spirit liked, shepherding Sharon and Noreen along. "I have a bad feeling this isn't over," she told the others quietly, when they finally got into the hall on the girls' floor.

"Yeah," Burke replied, his eyes going everywhere, as if he was looking for danger. Probably he was. Finally, they got into Addie's room, which was supernaturally neat. Addie closed the door, then the curtains, and lit a candle. And a good thing, too, because fifteen minutes later, the power went out *again,* and the fear descended.

Sharon and Noreen wailed for a moment then passed out on the bed.

Addie put the candle on the floor; the rest of them huddled over that candle like a campfire, staring at it as if it was their salvation—

Which it was. Somehow, with that light there, the fear wasn't able to get hold of them as thoroughly. They were able to think. It was Loch who began to recite this time. Recite, and then sing, hoarsely. And it was the filthiest song Spirit had ever heard in her life. The lyrics were so rude, and so funny, and so shocking, that her surprise even overcame the terror. She had *no* idea that Loch—proper, gentlemanly Loch—knew anything like that! She started to giggle.

Then when Loch finished the song, Addie started one— about some poor bricklayer having a really, really bad day.

Then, when she was done, Muirin started croaking out dirty limericks. They were much, *much* worse than Loch's song.

Burke was bright crimson. So was Addie, and even Muirin herself. Spirit had a pretty good idea that she was just as red— and she had *no* notion of what she could contribute, but after Muirin had recited about a dozen, suddenly the power came back up and the terror vanished again.

This time there was a knock on the door less than a minute after the lights came back on. It was Doc Mac and a couple of the Breakthrough people. They collected Sharon and Noreen and left without saying a word, leaving the five of them sitting on the floor with the candle still burning.

It was very quiet. "Do you think it's over now?" Muirin asked, in a small voice.

"Usually these things happen in odd numbers," Addie said, staring at the candle flame intently. "I don't know. I don't know if there's going to be a third wave and Doctor Ambrosius will manage to repel it. I—just don't know." She frowned with concentration. "Who's feeling brave enough to get up and get into one of my dresser drawers?"

Loch coughed. "I am," he said, before anyone else could answer.

"Left hand side, third down, behind the thermal shirts," Addie said. "There's a big rectangular box, it fits all across the drawer. I took advantage of the new rules. Get it and bring it here."

Loch did so, coming back with a box that looked expensive largely because, though it might have been cardboard, it was like no cardboard that Spirit had ever seen before. Glass-smooth, a deep, dark metallic brown, the word *Lavendula* was written in gold script across the top. Loch carried it as if it weighed ten pounds. He put it down next to the candle. Addie slid the top off. Inside were stacked squares wrapped in gold foil. Addie took one and unwrapped it.

"Chocolate?" Burke said doubtfully. "Did you body-swap with Muirin?"

"Ninety percent cacao dark chocolate infused with chamomile and lavender," Addie replied, a little grimly. "Best way to calm down that I know of short of liquor, and I don't have any booze. I found them in France and told the Trust that was what I *always* want for Christmas and birthdays. Usually my box is kept in the Admin office and I get a couple of pieces each Sunday, but . . ." Addie shrugged. "When everything started going crazy around here, I asked if I could have it, and they gave it to me. Help yourselves."

Gingerly, they all did. The chocolate was startlingly intense, and tasted a little like flowers. Spirit wasn't sure she really liked it, but one thing was sure: You knew you'd eaten chocolate when you'd finished a piece.

There was a knock on the door, and Doc Mac stuck his head in. His grim expression told them that this had been worse than the last time. "You kids stay here and stay together," he told them. "We're missing people. There's your group, and a couple of other knots of kids that managed to keep it together and huddle, but we know people went running out the doors in all directions. We have search parties out, but there's a lot of 'out there' out there. Don't leave this room till someone comes to tell you it's all right."

"Yes sir," Burke said. Doc Mac closed the door.

"Okay," Muirin said into the silence. "I'll say it. Spirit was right. The Gatekeepers are Lizzie's Shadow Knights. And they're *horrible* people. The only way this could have happened tonight was from the inside. . . ."

"We should run." Addie's hand was shaking as she reached for a square of chocolate.

"To where?" Loch retorted. "And how? Steal horses and ride

off to Billings? Even if we could get past Rider's goons, and ride horses for two days, what would we do when we got there? I pretty much doubt Muirin's and my secret charge cards are secret from Rider at this point."

Muirin colored. "I sort of, kind of, told Madison about mine," she muttered.

"We have to look insignificant," Spirit said quietly. "Like we're not worth bothering about. Us taking out the Hunt could have been a fluke—"

Burke nodded. "We didn't really go into any detail when we told Doctor A., it's true. We could have just gotten lucky. I don't think any of us have done anything particularly wonderful since. . . ."

"We have to keep our heads down," Loch said. "But how?"

"I know how," Spirit said. "There's more than one way to spread possible attention around. We need to get to some of the others, give them some idea of what to do when this happens again, and make them think it's *their* idea."

"You think this is going to happen again?" Addie began, then shook her head. "No, I'm being stupid. Of course it is, the only question is, when and why?"

"The Dance. It has to be the Dance," Spirit said firmly. "We're all together. Like Halloween. And New Year's. I just don't know how significant the date is."

Addie's brow wrinkled, but it was Loch who spoke up. "The dance is February Second. That's Imbolc," he said. "The Return of the Light. Except what if it doesn't? What if the power goes out and there's nothing but dark and cold and fear?"

Spirit snapped her fingers; "*That's* why the fear-thing has hit us twice so far!" she said "They've been practicing!"

The others nodded. It all made perfect sense. "We have to figure out how we can fight off that fear. . . ."

"It can't be a direct confrontation, not like the Hunt," Burke pointed out.

"Well, both times that the Shadow Knights have shown up in person, we've been pretty nonconfrontational," Muirin said sourly. "We just milled around like anyone else."

"So we *look* like we're milling around, but we do stuff." Spirit looked down at the candle. "You know, the candle didn't go out."

"You know what's better than anything . . ." Muirin began to smile, slowly. "A prank. We can get a lot of the kids in on a prank. All this military-school crap is starting to bite, and I'm not the only one that feels that way."

"So, against cold and dark . . . fire and light. Maybe some other stuff . . ." Spirit nodded. "And we probably have all night to figure out what we need to put together."

Addie got up and pulled some hoarded soda out of her refrigerator. "I've got the caffeine," she said. "Let's do this."

SIXTEEN

When the searches were finally called off, three teachers and twenty kids were still missing. The day after that, e-mails went out that claimed they'd been found in Radial, and were electing to leave Oakhurst under the protection of Breakthrough. When Spirit counted it up, that was four teachers and almost forty kids that she knew of who had "left" Oakhurst, including the kids who had been Tithed or driven crazy in the last two years. It was a staggering total of dead and just-as-good-as. She knew the kids who were left wanted desperately to believe the missing ones had really gone off somewhere; there was no point in trying to tell them otherwise.

More Breakthrough people came to replace the missing (dead) teachers. The new teachers meant a new round of discipline-tightening, more classes, even less free time, and more of Mark Rider's security goons prowling the campus, giving people the hairy eyeball, trying to chase them back to their rooms when they weren't in class. And that was where Mr. Rider made his big mistake.

Maybe he figured that kids would do what they were told. Maybe he figured they were so scared by now they'd agree to *anything* as long as they were safe. Spirit remembered her parents having long debates about that with their friends—how some people would put up with just about any restrictions as long as they thought they'd be safe.

The thing was . . . even if she didn't *like* a lot of them, Spirit knew that none of the kids at Oakhurst were stupid. Smart people tended to ask questions, and tended to resent it when they had to give up privileges and freedoms. She remembered her mom saying, "Stupid people are satisfied with *stuff*. Smart people can make themselves stupid by being willing to settle for *stuff*. It's all about what you're willing to settle for."

The kids didn't say anything openly—some of them were afraid to, truth to tell—but there was a *lot* of grumbling when Breakthrough people weren't there.

The Breakthrough people got wind of it, of course, and another e-mail went out reminding everyone that the dance was still on, and that "the goal of Breakthrough was to get things back to normal as quickly as possible, so relax and enjoy your evening." As if one of the Oakhurst dances was going to make up for being shadowed by a goon when you just wanted to take a walk and be alone for a while. As if the soda and otherwise-forbidden snacks would make up for *knowing* the Breakthrough geeks were monitoring every single keystroke when you chatted.

Combine the sort of strict regime that the kids brought up like Addie weren't used to and strongly resented with the tension of wondering when the next "incident" would happen, and you had a tightly wound bunch of kids who were just looking for an outlet for all that nervous energy. It didn't take much in the way of a hint here, a suggestion there, to get the "prank" rolling.

By the night of the dance, everything was primed to explode.

The best thing is," Addie observed, as she twined Spirit's hair into a loose French braid, "even if *nothing* happens, the prank will still go off, and Rider's people will have a hundred 'suspects' to watch. None of whom will be us."

"You don't really think that's likely, do you?" Spirit asked, staring into the mirror so she could look into Addie's reflected eyes.

"No," Addie admitted, and rubbed the back of her neck. "I can feel it. It's like a thunderstorm on the horizon."

This wasn't a formal dance, like New Year's, but Muirin had insisted they all wear something besides Oakhurst clothing, so Spirit had her new red sweater and a pair of black pants Muirin had whipped up out of some velour from the theater supplies, and Addie had a similar gray outfit she said was cashmere. Those outfits would have gotten really warm after a while at a normal dance, but none of them figured they would be in the gym long enough for it to matter.

As for dates, in the end, Spirit had asked Loch and Addie had asked Burke; Muirin went through with going with Dylan, "Because it would look weird if I backed out after I already asked him." Not that who you asked made any difference in the end, because they were all herded out to the gym in a group under the watchful eye of the Breakthrough guards. Even the real couples were looking resentful. It was pretty hard to get romantic when you had an expressionless Security Goon carefully not-staring at you.

No one had really known how to decorate for a "Sadie Hawkins Day Dance," so they'd done a sort of pre-Valentine's Day generic pink background of balloons and Mylar streamers with a disco ball in the middle. The usual soda-and-snacks tables were set up, but with a difference. Some of the Breakthrough geeks had made their own additions—a light show and a real DJ.

Much as Spirit hated to admit it . . . both were good. The light show was spectacular, and the DJ really knew his stuff.

Plus, he was playing music that was definitely *not* available in the Oakhurst official music libraries. Everyone started to relax when they realized there weren't any members of the Goon Squad in the gym and the music was going to be fantastic.

It's a good thing that this is all going to fall apart before the evening is over, or I'd be worried, because this kind of treatment is pretty tempting, Spirit thought. Loch got her a drink, then drifted away to the "spot" he was going to cover for a while. Dylan hauled Muirin out onto the dance floor right away, but he didn't even make it through two songs before Ovcharenko materialized out of the shadows and cut in. The DJ immediately faded into a ballad, which more or less forced Muirin into a slow dance with him. Loch moved out of his corner and onto the edge of the dance floor and made a little finger motion, since Dylan appeared to be too intimidated by Ovcharenko to cut back in. But Muirin shook her head, and Loch went back into his own little pool of shadow.

As Spirit stood there, nursing her soda, she felt someone come up close beside her. She turned. It was Mandy, the girl-geek from Breakthrough, and she had a guy with her. A guy who was pretty much a dead ringer for Jensen Ackles from *Supernatural*, except with a pair of wire-rim glasses that made him look even hotter. If that was possible. Spirit's Spidey-Sense went off the scale, because Breakthrough could not possibly have picked someone *more* like what her Dream Guy would have looked like . . . a year or two ago.

"Hey," Mandy said, far too casually. "This's Clark, he's another codehead. He saw you in the dining hall and wanted to meet you, so I said I'd introduce you. Clark, this is Spirit."

"Hey," Spirit said, forcing herself to look pleased. "My so-called date kind of ran off on me."

"Yeah, I saw," Clark said, with a far-too-ingratiating grin. "Well, it's supposed to be a Sadie Hawkins thing, right? So, can you pick someone else instead?"

Way to go with the subtle hints, bozo, she thought. "I don't know," she replied hesitantly. "I mean, he—"

"You do know he's gay, right?" Clark interrupted, getting a little closer as Mandy vanished into the crowd around the soda table. "I mean, I could tell when I walked in, and . . . uh, magician here. Sorry."

If Loch hadn't told her himself— If they all hadn't known what the Breakthrough people were doing— Spirit shut those thoughts away and concentrated on acting like this was a confusing—and unwelcome—surprise.

"Wait, what?" she said. "What do you mean? He's—"

"I mean, if you think he accepted your invite for any other reason than to drool over the other guys, Spirit, I'm sorry." Clark moved even closer. "Don't think I'm gay-bashing. I'm not. But I thought you had the right to know in case you were going to fall for him. And I think whatever the rules for this thing are, if he didn't tell you he wasn't really interested, that pretty much undoes you inviting him, doesn't it?"

Now Spirit was actually beginning to feel a little alarmed— first that this "Clark" was coming on so strong, and second that if she wasn't nice to him, he'd out Loch, right here at the dance. She really didn't know what to do, and her apparent confusion was very real.

"Come on, try me out with a dance," Clark coaxed. He took her hand and gave her no alternative other than to pull away— which was no alternative at all, if she wanted to keep up the pretense of being the shy little hippie chick.

Which was right when Burke swooped in from out of nowhere and saved her.

"Hi, this is my dance, I think," he said, cutting in. "Besides, I bet there are a lot of Breakthrough gals closer to your age who'd appreciate someone who can dance."

Clark colored a little. "Look, kid, just because you're one of the Big Bad Jocks—"

"Seriously, didn't anyone ever teach you that you don't try and make moves on a girl who's going steady?" Burke said, with a mocking tone to his voice Spirit had never heard before. "Oh wait—you're a code-monkey, and that sort of etiquette goes straight over your head, right? Well, here's your fast education. You don't haul someone else's girl off for a dance, and you don't *ever* mess with a jock's steady. Got it? Great. Buh-bye." He made a little finger-wiggle at Clark, who slunk away, muttering. Then he put his arms around Spirit and they started slow-dancing away from the Breakthrough geek corner. Before the crowd hid them, Spirit saw Clark arguing with Mandy.

"Um. Thanks," Spirit said, feeling awkward. "The only thing is, that wasn't true."

"I know," Burke replied, and flushed as he looked down at her. "But would you like it to be?"

All she could do was look up into his eyes and say, "Um—"

Which was precisely when the lights went out, the temperature dropped down to freezing, and the terror descended.

The terror wiped away her astonishment at Burke's question. Before the terror could take hold, she took a deep breath and yelled into the silence: *"Rave! RAVE!"*

Burke bellowed the same word as he seized her hand. He hauled her across the dance floor by memory to one of the preset spots where the decorating committee had stashed a cache of flashlights and chem-lights. They stumbled into a few people on the way, and the silence had been replaced by deafening noise, but this time the noise was less screaming in fear and more shouting *rave*. Loch was already passing out chem-lights and flashlights from his station. And Addie, with chem-necklaces aglow around her neck and fistfuls of more chem-lights, was opening the fire exit door to the outside.

Addie was supposed to jam it open with a cinder block that had been left outside; Spirit couldn't see if she had, because she was too busy handing out lights. Once she and Burke got that box started, they moved to one of the others—and by the time they got that one started, there was a huge *whoosh* outside, and the fire exit doorway lit up with a bright yellow light. The pranksters had been building an enormous bonfire in the sunken garden's drained fountain all week, and someone had just lit it. Muirin's illusion had fooled everyone not in on the scheme into thinking there was nothing in the sunken garden. She'd held that illusion 24/7 for days, and Spirit couldn't wait to really congratulate her for it.

Everyone who had lights streamed out into the now brightly lit night. The rest scrambled through the boxes frantically to get something. Within minutes of the power going out, everyone was heading for the fire—and that was when they set off Part Three of the Great Rave Prank.

A wall of sound erupted from the vicinity of the fire.

A sound system, powered by batteries stolen from idle Breakthrough construction equipment, bellowed out the most cheerful, high-energy songs that any of the pranksters could think of. There were six hours' worth of songs on the iPod that was running the show, and if the terror went on for more than six hours, well—it would be more than anyone could fight.

Everyone started dancing around the fire, which was easily fifteen, maybe twenty feet across, huge, and burning too high and hot for anyone to have a hope of putting it out, thanks to a five gallon jug of vegetable oil and a *lot* of candle-ends. Addie wasn't the only one who liked to have scented candles in her room, and the Christmas decorations had included hundreds of candles. As the terror closed in on them they translated their hysterical energy into equally hysterical dancing, and—

—and that was where things got weird. Spirit knew what the plan was—Loch and Addie were somehow supposed to be feeding Muirin and Burke with the emotions and energy they were getting, and Muirin and Burke were supposed to be turning that into a shield against the fear. But as Spirit hung on to Burke's hand as hard as she could, she could feel . . . something.

It was like there was this river flowing *through* her; not something she could stop, or do anything with, but—somehow, she needed to let this happen. Because somehow, what was flowing into her was much more powerful than what was flowing out of her. Which made no sense. So she hung on to Burke's hand and tried to focus on the bonfire, and the music, and the kids all dancing around like a bunch of barbarians in a Viking movie.

Then, out of nowhere, she knew, she *knew*, the terror wasn't all there was going to be this time. "They're coming—" she said, breathlessly, then tugged on Burke's hand, and repeated, more urgently, *"They're coming!"*

And a moment later, they were *there.*

Shadow Knights.

Some on horseback, some on foot, a few on ATVs and snowmobiles, they surrounded the bonfire and the Oakhurst kids. They were all wearing the same outfit the attackers who'd come after the endurance riders had been wearing: gray hooded parkas, gray scarves over their faces. This time, Spirit could tell that there were illusions on all of them to keep their faces in shadow, because the bonfire was throwing off so much light there was no way their faces could have been hidden otherwise.

The terror increased exponentially.

One of them charged the sound system; somehow he must have figured out where it was. It was one of the ones on a snowmobile; he gunned the engine, and the snowmobile careened toward the station. He just ran the machine over everything, ice forming ahead of the skids to give him a surface to drive on, his passenger whacking at everything in the way.

He managed to connect with something vital. The music cut off, alerting even the kids who were still dancing that something was wrong.

Silence and the fear descended.

But this time was different. This time they could all see, there was light, light that the Shadow Knights couldn't put out.

Before the Shadow Knights could move, Dylan grabbed a piece of burning wood, and charged the nearest Knights with a bellow of fury. The three Knights might have been ready to fight, but their horses weren't ready to face a screeching maniac flailing at them with fire. They bolted.

At that, almost the entire student body broke out into shouts of defiance and anger. The fear strengthened; people stopped shouting, and started to back away—but there was nowhere to back up to except the fire.

Do something! Spirit thought, desperately.

"What are you waiting for?" Dylan screeched, his voice sharp with hysteria. "Are you a bunch of sheep, or what?"

The Knights struck first. They raised their arms as one, and a howling wind filled with ice fragments sprung up behind them, cutting everyone off from anyone not around the fire.

"*Not this time!*" Kelly screamed, and picked up a snowball and threw it at one of the Knights. It hit him in the middle of his chest. He looked down at the splotch of snow. Looked up at her. Started to raise his hand.

Somehow that was the one thing that the paralyzed students needed. Kelly was as popular as anyone *could* be at Oakhurst; she was fair, and when you got caught at doing something minor, more often than not she would cut you a break.

Instead of hammering a helpless teenager with his magic, the Knight suddenly found himself and his friends the focus of a school full of terrified, but angry, young magicians. Again, Spirit felt that strange sensation of being the conduit for something—and it all erupted at once.

It was like being in the middle of that attack on the endurance riders, except this time, both sides were playing. Those who had Combat magic used it. Those who didn't looked for a weapon of any sort. Fueled by energy frantic for any sort of outlet, the Combat magicians of Oakhurst filled the air with spells. Fueled by—what? The fear? According to Ms. Groves, the fear of someone else was a great fuel for spells. Spears of ice, gouts of fire, deadly little tornados and fierce blasts of straight-line wind pummeled the Shadow Knights who'd been expecting to confront a huddle of terrified youngsters.

And at first, the unexpected attack worked. The Shadow Knights actually stood there, stunned, for a long moment. Then they were forced to duck for cover under the barrage of magical weaponry.

But a moment later the Shadow Knights were rallying. The ice-weapons were vaporized by shields of fire; fireballs impacted planes of force. And the little tornados found themselves sucked into a greater whirlwind. A hurricane-force wind whirled around the Oakhurst kids; the Air Mages were forced to give up their offense in order to keep the kids and the bonfire shielded from it.

Fireballs arced toward the Oakhurst line, joined by lightning out of the whirlwind. Spirit gasped as one kid was hit by lightning and went down; another had to drop and roll in the snow when a fireball struck him and set his coat ablaze. All around her, she could hear cries of pain, and screams.

The Breakthrough guards who were *supposed* to be keeping the kids safe were nowhere to be seen.

Of course. Some tiny, calm part of Spirit's mind wondered what excuse they would use for not being here.

But the Oakhurst students weren't down yet. Illusory copies of Dylan led the kids charging at the lines; kids who were throwing whatever came to hand found themselves with piles of perfectly round ice balls beside them. There must have been a couple of people who had Animal Telepathy and Animal Control, because the mounted Knights found their horses practically turning themselves inside out to be rid of their riders.

The Knights managed to deflect the magical weapons, but they did so at the expense of *not* deflecting the physical objects being hurled like missiles. And the Oakhurst kids had been getting a *lot* of target practice these past several weeks. It showed. Spirit had the satisfaction of seeing one of her own ice balls make a direct hit inside the hood of the Knight nearest her, and seeing him go down. Silence from the Shadow Knights turned to cries of fury and pain of their own.

Thank goodness they hadn't brought any physical weapons along!

Please, please, please let them NOT remember there are a lot of guns here!

Someone here could Jaunt—Spirit couldn't make out who it was in the chaos, just a kid-shaped blot against the bonfire. Just as her eyes fastened on him, he vanished—then returned a split second later with his arms full of kendo weapons and fencing sabers. He dropped them and vanished, returned again, and repeated the trip three more times in the space of a minute or so . . . but on the last return, he swayed and pitched over, exhausted. She pulled on Burke's arm and pointed.

Burke dropped her hand and they both ran for the pile of weapons. The barrage of fire, ice, and wind was falling off, as everyone reached the end of their energy.

There was a moment of utter stillness as the winds fell and the fire and ice stopped The circle of Knights faced the circle of kids again. It was deathly quiet.

One, then another, and another of the Knights revved their snarling snowmobile and ATV engines. The mounted Knights got their horses under control again.

Spirit's heart nearly stopped. *No—no—*

The terror swelled, pressing down on them. Someone sobbed.

And that was when some of the others, now with *real* weapons in their hands, turned to face the Knights.

Dylan stepped forward defiantly, head up. He didn't look cowed or frightened. In fact, he looked as if he was out for some blood.

"*CHARGE!*" Dylan screamed at the top of his lungs. He seized a kendo sword from someone next to him and brandished it over his head before bullrushing the line. His impromptu army, including Spirit and Burke, followed on his heels.

The Shadow Knights broke and ran. And the terror collapsed.

Those who could still control their horses picked up some of those on foot. The rest were snagged by those on ATVs and snowmobiles. There was no way the students could catch them on foot, but they pursued them out past the bounds of the campus, returning only when they were sure the Knights would not be back.

And that was when the party really started.

❊

There was no chance the teachers would be able to chase them back to their rooms before dawn, so no one even tried. Doc Mac and Lily Groves even made a raid on the kitchen and put sandwich fixings out with the drinks at the gym— probably to ensure the students didn't tear the kitchen apart looking for something to eat.

While Doctor Ambrosius didn't go out to the celebrants having a pagan war dance around the dying bonfire, he did go around to those who'd decided to go back to the gym where it was warmer. By the time he got around to Burke, Addie, and Spirit, the consensus was that this had all been Dylan's idea, from the "prank" to the defense of Oakhurst, a tale none of them intended to dispute.

Spirit felt as cratered as if she'd been on an all-day endurance ride, and when Burke suggested they move over to the lounge, she readily agreed. It wasn't as if she had any more energy for dancing.

"I'm starving," Burke said, looking with dismay at the food table in the gym, which seemed to have been attacked by swarms of locusts.

"I heard a rumor Doc Mac got someone to put food out on

the buffet line at the Refectory, too," Spirit told him. "Bet Murr-cat's there."

They headed back to the main building. "Bet the Break-through goons all have a good excuse for why they weren't around when the balloon went up," Burke observed sourly.

"Probably lots of excuses," she agreed. Burke reached out and took her hand halfway to the building. "And probably lots of doctored evidence 'proving' they were where they'll claim they were. But if Mr. Ovcharenko shows up tomorrow with a black eye, be sure to thank me." She had been pretty certain the guy she'd nailed with her ice ball had been Ovcharenko.

"One day it's going to be more than just a black eye," Burke muttered, then stopped, just as they reached the door. "And you never did answer my question."

Now she was confused. "What question?"

"You said me saying we were going steady wasn't true, and I asked you if you wanted it to be," Burke told her, pulling on her hand a little so she faced him.

Once again, Spirit felt as if she'd been stunned stupid. But she managed to stammer out something enough like "yes" that Burke pulled her into his arms for a kiss that lasted long enough that she started going weak in the knees.

Then his stomach growled loudly.

They both laughed. "I guess we'd better find you some food," she teased, and they went inside.

The rumors were true; anything leftover that could be made into a sandwich or thrown into the microwave had been put out on the line. To Burke's immense satisfaction, Spirit identified some bits of meat in a pan as the leftover steak from three nights ago, and the two of them made a plate of steak sandwiches, which they took into the lounge.

There they found the rest of their friends presiding over the remains of their own feast.

"We did it," Muirin said, in tones of disbelief. "We did it."

"And Dylan got all the credit," Loch grumbled.

"*Blame*," Spirit reminded him. "Believe me, this is one we don't want extra credit for."

"Mark and Madison are really not going to be happy about this," Muirin agreed. "And Dyl's going to be Anastus's little chew toy from now on."

"Better him than me," Burke muttered, then spoke up after inhaling half his sandwich. "So . . . now what? They lost this round, but they aren't going to give up."

"We keep our heads down until we find a good way to get out of here," Spirit said firmly. "We need somewhere safe to go, and we need a way to get there. Meanwhile, we hide right here."

Addie nodded; so did Loch. "My father had a lot of vacation properties," Loch said slowly. "I just need to remember where some of them are. We had a system of where we hid spare keys and I know all the alarm codes."

"We might be able to use the horses, or maybe steal a car," Addie said. "Once we get out and get somewhere safe, Loch and I can get to people on our Trusts." She got a sly look on her face. "I know just the person, too. He *hates* video games. All I have to say is that Breakthrough took over the school to get the kids hooked on games and he'll help us figure out what to do."

Spirit nodded. "Okay then. Until we get a plan and a way to get out of here, it's hide in plain sight. Don't fail anything, because we don't want them to cull us, but don't be outstanding, either. Just look absolutely normal and average."

Burke squeezed her hand. "Got it," he said, and cracked a small smile. "Just a regular guy and his steady girl. What could be more normal than that?"

Spirit almost giggled at the looks on the faces of the other three, and enjoyed her moment of happiness. Tomorrow they'd have to deal with the repercussions—and there *would* be repercussions. They'd have to figure out how to keep Mark Rider and Breakthrough from figuring out what they were doing. They'd have to find out how to get away. She'd have to decide if QUERCUS was a friend who could help, or a trap. And somehow, they would have to figure out who Mordred was—and where—and how to take him out for good. Because she knew in the depths of her soul that Mordred wasn't going to stop until they were all dead . . . or his servants.

But not this minute. She squeezed Burke's hand back. Tonight, at least, was going to be theirs.

*Don't miss the first young adult series
from bestselling authors*

Mercedes Lackey and Rosemary Edghill

SHADOW GRAIL #1:
LEGACIES
SHADOW GRAIL (#1 OF 4)

"*Shadow Grail #1: Legacies* is an
enchanting mixture of mystery,
romance, magic, and murder.
You'll never feel the same about
rural Montana again."

—Delia Sherman,
author of *Changeling*

In trade paperback
978-0-7653-1761-2

www.tor-forge.com

Read the entire collection from the *USA Today* and *New York Times* bestselling team

Mercedes Lackey and James Mallory

☙❧

The Outstretched Shadow
Book One of The Obsidian Trilogy

"In this captivating world conjured by veteran Lackey and classical scholar Mallory, there are three types of magic, each of which has its own rules, limits, and variables. The narrative speeds to the end, leaving the reader satisfied and wanting to know more." —*Publishers Weekly*

☙❧

To Light a Candle
Book Two of The Obsidian Trilogy

"Lackey and Mallory combine their talents for storytelling and world crafting into a panoramic effort." —*Library Journal*

Read the entire collection from the *USA Today*
and *New York Times* bestselling team

Mercedes Lackey
and James Mallory

* * *

When Darkness Falls
Book Three of The Obsidian Trilogy

"Highly readable . . . High-fantasy
fans should appreciate the intelligent
storytelling with an unmistakable
flavor of Andre Norton at her best."
—*Publishers Weekly*

* * *

The Phoenix Unchained
Book One of The Enduring Flame

"Sets a lavishly detailed stage peopled
with intriguing and well-developed
characters whose futures hold both
promise and peril. A good addition to
most fantasy collections."
—*Library Journal*

Read the entire collection from the *USA Today*
and *New York Times* bestselling team

**Mercedes Lackey
and James Mallory**

The Phoenix Endangered
Book Two of The Enduring Flame

"Readers can rest assured that Lackey
and Mallory will not let them down."
—*SFRevu*

The Phoenix Transformed
Book Three of The Enduring Flame

"[Lackey will] keep you up long past
your bedtime."   —Stephen King

www.tor-forge.com